Broken

AN UNLUCKY 13 NOVEL

ANDI JAXON

Cover Design: Rebel Ink Co.
Cover Model: Darren Birks
Interior Formatting: Ashley James and Andi Jaxon
Editing: Candace Royer (editor), Anette King (development editor), and Rumi Khan (proof)

Blurb

Welcome to Black Diamond Resort and Spa...
After years of drowning myself in parties, hook ups, and pain, all it takes is one viral sex tape to get me thrown on a remote island to disappear for a while.
That or lose my trust fund.
Having to share a room with the one man I let hurt me is my worst nightmare.
I'm the broken shell of the boy he walked away from on the single worst day of my life.
I hate him almost as much as I hate myself.
This island was supposed to be a place I could rest but instead I'm running.
From Asher Vaughn.
From myself.
From the scars on my heart that never healed.
It hurts to look at him and see all the things we never got to have.
But how am I supposed to keep him at arm's length when he watches me the way he used too?
When he touches me? When he calls me his?
We can't be together, not off this island.
The straight football star and the gay femme son of famous parents.
The media would rip us apart and ruin his career.
I barely survived the last time he left me, can I live through being deserted again?

Broken is a brother's best friend, mm romance with some praise kink, and a broken boy in desperate need of love.
This story has triggers which you can find on my website.

Dedication

For Melissa,
My newest bestie. I love you like Jordan loves Eli.

Playlist

THEME SONG:
"I'm Trying" by Alexander Stewart

"Hold On" by Chord Overstreet
"Please Don't Go" by Joel Adams
"Like I Do" by Rain City Drive
"If Our Love Is Wrong" by Calum Scott
"Till It Hurts" by JORDY
"Make Hate To Me" by Citizen Soldier
"No Right To Love You" by Rhys Lewis
"Fender Bender" by The Drama Scene
"Can You Hold Me" by NF, Britt Nicole
"Need Somebody" by Xuitcasecity
"Get You The Moon" by Kina, Snow
"Memories" by Shawn Mendes
"Monsters" by Timeflies, Katie Sky
"Chariot" by Jacob Lee
"River of Tears" by Alessia Cara

"Turn Back Time" by Daniel Schulz
"I Don't Want To Love You" by Taylor Matthews
"Lost In The Moment" by NF, Andreas Moss
"Beautiful Addiction" by Nate Feuerstein
"I Tried" by Camylio
"Quiet Hours" by Letdown.
"Silhouette" by Caleb Hearn
"Good To You" by Marianas Trench
"Fallout" by Marianas Trench
"Bitter" by Citizen Soldier
"Dial-Tone" by Catch Your Breath
"Stitches" by Shawn Mendes
"Another Reason" by Grant Knoche
"How Are You?" by Dylan Brady
"All I Know So Far" by P!nk
"Dancing All Alone" by Clinton Kane
"Scars" by Keenan Te
"Outsider" by Rachel Grae

Authors Note

This book does include triggers, mostly surrounding mental health. For a list of triggers, please check my website under the Trigger Warning tab.

Welcome To Black Diamond Resort and Spa

Since our founding in 2001 by the Diamond family, we've strived to provide a unique experience to those who live in the public eye. Privacy and discretion is of the utmost importance to us so you won't find paparazzi or journalists looking for a juicy story on our shores, only the relaxing lapping of waves and delicious drinks.

Enjoy the all inclusive, private, resort built exclusively for the elite. From luxury villas to gorgeous white sand beaches, there's something here for everyone on the island. Water sports, hiking, massages, and 5 star gourmet meals will have you never wanting to leave.

So take a deep breath and let us handle the rest.

Prologue

ASHER

The sun burns hot on my skin as Marcus and I wait for his younger brother to climb the path from the water back up to the jump-off spot. We've been coming out here since we were kids, before life knocked me down and stomped on me just for good measure. Before sexuality mattered, when my family was still whole, and Marcus's parents pretended to give a shit about him and Elliot.

Out here there's nothing but water, adrenaline, and friendship.

Liar. You have more secrets than you know what to do with.

I can't stop myself from watching him. Eli. The seventeen-year-old little brother of my best friend. Even though I've known him longer than not, over the last year something changed. I kissed him on New Year's, and since then, when I'm home from college, we find minutes to sneak away when Marcus is distracted.

Usually I have better control, I can pretend I'm not

watching him, but not today. He's dripping wet with no shirt, and his board shorts are riding low on his hips. His mop of curly blond hair that's normally rioting around his face is plastered to his head. My cock throbs as he grabs a towel and dries his face. Those soaked shorts are clinging his ass so perfectly it should be illegal. Fucking him *is* illegal. Not to mention Marcus would murder me.

Taking care of Eli has been Marcus's job since before I met him. Their parents are always off gallivanting around the world, filming and shit. They've left the raising of their kids to nannies and Marcus. We're three years older than Eli, but we've taken our job to protect him very seriously. The hardest part of going away to college was not being able to protect Eli anymore.

Marcus stands and prepares to run and jump from the cliff face as Eli and I watch. He counts down from three and launches himself over the edge. Eli and I both step forward and watch Marcus hit the water, then grab for each other. We have about two minutes before Marcus makes it back to the top and can see us.

I wrap an arm around Eli's waist and pull his chest flush against mine. Finally, skin to skin. Goose bumps erupt across my flesh at the contact. Eli wraps his arm around my neck and crushes our lips together in a hungry, heated kiss. We know we don't have long, so we don't waste a second with small talk or hesitation. Guilt threatens to ruin this moment. I have shit to tell him that I've been putting off for months, but I don't want to see the hurt on his face when I do.

I bite his plump lower lip and suck it into my mouth. My damn heart beats for this boy. It's a blessing and a fucking curse to need what you can't have. He's one of the few people that know I'm bi. Most think I'm straight, Marcus included.

Eli groans, and I quickly shush him before crashing my lips to his again. I crave him. I'm desperate for him. Only him.

I slide a hand down the length of Eli's back and cup his bubble butt in my palm, kneading the muscled flesh. He grinds against me, his dick just as hard as mine.

"Fuck," he mutters against my lips. "How much longer do we have?"

Footsteps and sliding pebbles on the path answer for me, and we jump apart. Eli sits on a boulder with his towel balled up in his lap and picks up his phone. I tuck my dick into the waistband of my swimming trunks and pray to the god of hard-ons that mine goes away quickly.

Marcus's smiling face appears a few seconds later.

"That was awesome. You're up, Asher." He nods at me, but I'm not feeling it.

"I'm going to head out." Eli stands up and slips his feet into his sandals.

"Where are you going?" I demand, more forceful than I should.

"Some of my friends are having a bonfire at Colin's." He lifts an eyebrow and shrugs with one shoulder.

Marcus smirks at his brother while I seethe. Fucking Colin. He's had a crush on Eli for months.

"You finally going to give Colin a shot?" Marcus asks, wagging his eyebrows. I clench my hands into fists and try to control my breathing as jealousy races through me.

Abso-fucking-lutely not.

"I don't know." Eli glances quickly at me, then away again.

He turns and picks up his stuff. I start to panic, needing more time with him. I leave to go back to school next week, so I need every minute with him I can get. My heart is racing at the idea of Eli leaving when I have such a finite amount of time left.

"You don't want to jump?" Marcus asks me, oblivious to the internal fight I'm having.

I clear my throat. "No, I'll walk Eli out."

Marcus runs and jumps again. Eli and I wait to make sure he surfaces, then head up the path to the little parking spot along the side of the road. Out here, we're just people. There's no celebrity status, no cameras, no expectations. Eli can be himself and not hide his truth from a world that would judge him for it.

It's a quick walk to the road, and Eli unlocks his black G-Wagon. He drops his stuff onto the passenger seat and turns to me. My heart sputters in my chest. Stepping in close, I lean my forehead to his and close my eyes. That one spot is the only point of contact between our bodies.

"I'm sorry." I whisper the words, but I'm not sure what I'm apologizing for. For not being man enough to tell Marcus that I'm in love with Eli? For forcing him to stay in the closet because my future as a football player depends on it? For needing every second of him I can get?

His lips brush mine softly, and one of his hands threads our fingers together.

I open my eyes and see him smiling up at me, the light sparkling in his bright blue eyes. He must think I'm apologizing for almost getting us caught. In moments like this, I don't want to go back to school. I fucking love playing football, but I love this stolen time I have with Eli too.

I kiss his lips again and step back, letting our fingers linger for a second longer.

"I'll see you later?" The hopeful expression on his face almost breaks me.

"Yeah." I nod and watch him get into the car and pull away. I suck in a deep breath and turn to find Marcus staring at me with fury in his eyes.

"What the fuck?" His words are cold, quiet, and calm. Fuck.

"Marcus," I start, stepping toward him, needing him to understand but not having the words to explain it.

"Don't you dare!" he roars, stomping away from me back toward the cliff edge. "I trusted you! Eli trusted you! You lied to me!" He whirls around on me, eyes wide and face flushed with anger and hurt. "You're fucking my little brother!"

"No, I'm not!" I shout back, determined for him to not hate me. "I've kissed him but never anything else. I love him." *And I'm not trying to go to jail.*

"Since when? Huh? When did you decide you liked dick? Or is it just Eli and not any other dude? Why *my* brother?" he demands, pacing like a caged animal.

"I'm bi. I've known for years, but I didn't think it would matter to you, so I never said anything." Helpless. This is what it feels like to be helpless. It's the worst feeling in the world. Knowing someone you love is suffering and can do nothing about it. Like watching my mother die of cancer and my father lose his mind right along with her.

"I kissed him on New Year's. It was supposed to be a one-time thing. He was upset he didn't have anyone to kiss." I shake my head, realizing how fucking stupid it sounds now. "I don't know what to say. I just want to be with him."

Marcus stops pacing. "You're playing football! You're condemning him to a life in the fucking closet!"

"You don't know that, man! Times are changing. Being anything other than straight is more accepted." I shrug lamely. I desperately want it to be true.

The only sound is the occasional car passing on the road. I swear I stop breathing as I wait for Marcus to say something.

"How many times have you heard homosexual slurs in the locker room?" Marcus gets in my face and demands an answer. The fucked-up part? He's right. Slurs are thrown around all the fucking time. Toxic masculinity runs rampant through sports. Even today there's only one out player in the league.

I open my mouth to speak, but nothing comes. There are no walls up; every emotion fighting through my body is written on my face, and I know he can read them. He's known me long enough to see each and every one.

Finally, I lift my hands and drop them back down to my sides. It's all I can do. My heart is breaking, and there's nothing I can do about it. Being with me will force Eli to hide who he really is, and I don't want that life for him. He deserves so much more than that. The confusion on Marcus's face morphs into rage, and he rushes me. I don't try to stop it since I deserve to get my ass kicked. He deserves to get a few good punches in to defend Eli.

He tackles me, and we hit the ground, rolling around in the dirt as he swings at me. I don't fight him at first, letting him land a few hits before I start blocking them, but I never return them.

"Then stay!" he screams in my face. "Fight for him!"

I can't. How can he not see that I can't?

I have to walk away from both of them, not because I want to, but because I *have* to. There's no life for me here. My only way out is football. I was suffocating here. Watching my father work himself to death just so he doesn't have to look at me. So he doesn't have to come home where memories of my mother still linger. I'm in love with a boy I can't have, and it's killing me.

"I'm sorry." The words rip from my face as we roll again, and I manage to get to my feet.

Marcus jumps up and rushes for me again but slips. In slow motion but the blink of an eye, Marcus hits his head on a rock and falls over the edge of the cliff.

Like a horror movie, I watch but can't move, can't stop him.

I scramble to the edge and watch his lifeless body hit the water between the boulders jutting up from the lake bed. It's why we run and jump, to get away from the rocks.

My heart is in my throat and panic makes my body tremble as I stumble to my feet, then run toward the edge. I have to save him.

I hit the water and immediately kick toward the surface. Once I break through, I reorient myself and swim as hard as I can toward the rocks.

Hurry.

He can't die.

Save him.

I force my body to move as fast as it can, adrenaline and fear working my muscles harder than they ever have before.

Where the fuck is he?

"Marcus!" My voice is drowned out by the sound of water lapping against the stones blocking me from finding my best friend. "Marcus!"

I get into the area with boulders and search while the waves drive me into the rocks.

"Marcus!" The sun reflects off the water, blinding me for a minute as I try to locate him.

A wake from a speedboat crashes into me hard, making me hit the side of my head against a boulder. I'm dazed for a second and shake my head to clear it, but from the edge of my peripheral I see an arm. Focusing all my energy, I manage to get away from the boulder and around it to the next one where Marcus has gotten caught.

"Marcus!" I grab for him, but he doesn't open his eyes or move at all. "Marcus, wake up!" There's a deep gouge on his temple, and he looks pale. Is it from being in the water?

It takes a minute, but I pull his back against my chest and try to pull him to the small bank, but I can't. Something is holding him here.

"Fuck!" I scream as loud as I can with frustration and fear and guilt. This is my goddamn fault.

"Come on, Marcus." Tears form a knot in my throat as I try to get enough leverage to pull him loose, but whatever it is doesn't give. Eventually, I stop trying and just hold him to me, letting the waves move us where it will. My body is tired, and some small part of me knows he's not going to wake up. He's gotten colder since I came out here, his skin turning blue, but I can't give up.

"I'm sorry." A tear streaks down my face, hot against the cold fear that's dug its claws into me. "I should have told you on New Year's when I kissed him. I should have told you that I was falling in love with him. I should have told you that I left to play football because I feel invisible in my own house since my mom died and that my dad is working himself to death and there's nothing I can do about it. He won't take his own life, but he misses Mom so much he's killing himself so he can join her." Tears fall freely down my face now as I hug my best friend's body to my chest. My arm wrapped around him to keep him with me. I can't leave him. I'm a shit friend, but I can't let Eli lose him. Eli deserves to be able to bury his brother. The only family he's ever had that gave a shit about him.

I don't know how long we're out here, but the sun starts sinking on the horizon, and I start to shiver in the shadows. Logically, I know I should leave, go find my phone, and call for help, but it hurts so much to give up on him. I can't even get him out of the water. My throat is raw from yelling for help in the hope that someone walking past on the road would hear me, but no one came. I'm alone.

"I'm sorry I'm not enough for Eli. I'm not now, but I'll learn how to be, and I'll come back for him. I promise I'll come back for him." I have to go, or I'll die out here too. It's nothing less than I deserve, but I made a promise, and I'll keep it.

With a sob, I kiss Marcus's uninjured temple, squeeze him tightly, and apologize again, then let him go and swim for the shore. I'm weak from the mental load of what's just happened and physically from fighting off the waves for hours, but determination keeps me moving.

By some miracle I make it to the shore and up the steep trail to the clearing. I don't look back at the water. I don't know what would be worse, seeing him or not. Gathering our things, I finally get to the road, put his stuff in his car, and call 911 to report a drowning.

I tell the operator what happened and even though my body is ready to drop, I wait for the police to show up. It's hours of answering questions, my dad getting called, the Cushings getting called overseas, before I'm able to leave. I'm emotionally drained, physically exhausted, and numb when I call for a ride to the airport.

With every step, my legs beg for a break. I don't know how I'm going to move tomorrow, but I'll find a way. I have to. I'm flying back to school tonight instead of next week and ending this with Eli so he can find someone worthy of him.

My ride shows, and I drop into the back seat.

"Where to, kid?" the guy asks, and I rattle off my address.

I shouldn't go home, Eli will come looking for me, but I won't stay long, just grab a few things I need for school, then head to the airport.

Flipping through my phone, I find my messages and bring up Eli's chat. I stare at his small picture, tears once again filling my eyes, and I type out a message.

ASHER

I'm sorry.

One

ELLIOTT

I'm awake when my phone vibrates at midnight. My bed is calling me, but Jordan, my pink-haired, feisty friend, dragged me out of my apartment for the first time in months. These days I don't have to leave my cave. Groceries can be delivered, and I can order anything off the internet, and I can have meals delivered too so I don't even have to cook. Not that I'm hungry much these days. My days mostly consist of laying around the house in the silence of my life, too exhausted to put on a mask convincing enough to leave. Somewhere along the way, I've lost my easy smile, my laugh.

"Come on!" Jordan grabs my hand and pulls me toward the band performing on stage. NF, I think she said? I don't know. It's loud, the lyrics rip at your heart, while the drums pound out a beat you can feel in your bones.

The noise and number of people makes me anxious, but it's also amazing to get lost in the crowd. I'm not Elliot Cushings, son of Grammy-winning parents with a dead brother.

Yes, it's all very tragic. But right here, right now, I'm just a person. There are no cameras in my face. No paparazzi shouting questions about my sexuality or lack of dating history.

It's dark, loud, and humid, but Elliot Cushings doesn't exist. Not here. I don't matter. I don't have to wear a mask because no one is looking at me.

Stumbling after Jordan as she yanks me through the crowd toward the front, I let the anonymity of the situation wash over me and relax for the first time in hours. We get shoved into the barrier, but that's fine. I stand behind her to protect her from anyone who tries to get handsy, but let's be honest—she's my protector, not the other way around. Her ripped jeans, tattoos, and combat boots are a lot tougher than my skinny jeans and pearl necklace, but whatever. I'm used to getting felt up by strangers in the dark.

She screams and throws her hands in the air as her favorite song comes on, "Lie." I try to get swept up in the energy of the space, but I know what that message on my phone says and who it's from. He haunts me. Every year, on my birthday and Christmas, I get a text from the only boy I've ever let close enough to hurt me. Asher Vaughn. I've never responded, but he sends them anyway. I leave him on read. It hurts to pretend like he didn't leave a gaping, bleeding wound in my chest when he left. Then had the audacity to succeed in his dreams. Dreams I never would have been able to stand next to him for. No, I would have been relegated to "just the roommate" in the public to protect his image while rumors spin about him fucking the fem twink he claims he isn't in love with. He left me for the NFL. Football meant more to him than our ten years of friendship. Would he have walked away from Marcus too? Was that his plan when he came home that summer?

I shake my head to stop my thoughts from spiraling down that dark path any further. I don't have the energy to pull myself back out of that all-consuming, painful pit.

No one really knows about him, about how he disappeared the night my brother died with nothing more than an "I'm sorry" text. Jordan knows that I grew up with the San Diego Thunderbolts star running back, but only that he was my brother's best friend. It shouldn't still hurt. Not after six years, but it does. He abandoned me on the worst night of my life. Left me to find out about my brother's death while I was alone in the house for days before my parents showed up. For three days, I sat in Marcus's room and did nothing. Just hoped he would show up and tell me the police were wrong.

I called both of them so many times, but no one answered. Ever.

There was an investigation, of course, but Asher's dad stepped in and got things *handled,* I guess. Marcus's death was marked an accident and everyone's lives went on as normal while I tried to pick up the shambles of my world. My parents told me he drowned at the lake, so I never went out there again.

I clear my throat, trying to get rid of the ache at the back and shake off the memories of that first week without the most important people in my life. Of the interviews with the police. Of Asher's father telling me not to speak to anyone without him present. It was the most I had ever seen him in the ten years I had been friends with Asher. I wasn't allowed to know anything that was going on or what they found out.

Mr. Vaughn managed to block me at every turn like it was a national fucking secret. The not knowing hurts almost as bad as being abandoned by everyone that loved me.

The song comes to an end, and Jordan spins around, forcing me to plaster a fake smile on my face. The band bows and thanks the crowd, then leaves the stage. The lights turn on, and everyone flinches at the shock to their eyes.

Jordan is flushed and beaming. I'm glad she enjoyed this, and I'm glad I got to see it, but all it does is remind me of how empty I am. All the fucking time.

"That was amazing!" she hollers, wrapping her arms around me in a hug I try not to cringe from. I'm a huge cuddler. I live for hugs and lazy days on the couch, curled up watching movies together, but I don't let myself have it. Not anymore. Not since the only person I ever wanted to touch me walked away without looking back. I can't afford to be hurt like that again, so it's easier to just tell myself I don't want it.

We stand shoulder to shoulder, both of us barely five-foot-six, and move with the crowd toward the doors. Since we were so close to the stage, it'll be a minute before we get out of here.

Jordan pulls her phone out of her pocket and smiles at her screen before shoving it back in her pocket.

"What's got you smiling like that?" I yell over the buzzing in my ears.

"You'll see." She winks and wraps an arm around my waist to keep me close to her while we move through the first set of doors.

Dread drops into my stomach like a lead rock. That doesn't sound fun to me. Fuck. I need to hide in my apartment for at least a week after this. How does she have an endless supply of energy?

Jordan's dad is a rock god, so she grew up touring with her parents. She's always on the go, ready for an adventure at any time. I adore her, but I can't keep up. She's usually a lover, but she can brawl with the best of them, can drink hulking men under the table, and knows more about music than anyone I know. The woman plays like five instruments too, but fame isn't what she wanted.

We finally make it out of the arena and to the parking lot. It doesn't take us long to get to my old G-Wagon and climb in. I should have sold it years ago, but it holds too many memories. Sometimes they're suffocating, sometimes they're comforting, and I never know which one it'll be until I climb inside.

Jordan turns on the radio and reconnects her phone to the Bluetooth to blast music through the speakers. It's a mix of bands, most of them are familiar, but I don't know all the words like she does. As we drive down the freeway, she rolls down her window and hangs out of it. I chuckle at her but am not surprised. She's pumped up from the energy of the concert. The same energy that drained me further than I already was.

A few songs play, the wind drying the sweat that was dotting my skin and unsticking my curls from my forehead and neck. My thumbs tap out the beat on the steering wheel as I head to her house. Hopefully, I can drop her off and head home without having to stay.

I pull onto her street, and she shuts off the music and rolls up the window.

"I know you're exhausted, so I'm not going to ask you to

stay. You are always welcome to, though." She looks at me seriously for a moment, and I panic as I fear my mask has slipped. "I know your depression has gotten worse, bestie. I see it."

Tears prick at my eyes, and I chew on one side of my lower lip to keep from blubbering like a baby.

"I love you," she says as I pull up into her driveway and put the car in park. Jordan reaches for my face and cups my cheeks, resting her forehead against mine. "I love you. So, if you aren't taking care of the depression, I will hound you until you do. If I could make those appointments for you, I would."

A tear slips down my cheek, and she brushes it away.

"I know it's hard and overwhelming, but you can do it." She wraps her arms around me, and I collapse into her, sobbing into her shoulder. Jordan rubs my back and tells me it's going to be okay.

It takes a few minutes, and my throat feels raw, but I'm able to pull it back and shove it back behind the door in my mind. I sit up, and she wipes my face.

"Get some rest tonight, then come out with me tomorrow."

I sag in my seat, already exhausted. "Tomorrow? I won't be recovered from today!" I'm whiny, and I know it.

"Yup. We're going to eat breakfast and go do something fun for your birthday." The mischief in her eyes makes me nervous.

"I'm locking my door," I grumble at her.

She laughs and kisses my cheek. "You gave me a key."

"Ugh!" I drop my head back on the headrest dramatically.

Jordan climbs out and closes the car door. I wait in her driveway until she's inside, then back out and head to my condo. My body is weak with exhaustion, both physically and mentally drained. My face a blank shell of who I am as I navigate the streets to my underground parking lot. Thankfully, my head is empty too.

I drag my ass to my place and fall face first onto my unmade bed, passing out in a blissful black void.

SOMETHING HITS MY FOOT, and I'm jerked out of slumber.

"Hey. Wake up, birthday boy," Jordan says much louder than necessary.

"Go away," I grumble and shove my head under my pillow.

"Get up and go shower. Now." That's the no-nonsense voice. The "do what I say, or I'll make you" tone.

My brain is begging me to stay in bed, to sleep for the rest of the day and maybe tomorrow, but I throw my pillow and glare at my friend. "I hate you."

She's standing next to my bed with her arms crossed, a hip cocked, and an eyebrow raised. The set line of her lips means she's about to read me the riot act too. Fuck me.

I roll my eyes and force my body up. "Fine."

Sliding my feet to the floor, I realize I still have my shoes on. Ugh. Gross. Now there's concert floor in my bed. When does the cleaner come? Has to be soon, right? Aren't they supposed to come like twice a week?

I glance around my room and notice my doom piles,

clothes on the floor, dishes and half-empty water bottles littered all over the place.

"Don't you still have a cleaner?" Jordan asks.

"Of course, I do," I snap as I untie my shoes and kick them off, then pull off my socks.

"From the look of this place, they haven't been here in months. They better not be getting paid for doing nothing."

My gut sinks with embarrassment, and I suck the inside of my lip between my teeth. I shrug but don't reply.

"Seriously, who do you use? You need to call them."

I stand and start for the bathroom with my head ducked toward the floor. I can't look her in the eye. My place is awful. It's a disgusting mess.

"I don't know," I mutter, shoving my hands in the pockets of my jeans. "My parents hired someone."

"You should ask them for the contact information," she reiterates.

I close the bathroom door before stripping out of my clothes and getting under the spray. The hot water boils the sweat and exhaustion from my body. My hair is crunchy with product and sweat, but I don't have the energy to deal with it, so I just get it wet and hope for the best before I get out of the shower.

When I open the bathroom door, I open it just a crack to peek into my room, and breathe a sigh of relief Jordan isn't still standing there. I hurry to my huge closet and pull on another pair of jeans and a crop top T-shirt. I gaze at my pleated skirts longingly, but I don't have the mental capacity to wear one today. At my jewelry drawer, I select a pearl necklace and put it on.

In the mirror, I lightly caress the pearls with the tips of

my fingers. This necklace belonged to Asher's mother. She left me a few strings of them in her will when she died. The woman was an amazing human. She looked after Marcus and me when she could, loved Asher fiercely, and was a ray of sunshine and maternal comfort in our gray world. Maggie loved pearls, and I used to stare at them when she wore them, which she did often. This string is slightly pink with a gold clasp and hangs to just past my collarbone. It's my favorite one. She would wear this one when she baked chocolate chip cookies. I smile slightly at the memories of warm baked cookies and mom hugs.

My face falls when her ashen face pops into my head. The cancer was so cruel. Aggressive and all-encompassing. It sucked the life right out of her, before our very eyes. The last month she was alive, we weren't allowed to see her. Mr. Vaughn banned us from the house. Even Asher. We all slept in a pile in Marcus's room. Well, when we could sleep. Most nights we just held on to Asher as he cried or sat back as he yelled and punched the walls until the tears came again.

I hate that I still care. That I still follow his career and keep tabs on him. I've locked up my feelings for him in a lead-lined coffin and buried it as deep as I was able to. Forced myself to shut my feelings off where he's concerned, but sometimes, memories of his mom or Marcus bring them to the surface, and it hurts just as badly as when he walked away. I thought time healed all wounds, but after six years, this one still bleeds.

Jordan's voice carries down the hallway as she paces while on the phone. I swear she can't sit still for very long.

"How long has it been since you've sent someone over

here?" She pauses as she waits for the answer. "And why did they stop coming?" Another pause. "I see."

I pull on a pair of ankle boots and scrunch my fingers in my hair a few times with a microfiber towel, then leave my room.

"And when can someone come in? We're going to need a deep clean." Jordan turns when she hears me. "Sounds good, thank you."

She hangs up the phone and looks at me. "They'll be in next week. Apparently, about four months ago, you told them to fuck off and never come back."

Four months?

I shuffle my feet and chew on my lip again as I look around my living room and kitchen. They aren't as bad as my room, but that's because I spend most of my time in there. These rooms aren't good, though.

"Come on, let's get out of here. I'm starving." Jordan reaches for my fidgeting fingers and links hers with mine, picks up a grocery bag sitting by the front door, and pulls me from the space.

"I'm sorry," I mumble as we wait for the elevator.

"Nothing to be sorry about. We'll get it handled." She rubs my back with a comforting hand and a nod. "Depression can cause time blindness. I doubt you remember telling the cleaning company not to come back and definitely didn't realize it was four months ago."

Since Jordan drove my car, which isn't abnormal for us, we end up at a place that serves breakfast that only Jordan loves, and I drink a basic bitch Frappuccino while picking at my eggs.

"Seriously, you need to eat. I know you don't feel hungry,

but you need to nourish your body." She looks between my plate and my face. "Part of the reason you're tired is because you aren't taking care of yourself."

She cuts her hash browns in half and pushes some onto my plate. Why are fried potatoes so tasty? Jordan hands me some hot sauce, and I put some on the hash browns and eggs, then eat about half of both. My stomach feels like it's going to explode.

"I'm done." I push the plate away, and Jordan gives me a smile.

"Good. Thank you for eating."

Two

ELLIOTT

Jordan navigates my car to a high school parking lot and parks in an empty space. I lift an eyebrow at her in confusion, but she just smiles at me and jumps out. With a resigned sigh, I follow her and leave the safety of my car. She grabs the grocery bag from the back and hooks her arm through mine, leading me toward the throng of people moving toward the football field.

Outside the entrance is a bunch of signs announcing a food drive. My girl Jordan is a giving soul, so it doesn't surprise me that she is donating to a canned food drive, but why am I here?

"Is this the fun thing you wanted to do for my birthday?" I ask.

She gives me a shit-eating grin and wags her eyebrows at me. "Yup."

"You're making me nervous." I glance around, looking for some clue as to what she wants me here for. What is so exciting about a food drive?

My eyes zero in on some news vans. Okay, that's not too weird. More publicity means more people will come out and donate, which means more people will be helped. I scan the crowd and don't see anyone that I recognize, but are there more Thunderbolt jerseys than normal? Like, a lot more? The team is based in San Diego, but we have a big fan base here, so seeing the team's T-shirts or hats is common, but this is almost everyone. What the hell?

As we get closer to the field, I overhear someone say something about getting a signature from the quarterback Ryan Thomas.

Oh no.

My heart starts pounding, and my skin chills even though we're standing in the sun. I wipe my palms on my jeans to get rid of the clammy feeling.

I can't see Asher. I fucking can't.

There's a pressure on my chest, and my hands start to shake as Jordan pulls me forward. Buzzing in my ears blocks out whatever is being said around me, overwhelming my head until I want to scream.

"I can't—" Every muscle in my body is screaming with tension and the urge to run. I can't breathe.

"Elliot." Jordan's voice cuts through the panic just enough for me to hear it but not enough to respond.

My arms are wrapped around my torso as I rock and shake my head. *Make it stop. Just let me breathe. Please.*

I can't see *him*. I can't do it. Face the man who ripped my heart out and left it on the floor to rot. I was forced to pick up the tattered shreds he left and stitch myself back together. I can't do it again. I'm not strong enough.

Home. Get home. Home safe. Safe. Need safe.

I clench my eyes closed, trying to stop some of the overwhelming input flooding my brain. My knees give, and I drop into a crouch, wrapping my arms around my head to block out the onslaught of torment.

Asher. Not Asher. Safe. No.

Pain. Asher hurts.

Asher comforts.

Asher isn't safe anymore.

"Eli?" That name in that voice is a physical blow to my body that I recoil from. Only two people in the world have ever called me that, and one of them is dead. The fragile scars the other one left on my heart rip open to bleed at my feet because he won't stay, and I never got over him.

Strong arms surround me, so different but so familiar. A chest that's bigger, harder than I knew but still holding a flame that could never be a stranger. Too weak to fight the desire, I cling to him. My arms circle around his neck, my face buried in the warm softness of his throat, and my legs wrapping around his body. He holds me just as tightly, and for a second, I'm a child again. Desperate for my parents to show some kind of interest in my life.

"Hey, sweet boy. You're okay." His calm voice in my ear makes me sob. It's everything I've needed in the years since he left. I hate him for it. I hate myself for how quickly I let him take control of me. He was my home. My safety. My comfort. But he took it away and left me to fend for myself at seventeen, heartbroken, mourning, and lost. I loved him more than I loved myself or my brother, and he walked away with nothing but a fucking text.

With me wrapped around his body, clinging to him like the headcase I am, he lifts me and walks us somewhere. I don't look to see where we're going. It doesn't matter. For just a second, I allow myself to be consumed by his warmth, to let myself accept his comfort. He's so familiar. He's home. Most of my life, Asher protected me, and falling back into it is second nature.

How did we get here? How is this my life? I loved him so completely, and now I can't even see him without falling apart. When he left, I was able to shove him behind a door in my head. I buried my feelings and memories, but they've been ripped out so violently I can't put them back because my emotions are like water escaping my fingers as I desperately try to scoop them back in the box.

But it's useless.

I'm sure the gossip rags will be all over this, spreading more rumors and blasting my mental instability on the front page. Probably print that I'm fucking Asher because how else would we be this physically comfortable with each other. They'll dig up our family's connection, rehash my brother's death, and splash our pictures everywhere. Once again, I won't be able to hide from him.

Fuck!

Immediately, I'm struggling against him. Shoving against his chest and trying to get my feet to the ground.

"Put me down!" I yell louder than I should.

"Whoa, whoa. Eli, you're okay. Relax." He scoops me back up with an arm under my ass and one huge hand splayed on my back to keep me against him.

"He said let him go!" Jordan demands, probably standing in front of Asher to make him stop walking.

"He's in the middle of a panic attack—"

"You think I don't know that? Who do you think usually

helps him? He doesn't like to be touched when he's freaked out. Put. Him. Down." That tone in her voice is dangerous. She's about to fuck shit up; even in my half-out-of-it head, I know that.

I push against him again, but he tightens his arms around me. It rips my heart open how easily he fell back into comforting me. No hesitation, just accepted me wrapping myself around him like no time has passed. How desperately I wish that were true.

"You're safe, Eli. Deep breaths, it's okay." His tone is soft and soothing as his lips brush over my ear when he speaks. A shudder zings up my spine, and it takes all the strength I have left to not melt into him. Angry tears well up in my eyes, and my throat clogs at how hard I have to fight this.

"Put me down," I say more calmly this time. "There are reporters."

Forcing myself to pull my face from his skin, I put as much space between us as I can while he's holding me against him.

"Now. Vaughn," Jordan demands.

Asher looks at me, but I can't lift my head to meet his eyes, choosing to stare at the button of his Thunderbolts polo. His lips brush my forehead, and a tear streaks down my face. The emotions clogging my throat burn with the need to break down again.

My feet touch the ground, and I scramble back away from him, putting Jordan between us. With my head ducked, I gaze around us to see we're under a pop-up tent with some kind of temporary wall shielding us from the public. I quickly wipe at my face.

"You lied to me." Jordan steps right up into Asher's space

and shoves him back a step. A flash of surprise crosses his face, clearly caught off guard since she was able to move him. She's tiny compared to him, but she's furious. "You didn't tell me he was terrified of you. If I had even an inkling, I never would have brought him! Stay away from him! It's his fucking birthday!"

My arms wrap around my middle again, needing to be held, and chew on my inner lip.

Asher crosses his thick arms and raises an eyebrow at her. "You think I don't know it's his birthday? I've known him since he was seven."

"Yet the only thing he's ever mentioned about you is that you were his brother's friend," she throws back. "I've been friends with him for years, and I've never seen you around, heard about you calling or texting or hanging out. Nothing. You don't know shit about him anymore."

Asher squares his shoulders and looks down at her with a look that oozes intimidation, but Jordan is so used to it that it doesn't faze her.

"My relationship with Eli is none of your business." His growl sends shivers up my spine.

"Stop calling me that," I snap, finding some of my backbone. "You lost the right to call me that when you left."

Asher's eyes flick over to meet mine.

"I want to go home, Jordan." My eyes stay on Asher's. "There's nothing for me here."

One of his eyes twitches at my words.

Good. I hope it hurts. I shouldn't be the only one maimed by his abandonment.

"Absolutely." Jordan grabs my hand and pulls me from the shelter.

Reporters are waiting for us, yelling questions about how I know Asher Vaughn and if I'm in a secret relationship with him. Jordan pushes right through them, pulling me along with her, completely ignoring the mess of people. At the car, she opens my door and closes it for me before climbing into the driver's seat.

She gets us away from the school before she speaks, but I know the questions are coming. My foot is bouncing as I lean my forehead against the glass and focus on my breathing.

Calm. Slow inhale. Controlled exhale.

"So, you really *know* Asher Vaughn."

My phone buzzes in my pocket. My best guess is it's Asher, and I can't with him right now. I can't even be in my own head right now, dealing with the tornado that just unearthed the disfigured crater where my soul used to live. The sunlight that once hummed through my veins is now nothing but empty darkness with monsters living in the deep shadows.

I miss who I was.

Three

ELLIOTT

In my apartment, Jordan sits on the couch and pulls my head into her lap, running her hands through my hair. A single tear slips from my eye and soaks into her jean-clad thigh.

"Tell me about him," she says softly.

I close my eyes and let out a shuddering breath.

"I loved him." My voice is broken and sad, even to my own ears. I don't think I've ever said those words out loud. At least not where anyone could hear me. It forces light onto the wreckage inside my rib cage. My heart beats in an irregular pattern of scar tissue and broken heartstrings that never healed. I'm so tired of hurting. Of hiding it.

Jordan's nails scrape lightly over my scalp, setting off chills across my skin.

"I'm sorry I ruined your birthday."

I shake my head as much as I can with my face against her leg. "You didn't. It's the thought that counts."

"He lied to me." She takes a deep breath, and from the

movement of her body, she dropped her head back onto the couch. "He sent me a message on Insta, told me he was going to be in the area on your birthday, and surprising you would be the best present. Looking back, he was either vague or just gave me bullshit answers to the questions I asked, but this picture kind of sealed the deal for me." She lifts her phone and finds something before showing me a picture.

My hand covers my mouth as I look at the smiling faces of Marcus, Asher, and me just a few weeks before my life flipped upside down. I remember when he took that picture out at the cliff. It was so hot that day, and my parents had come back to town for a while, so there were people everywhere at the house. It was loud and crowded, so we left to get away from it.

Marcus has his arm around my shoulders with his tongue hanging out, Asher ducked down in front of us with that devastating smile. Our eyes had met on the screen just as he hit the shutter button. It's clear in this image how much I loved him. It was etched into my face, but I'm not sure I see it in his. Was he faking it? Was he just better at hiding it than I was?

I thought I had run out of tears for him, but apparently not. The knot in my throat grows until I can't breathe as I sit up and hold her phone in my hand, staring at the screen through bleary eyes.

"I looked him up, did some research to make sure there hadn't been a big falling out, but any time he mentioned your family in interviews, it was good. He obviously loved your family, and it sounded like you had just grown apart when life got busy." Jordan puts her arm over my shoulder and pulls my head to hers so her forehead rests against my temple. "I'm so sorry, Elliot."

"Don't be sorry. It's my fault for not telling you the whole truth."

"Can you tell me now?" Her breath tickles my cheek.

I give her the phone back and move out of her hold, needing the space to tell her the story. "He was my brother's best friend. His family moved in next to us when I was seven; he and Marcus were ten. My parents weren't around much, chasing their dreams of being famous, so we were left with nannies." I drop my head back onto the couch and stare at the ceiling. "Asher's mom was amazing and had us over all the time, but we were also left alone a lot after she died a few years later. Marcus and Asher raised me more than anyone else." I suck in a deep breath and hold it for a second, the pressure on my chest so fucking tight I rub at it with the heel of my hand.

"On New Year's when I was sixteen, he kissed me at midnight." A tear slips out to trail into my hair. Jordan reaches for my hand and gives me an encouraging squeeze. "After that, we had these little stolen moments when Marcus was distracted and Asher was home from school. He came home for a while during the summer before camp started for his third year. We spent every day together, sneaking kisses and quick make-out sessions. About a week before he was supposed to go back to school, we were out at our favorite spot at the lake, and I left early to hang out with some friends. He walked me to my car, kissed me, and I never saw him or Marcus again."

"Jesus," Jordan whispers, running her hand through her bright pink hair. "That's awful."

All I can do is nod as I chew on my lip, trying so hard to keep the memories from overwhelming me.

"Why don't we watch a movie, eat some junk food, or order lunch?"

Doing nothing sounds absolutely amazing. But I don't want company.

I nod at her anyway, and she finds the remote for the TV. She browses the different streaming services and decides on *Spiderman* with Andrew Garfield. I have to admit that it's not hard to watch him in that tight suit. Looking around, I find a blanket on the floor and wrap it around myself, kick my shoes off, and curl up against the arm of the couch.

"Are you hungry?" Jordan asks about halfway through the movie.

"Sure." I shrug.

She eyes me but calls a little pizza place we like down the street from my apartment. She knows the way to my heart and orders a pepperoni and pineapple pizza.

Warm and semi comfortable, I fall asleep in the safety of my apartment.

When I wake up, the apartment is dark and the TV is off. I sit up and look around, but Jordan is gone, and now I feel like a dick. She just wanted to spend my birthday with me, and I ruined it.

Guilt eats at me as I stand and see the light over the stove on with a note. Padding across the cold wood floor, I see the oven is on a very low temperature. Jordan put my pizza in there to stay warm for me, and apparently put the fixings for strawberry shortcake in the fridge. My favorite dessert.

I shut off the oven but don't pull the pizza out. I'm not hungry. Leaning against the oven handle, I look around my apartment and notice she cleaned as well. God, I'm a lazy piece of shit. What a shitty friend I am. Why does she even stick around? What can she possibly be getting out of this friendship?

Grabbing my phone from the counter where I dropped it when I walked in, I turn it on, and it buzzes with notifications. A few happy birthday texts, about a dozen missed calls from Asher, and ten texts from him as well. I clear all of them without looking at them and text Jordan.

ELLIOT

I'm sorry I fell asleep.

She immediately responds.

JORDAN

It's all good, sweets, I'm glad you got some rest. Are you in for the night, or do you want to meet up somewhere?

I need out of my head, an escape, and I can't do that when I'm with her, so I lie to her, and the guilt just keeps packing on.

ELLIOT

I think I'm in for the night. Thank you for everything today.

JORDAN

I wish it had worked out better, but you're welcome.

Flipping to another text thread, I find Colin.

ELLIOT

Meet me at the club?

I slide the phone into my pocket and make my way to the bathroom to freshen up while I wait for him to respond. Fucking Colin. I dislike him as a human, but he works for what I need. A quick fuck to get off without strings or questions. He's a selfish prick, but over the years, I've learned how to use him to get what I want when I need it. It's been months since I reached out and wanted anything from him, months since I went out to a bar. Fuck, going out with Jordan last night was the first time I left my apartment in weeks in general. After I put on fresh deodorant and spray some cologne on, my phone buzzes in my pocket. I check the message without looking to see who it is.

ASHER

Eli, please talk to me.

My heart rate skyrockets as the frigid waters of dread crash over me. I need to get over this. I can't let seeing his name have this effect on me anymore. A text comes through from Colin with just a thumbs-up, and I finish getting ready.

Can I get out without having a babysitter follow me? They leave me alone if I'm with Jordan, but the damn security guards hound me when I'm alone.

A smirk lifts one side of my lips at the idea of dodging them and making them come find me. It's been a while since I've really messed with them, and tonight, I have no fucks left to give. I need to stop feeling, and I know just where to find that.

Four

ASHER

E li melting down is not how I expected to see him for the first time in six years. I've missed him every fucking day. Hated myself for walking away, but I had to. He deserves better than who I was, and I can't ask him to hide who he is for my career. While the world is getting more accepting, it only takes one convincing homophobe to turn a locker room toxic. Mob mentally takes over, and I would be attacked, either physically or mentally, and they would fuck with me on the field. I can't afford that.

Luckily, our team staff was able to get the situation with the reporters under control really quickly, telling them it was a fan who had a panic attack, nothing to write home about. I'm sure there were some actual fans who saw it or even recorded it; my boy having a meltdown and wrapping himself around me. I'm hoping for once they keep it to themselves. It's doubtful, but nothing has gone viral or been brought to my attention yet.

I wasn't expecting my career to take off as soon as it did.

My rookie year, the team was crippled by injuries and left without many options, so I was sent out to play. And I kicked ass. I've been kicking ass since. For four years, I've been better than the year before. I know my time is limited, and at some point, my body will give out or I'll get injured, and it'll all be over. I'm doing everything I can to be smart and stay in shape, but every year that I have to hide who I am is harder to swallow than the last.

I identify as bi, but I've never had anyone make me feel the way Eli does. It's only ever been Eli. Like I'm Eli-sexual or something. I've known since I was thirteen that he was it for me. While I find some men physically attractive, I don't let myself explore it. I guess it's my punishment for leaving. I don't allow myself to have what I could have had with him.

It gutted me to go, to not answer his calls or texts, but I'm the reason his brother is dead. I couldn't tell him that. I couldn't take the look on his face when he realized it was my fault.

If I'm being really honest with myself, tonight I wanted to touch him before I told him about Marcus. I lost a boy I considered my brother that night, my best friend, and I had to walk away from the boy who filled the cracks in my soul with his goodness and light.

I've ruined him. Today was proof of that. I've never seen him like that, so broken. Add that to the list of things I've fucked up.

Staring out the bus window on our way back to San Diego, my knee is bouncing while I replay the few minutes I had with him through my head on repeat. The way he clung to me.

"Hey." My teammate, Aaron, bumps my knee, and I pull my AirPod out of my ear.

"What?" I snap at him, though it's not his fault I'm angry.

"Who was the chick today?"

"Jordan? She's friends with someone I used to know." The confused look on his face has me stopping from putting the pod back in my ear. "What?"

"Not the pink-haired chick, the one who wrapped themselves around you like an octopus."

I blink at him for a minute. Do I lie and let him believe it was a girl, or do I correct him and have him question my sexuality? The locker room isn't too bad with homosexual bias, but it isn't exactly queer-friendly either. I've worked very hard to keep a straight image, to not give anyone a reason to question it.

He looks at me expectantly, and even though it physically hurts, the words fall from my lips so much easier than they should.

"El," I tell him and hate myself for it. "Been a long time since we saw each other."

He nods. "She live in LA? You should send her tickets for a game." I have to force myself not to cringe at the misgendering of Eli. Shame turns my stomach sour, and I work to keep it off my face.

"Good idea," I tell him and turn back to my phone to hide the guilt and anger coursing through me. I need to get fucked up tonight, or I'm going to explode.

"You ever get with her?" Aaron asks a few minutes later.

"What? Why?" Dread sinks into my stomach like a lead weight. Even I can tell my eyes are too wide.

"Every girl I've seen you go after looks like her. Slim,

curly blonde hair." He shrugs and watches me as I stumble over that bomb he just dropped.

Do I really do that? Yeah, I like small blonde girls, but it has nothing to do with Eli. *Does it?*

"I've never thought about it, I guess," I finally answer. In my head, I flip through the girls I remember, and fuck if he isn't right. It's rare for me to date anyone who doesn't look like him. Slim, not curvy, curly light hair. *Fuck.*

As the bus makes its way down the freeway, I pick apart that fact and hate myself a little more. Since I couldn't have him, I found girls who looked like him. They were as close to him as I could get, probably another way to punish myself.

More times than I want to admit, I think about him while I fuck them too.

I scrub a hand down my face and send another text message to Eli.

ASHER

Eli, please talk to me.

The icon updates, saying it's been read, but he doesn't respond. Goddamn it!

By the time we get back to town, I'm ashamed, angry, and looking for an outlet. From the field where the buses drop us off, I head home to drown in liquor. Aaron offered to hang, but I told him I wasn't in the mood. Which I'm not. I need to figure out my fucking life and find a way to get Eli to talk to me.

It doesn't take me long after I get home and find the bottom of a bottle of scotch. It wasn't full, and there wasn't enough in it to get drunk but enough to get a good buzz going.

I swear I keep getting whiffs of the scent of his hair, that almost-there smell, just enough to make me turn my head to look for him.

I need out of the house. Sliding my shoes on, I leave the building to go for a walk. It's what we did growing up when we needed to work something out. We went swimming, hiking, or walking. Used physical exertion to clear the fog from our heads and find the answer or make a plan.

The sun is setting over the horizon, turning the sky pink and purple when I find myself at a bar I didn't know was here. How far did I walk? It's a smaller space, tucked into a little shopping center with a dentist's office on one side. There aren't many people inside, so I head to the bar and wait while the bartender finishes up with his customer.

"Oh hey." He smiles when he recognizes me. "What can I get you, man?"

"What have you got for good tequila?" Should I be drinking tequila? Not a fucking chance. Do I have to work out tomorrow? Yup. Am I going to be hungover and miserable? Most definitely.

"I've got a Don Julio 1942," he says, pointing to the bottle on the top shelf.

"That'll work. Neat, three fingers."

He grabs the bottle, pours the drink, and takes my debit card to run. That's not a cheap drink, and honestly, I'm surprised this tiny bar even has it. I was expecting Patrón.

Grabbing the glass, I find a stool at the end of the bar and torture myself by flipping through Jordan's Instagram to find pictures of Eli while I take a drink of the liquor. He has an account but doesn't use it. I stumbled across hers by accident when I was searching for her dad's band. She has pictures of her and Eli, and I messaged her. I needed to know something about his life. To know he was okay. Before I realized it, I was convincing her to surprise him with coming to see me, and I'm a grade-A asshole for it.

I hate the dark circles around his eyes in these pictures, the forced smiles he's trying so hard to hide behind.

I swallow the last mouthful of the tequila and set my glass on the bartop. The warmth of the liquor hits my empty stomach and unravels through my body until my head is almost fuzzy. I keep scrolling through the fucking app, a glutton for punishment.

Needing to piss, I head to the bathroom and come face to face with a dude in a black T-shirt and board shorts. He sways a bit toward me, caught off guard by the door opening.

"Are you? Uh." He staggers again, and I give him a hard stare. "Are you Vaughn?"

I let out a sigh, not wanting to deal with whatever this is. I'm not in the mood to put on a smile for a fan or keep it cool with a hater.

"Yes, excuse me." I try to push past him into the bathroom, but he moves to block me. I stand at my full height, a good four inches taller than him, but he's too drunk or too stupid to recognize the warning signs.

"Why are they calling you the best?" he scoffs, and I clench my fists to keep from ripping his head off. I've already been in a few fights this off-season, and my agent will murder me if I get into another one. Not to mention what the team will do if I'm in the headlines for another bar fight.

"Since I'm not the one saying it, I don't know. Now—" I shove past him. "Excuse me."

He grabs me, and I've had it.

"Don't fucking touch me," I growl at him. "Get the fuck away from me."

"What are you gonna do?" He tries to pull himself straight but fails. "You're just an over-hyped pussy."

My fist connects with his face before I've thought it all the way through. The tequila making me more impulsive and quick-tempered. I fucking knew better, but it's too late now.

He goes down quickly, barely protecting himself since his reflexes are shit at this point. But my rage-filled muscles don't care, I hit him again and again until someone pulls me off. I'm shoved into the wall, and my body sags against the cold tile.

Fuck.

The bathroom is swarmed with people, someone yells about calling an ambulance, and I close my eyes and knock my head against the wall. My hands ache, and something trickles down my chin. Swiping at it, I look at my hand to find blood.

Did he get a hit in?

Turning to look in the mirror, I find my lip bleeding, but I can't tell how bad it is from here. I don't remember him hitting me, but obviously he did.

I need to get out of here before I'm handed my ass by the team. Fucking shit.

Five

ELLIOTT

The bass pumping through the speakers pulses in my body as I move to the music. Alcohol and cocaine flowing through me and most of the crowd in this nightclub. It's my escape just like everyone else who indulges. A way to hide from the real world, to get lost in the false narrative that's a happier place. No pain or past or trauma. Just this moment.

A warm, strong body presses against my back as a husky voice hollers in my ear over the music. "Bathroom, five minutes."

Colin. He's one of the safe ones. Sort of.

We've fucked more times than I can count, and he's discreet while not becoming a stage-five clinger. All the boxes are checked, and I'm able to get my rocks off. If only he liked it when I wore a skirt. I love short skirts and sexy panties, but I can't wear that here, in the open.

I lift the beer bottle in my hand to my lips and take a

drink, a secret code we've developed over the years that lets him know I heard him.

Not long after Asher disappeared and Marcus was buried, I stopped hiding who I was from the public. I'm more lenient about what I wear, dressing more feminine with lace and pearls, but skirts stay inside, and no one has seen them besides Jordan. I wear what I want, when I want, am seen with who I want to be seen with, and fuck the media. Now I make a scene when I go out just for the hell of it. Dance on tables, fuck up hotel rooms, I don't care. Nothing matters. I'm unloved and I have no one left to disappoint, so who cares what I do?

I stumble my way toward the bathroom and trip over my own feet when I push the door open, but Colin is there and catches me, so I don't face-plant on the disgusting floor. My skin hums with my high, tingly and warm and happy.

"You're a mess tonight," Colin says with a chastising tone, but my addled brain isn't offended.

"Make me a bigger mess." I rub myself against him like a cat in heat. It's not far from the truth. Cocaine makes me horny, makes me hungry for an orgasm, but I can already feel the crash coming. The apathy of not being fulfilled by the life I've been living tinging the edges of my high.

"Jesus." He grabs my arm and pulls me back into the hallway and out into the alleyway behind the club. My back hits the brick wall, and Colin's lips brush against my neck. I reach for his head and try to pull his mouth to mine, but he dodges me. I love kisses, and he knows it, but he's an asshole and doesn't give them to me.

His hands are on my too tight jeans, pulling them open and shoving them down. I'm on the verge of coming already just from the hum of the drugs and the way he manhandles me.

This is what I need. To be used. For a few minutes I'm wanted. There's no one in my life that needs me for anything else. I'm the "throw away friend" or the "after-thought friend". No one cares what I'm doing or where I go, no one except the media, that is. They love to post pictures and videos of me stumbling out of clubs, grabbing lunch by my-fucking-self, and contemplating why I'm not dating. Don't they get it? I'm not worth dating.

Colin spins me, and my face hits the brick since my reflexes are shit. He chuckles and steps in close, sliding his fingers between my ass cheeks and finding my hole already lubed.

"You're such a little whore," he growls in my ear with his hand around my throat. "Did you already get fucked tonight?"

I whimper as I shake my head.

"Hmm. You prepped for me?" I can feel his lips smiling against my skin as he slides two fingers into me, thrusting a few times before he drags his cock between my cheeks.

"Yessss," I hiss as he pushes in, one of his hands gripping my hip. A shudder makes my body tremble, and I reach for my dick.

"You're such a slut." Colin fucks me quickly, needing to get us out of this alley sooner rather than later and not wanting to spend more time with me than he needs to get off.

Colin grunts in my ear, and his thrusts speed up. I jerk myself faster, coming with a tremor, and spray my orgasm on the brick. My ass clenches around him, and he comes with a muffled moan. His mouth is suctioned to my neck, and I sag in his arms, just wanting to be held for a few minutes longer, but he pulls out and zips up. I lean heavily against the wall and pull my clothes back on correctly, watching him walk away without a backward glance. He never gives me a second glance.

Why do I keep doing this?

It takes longer than it should to get my pants buttoned, but somehow, I manage it and shuffle my way out of the alley to get an Uber.

"Elliot!" My bodyguard, Ian, catches my arm and pulls me back into the alley. "What the fuck? I can't protect you if you disappear on me."

"I don't need a babysitter!" I shove at him, but the wall of muscle doesn't budge. Bastard. "My parents pay you to keep me out of trouble, not to protect me! Fuck off!"

"Jesus. You're wasted already, and it's not even midnight." The brute of a man scrubs a hand down his face, pulls his phone from his pocket, and types out a message.

Tears fill my eyes, but he ignores them. That's fine. I don't really want him to acknowledge my weakness anyway.

"It's time to go home," he says in a tone that means business. Luckily for him, I just want to go home, so I don't fight him. A black car appears on the street next to us, and he ushers me inside. The warm, tan leather surrounds me, and I wish I could fall asleep, but the high of the drugs means I can't. Not yet.

"Your parents are going to cut you off. You realize that, right?" Ian says from the front passenger seat. The driver looks in the rearview mirror, his eyes meeting mine for just a minute. I think he's driven me before, but I don't care enough to figure it out. I have zero direction in my life. No plans or ideas of what I want to do when I grow up. Honestly, I don't know that I will live that long.

"Like you give a shit." The words tumble from my lips as the car starts moving.

"I do give a shit. Not only is it my job to care, but I'm also a half-decent person." He looks at the door I'm sitting next to. "Hydrate."

The streetlights illuminate a bottle of water in the cupholder in the door. I reach for it and chug half the bottle, wiping away the dribble that leaks from the side of my mouth with the back of my hand.

My gaze swings back to Ian, but all I can see is the dark hair he keeps in a short military cut and his massive arm.

Memories flood my head. Marcus, Asher, and I at our little hideout spot on the cliff. Road trips to the desert, listening to comedians in the car, and laughing until our stomachs hurt. Stolen moments with Asher, baking cookies for him, sleepovers in the media room at my parents' house. A life that was ripped away from me in a single night.

My brother's dead, and my first love disappeared at the same time.

Closing my eyes, I lift the bottle and take a deep pull from it with tears trailing down my face.

I hate my life.

The only person who loved me left. I don't even know what happened to Marcus. The police report said someone called in a drowning. Asher sent me a text message that just said, "I'm sorry," then nothing except for birthday and Christmas texts, which I refuse to respond to. What is he sorry for? Not having the answer still haunts me. But it doesn't stop me from stalking his career, watching his games and interviews. I hate him, but I can't stop myself from wondering if he thinks about me. If he regrets the way he disappeared on me.

The driver pulls into the underground parking garage of my building and stops next to the elevator. Ian gets out, the big man making me feel like a child next to him, opens my door, and hits the button to call the elevator. The car pulls away, and I assume the driver is going to park, then disappear into the security apartment that my parents pay for. He's not my problem.

"You need to be more careful before one of the vultures gets pictures of you that puts you back on your parents' radar." Ian stands in the small space with me, our reflection staring back at us in the perfectly polished mirrored walls. Despite the long black sleeves of his button-up shirt, I can see peeks of ink poking out at the wrists and collar. He hasn't been following me around for very long, six months maybe. Pretty sure that's a record.

Since Marcus died, my parents stuck me with a babysitter, and I've made it my life's mission to get them to quit. I guess I'm losing my touch.

The doors slide open, and I walk away from the hulking man with a body that screams military and badass. The exact opposite of me. Maybe if I had joined the military or gone to college, my parents would be proud of me or care at all. I unlock my door and close it in Ian's face. I don't have the energy for him tonight.

"Good night, babysitter!" I yell through the door with my back leaned against it. I can hear him sigh and walk away. With an exhausted breath, I drop my keys on the counter and head toward my room to shower. I toss my phone on the unmade bed and strip my clothes off before fumbling my way into the connected bathroom. I've lived in this apartment since I turned eighteen and haven't changed anything. The walls in my room are dark blue with white trim, the bed a tangled mess of blue sheets and what used to be a white comforter. I don't care enough to buy a new one.

There's no motivation in my body to take care of anything anymore. Not even my kitchen, which used to be my pride and joy. Cooking made me happy, but who do I have to cook for now? My kitchen is a mess of crumbs and take-out trash.

When did Jordan say the cleaner comes again?

It just makes me more aware of being completely alone.

The water pounds in the glass-walled shower, steam billowing from it. I slide the door open and step inside, dropping to the pebbled stone floor and letting it beat some heat into my chilled body. What's the point? With one arm around my knees, pressing into my chest, my other hand finds the scars on my inner thigh and traces them. It's been a while since I added another tally to my body. The need haunts the back of my subconscious, but it's not overwhelming. Yet. I could do it, cut my skin and watch it bleed, but I don't *need* it. Not yet.

I drop my head back against the wall, the water hitting me in the chest and running down my body. It takes a while, but the heat seeps in, and I'm able to relax enough to possibly sleep. I manage to force myself off the floor of the shower and find a towel. All the energy I had is gone, so I do a shitty job of drying off and fall face first onto my mattress.

Six

ASHER

Sweat drips down my face, making my beard itch as I do the damn burpees that I hate so fucking much. Jump. Drop to the floor. Push-up. Up into a jump. Over and over. My home gym gets a lot of use in the off-season, and today is no exception. With training camp coming up, I need to push my workouts harder so I can keep up. I'm sure my downstairs neighbors hate me, but I really don't give a fuck.

The bruises on my knuckles from the fight yesterday ache every time my hands hit the ground. The split in my lip pulls as I breathe. Fuck that guy.

I ended up spending a night in jail but was released this morning. My agent pulled whatever fucking magic he does and is not happy with me, but look how much I don't give a shit.

Breaking Benjamin blasts in my ears as I push my body to keep going. To use the anger at being called an over-hyped pussy by some asshole in a bar for something productive.

Air is rushing in and out of my lungs as I start my last set. I'm halfway through a push-up when the overhead lights flash.

Great. My fucking agent is here, probably to yell at me for being a testosterone-driven dumbass.

I get up and pull my AirPods out of my ears, breathing hard as I reach for a water bottle.

"Are you trying to get fired? Traded?" The buzzkill in a suit has his arms folded, and if looks could kill, I would be bloody on the floor. He fucking hates me, but I pay him to put up with me, so he does. The slim redhead has his own explosive temper when he's behind closed doors.

I wipe the sweat from my face before I respond. "Dude had it coming."

"He's in the hospital with a concussion and broken cheekbone!" Franklin yells. "You broke his face!"

Okay, that was probably overkill.

"Oops."

"You're going to be the death of me. Do you have any idea the shitstorm that's just fell into my lap because of this?" He storms over to me and slaps my chest with a newspaper. The headline reads ASHER VAUGHN IS OUT OF CONTROL with a picture of an ambulance outside of the bar I was at last night.

"Look, dudes with bones made of glass should keep their fucking mouths shut." I should probably feel bad for this, but I don't. "We all have problems, and just because money isn't mine doesn't mean I'm an easy target. Dude ran his mouth to the wrong person at the wrong time."

"You're going to Black Diamond to stay out of the spot-light, or the team is trading you." The fury coursing through him almost makes him vibrate. "The story is you're going for anger management. You're welcome."

I lift an eyebrow. "What am I supposed to be thanking you for, exactly?" I toss the newspaper aside and stare him down.

"I convinced the team to allow you another chance if you went away quietly for a few weeks and came back with a better attitude. You won't get that chance again, so don't fuck it up or you can find yourself another agent as well." He storms out of the gym, and I can't help myself from watching his ass as he goes.

Knock it off.

I shake my head and turn away from the surprisingly round globes of my agent's ass and stare at myself in the mirror. I need to get my shit together.

Forcing myself to the shower, I strip out of my sweaty clothes and blast the hot water. Today I allow myself to indulge in my guilty pleasure: thinking about Eli.

His sweet face and unruly golden curls as he shoots me a secret smile where Marcus couldn't see him. I shouldn't have wanted him. He was my best friend's little brother. A boy I helped take care of and raise even though he was only three years younger than me. My mom loved them, Marcus and Eli.

Even she left them, though. Left me. I'm alone now too, and it fucking hurts. Having to wear this fake persona when I leave the house. Pretend like the only emotion I have anymore isn't anger. I'm tired. Tired of hiding. Tired of running.

Wrapping my hand around my dick, I picture Eli. His slim frame pressed against me in the pantry of his parents' kitchen, his lips working mine just as aggressively as I did his. Him being smaller than me fulfilled some part of me that no one else ever has. He's the only boy I've ever touched, and I still crave him six years later. I knew he would keep my secret.

Now I can't imagine the scandal that would unfold if I were caught with a man. The team might just cut me loose, pay out my contract just to get rid of me.

I squeeze my eyes tight, remembering Eli and imagining the things we didn't get to experience. What it would feel like to sink into him, hear him moan my name. My cock pulses in my hand as I work myself over. Tingles have goose bumps breaking out across my skin as my orgasm hits, leaving me shuddering and weak.

Enough. Man up.

Leaning both palms on the wall of the shower, I breathe deeply and clear my head. Eli is a dream I can't ever have. Wishing my circumstances were different won't get me anywhere. Setting my shoulders, I turn off the water and dry off before heading to my bedroom to pack. It's bullshit that I have to go, but Black Diamond isn't the worst place to be sent to. I'll miss some of the organized team activities, but I'm sure I'll be back by the time training camp starts.

I pull on some underwear and grab a suitcase, shoving clothes, headphones, my toiletries, laptop, and chargers into it before zipping it closed. Knowing Franklin, I'm sure there's an itinerary already printed out and ready to go. My flight will have been booked for some time in the next two days as well.

I should call my dad.

Why? He never notices when you don't call.

With a bone-weary huff, I pull up my old man's office number and call his secretary. There's no point in calling his cell phone, he won't answer it.

"Good afternoon, Mathew Vaughn's office. Alice speaking." The no-nonsense voice of the woman who's worked for him since my mom was alive comes across the line.

"Good afternoon, Alice. How's the old man?" Honestly, I speak to her more often than I do to my father. He rarely accepts my calls these last few years.

"Asher, how are you? He's busy as usual and as cranky as the day is long," she says, but I can hear her nails clicking on the keyboard as she multitasks to keep up with him.

"I just wanted to let him know I'll be out of the country for a month or so. If he needs me for something, email will probably be the best bet since he doesn't text." I try to keep the frustration out of my voice, but I'm sure she heard it anyway.

"I see," she says in that disappointed tone that never fails to leave me feeling chastised. "Your father had some choice things to say about last night's situation."

I carry my bag to the front door and look around for the flight information I'm sure is here somewhere.

"I'm sure he did, yet he didn't call to make sure his only son was all right. Didn't reach out to see if I needed anything or even to call me a dumbass." I find the folder with the information for Black Diamond and my travel plans. Looking at my phone quickly to see what time it is, I curse. "I'm sorry to cut this short but I have to go. I'm flying out in a few hours."

"I'll pass the message on to your father. Safe travels."

The call ends, and I shove my phone into my pocket before racing back to my room for a shirt and shoes. Fucking Franklin. He could have given me some goddamn warning.

I pull a T-shirt on, find some jeans, and slide my shoes on. I grab a sideline hat that's light blue and yellow with the team logo on it and head downstairs. I pull up the app to call an Uber to take me to the airport but stop short when Franklin's BMW X5 is parked in front of my building. Walking over, I open the passenger door of the black car and lean down to look at him.

"What are you doing here still?"

He lifts a carefully manicured eyebrow at me. "Making sure you get to the airport."

"You're babysitting me."

He nods. "Yes. Put your bag in the back, let's go. Traffic on the 15 is going to slow us down."

I roll my eyes but put my bag in the back seat and climb in.

As I sit in the silence of the car, I scroll through my phone and immediately am bombarded with videos and articles of Elliot Cushings having sex in an alley behind a gay bar.

What. The. Actual. Fuck.

Even though I know I shouldn't, I don't hesitate to click on the first link and find the video. While the camera isn't the best quality, I can see it's him. With his face against the wall, pants around his knees, and some asshole pumping against his ass. I'm furious.

I have no fucking right to be, but I am. Fist clenching,

face flushing, angry. I want to punch someone, namely that fuckhead who's got his dick in my boy.

He hasn't been yours in years.

That fact doesn't fucking matter. Who the hell is this guy? Is this the type of shit Eli is into these days? Semi-public sex with strangers? The dude finishes and quickly pulls out, does up his pants, and leaves Eli there alone. I don't need a crystal-clear picture to see the hurt on his face before he turns his head to watch that prick walk away.

"What? You aren't about to go on a face-breaking rampage, are you?" Franklin's question pulls me away from the video, and I shut my screen off to stare out the window with my teeth clenched and my knee bouncing.

"Hello? Earth to Asher? What's your problem now?" My annoying agent waves his hand in front of me.

"None of your business," I snap.

"With all the trouble you're in right now, and me being the one trying to save your ass, *everything* in your life is my business. Out with it," Franklin snaps.

Seeing a leaked video of Eli shouldn't affect you that badly. You left him. Get your shit together.

"Nothing to do with me," I bite out, bitter that it's true. Sometimes I wish I could go back to that last summer and relive it, even though it ended in the worst possible way.

We drive through Little Italy and past the marina on our way to the airport. From this angle it looks like the planes are almost touching the water when they land.

Franklin drops me off in front of the airport, and I get my bag checked for the flight, then through security. It's busy enough that not too many people hound me, but a few ask for a picture or an autograph. I'm not in the headspace for it, but I do it anyway so I don't have to hear Franklin bitch at me for being rude to fans later.

Seven

ELLIOTT

My phone will not fuck off. The noise won't stop.

Jesus. Fucking. Christ.

My head is pounding, my body aches, and I may throw up. It's fine. This is fine.

Why do I keep doing this to myself? It's so fun.

Keeping my eyes closed, I slap around the bed until I find the offending device and crack an eye open to look at the screen.

My parents?

I accept the video call and throw my arm over my eyes to block out the light.

"Well, you really did it this time, Elliot Martin."

"Good morning, Mother. How are you this fine morning? I'm well, thank you for asking. Call again soon." I fake a chipper tone even though I feel like shit. How long has it been since she even sent a text message to check in? A month? Three months? I can't remember.

"You're going to Black Diamond." Her tone grates on my nerves but gets my attention.

"What?" I look at the screen. My mother's disappointed, angry face staring back at me. Cold, clawing fear wraps itself around my insides. "What the hell are you talking about?"

"There's a video all over the internet of you having sex with a *man* in a filthy alley behind a gay bar! A *gay* bar! I swear you don't care at all about how any of this looks on the rest of us," she shrieks, and my heart flutters somewhere behind my belly button. "So, you're going to Black Diamond, right now! You're going to hide out until this isn't news anymore! The official story is you're going to rehab, so don't do anything else fucking stupid, or I'll shut off your goddamn phone too!"

My hushed "What?" doesn't stop her tirade as she really gets going. Threatening to cut me off and telling me how much of an embarrassment I am to the family and to Marcus's memory.

I've been recorded doing a lot of shit over the last few years, faced homophobes and hate, had microphones shoved in my face while being asked all kinds of atrocious shit, but I've never had a sex tape go public. Never had a picture of my dick or anything like that be posted. I feel violated. My privacy was violated in the worst way, and *she's* mad.

Mom is still ranting, but it's just noise. I disconnect the call and head to the bathroom. Nausea rolling through me, the headache screaming, and the congestion making me want to cry is too much on top of this.

My body is tense and flushed, my chest tight like there's a

weight on it. Tears fill my eyes at the racing thoughts, and the anxiety spirals.

I can't leave my house anymore. I'll be attacked; the vultures will be even worse now, yelling questions at me in public that they have no business asking, hounding me even more about my parents and dating.

With a racing heart and busy head, I find my kit in the bathroom taped to the underside of the sink and sit on the floor. Tears stream down my face, my sobs hiccupping in my chest as I pull out the small black knife Asher gave me on my seventeenth birthday. It's all scratched up from me learning to sharpen blades on a wet stone, but I can't be without it long enough to send it out to be sharpened. Just having it makes me feel better. Knowing it's there is comforting. And it's all I have left of him.

My inner thigh is a mess of scarred lines, climbing like a ladder to the only part of me anyone cares about. Placing the tip of the blade against my flesh, I pierce my skin with just a little pressure and drag. The burn and welling up of blood dripping down my leg focuses me. Makes the buzzing in my head quiet, and it's just as intoxicating as the high of cocaine.

I sit until the tile under me warms, the knife still in my hand, but the bleeding has stopped. My body has sagged against the wall, letting the heaviness in my chest ease just a little with the adrenaline of the moment sweeping it away. The pressure lessons until I feel like I can breathe again.

Forcing my eyes open, I grab a wipe from my kit and clean the blade and blood from the floor, then put it all away and get in the shower. The hot water is beating at my sore and exhausted body. I'm tired of fighting. Tired of fighting to be seen, fighting to be enough, fighting to be loved or even just liked. Is life this hard for everyone, or am I just a big baby? Is everyone else just better at pretending?

I don't want to live like this anymore. Beaten down and lifeless. My life is jumbled shades of gray and has been for so long I don't remember what anything else feels like. I don't know how to find the bright colors anymore. The ghosts of my past dim the light of the flowers and the sun until all I see are the shadows left behind.

By the time I'm clean-ish and leave the shower, I'm numb. All I want to do is go back to bed. Through the open door, I can see my room but barely notice the mess of clothes thrown on the floor. When was the last time I did laundry? Or took a shower?

I find a baggy T-shirt that was Marcus's and pull it on with some shorts. I'm almost back to my bed when someone bangs on the front door. Ugh. Who is bothering me now? Why can't I just disappear into my head for a while?

"Elliot!" Ian's voice carries through the apartment once he's opened the door and come inside.

I drop heavily onto my bed and watch my bedroom door for him to come in.

"If you aren't decent, cover up," he says about five seconds before he opens the door to find me sitting on my messy bed. His shoulders droop when he sees me. "Time to pack. You have a plane to catch."

Eight

ELLIOTT

After hours on a plane I didn't want to be on, we finally land on the private airstrip at Black Diamond—one of the previously uninhabited islands in the Windward Islands—and I'm past exhausted. I barely see the reception desk of the resort or remember the number of my villa, but the guy taking me out to it via fucking boat apparently knows. Why I have to take the stupid boat instead of walking down the dock, I have no damn idea. Ian got me on the plane, followed me to the island, and now that I'm checked in, he left. Fucker.

The driver is friendly enough, I guess. I don't care. He's talking about amenities or whatever, but I'm not paying attention. After a few minutes, he pulls up to a private dock and unloads my bag. I climb the few wooden steps to the entrance, shove my keyless entry wristband at the electronic lock, and shove open the door.

I make a beeline for the king-sized bed in the next room and face-plant onto it where I promptly fall asleep.

When my eyes open again, it's because the lights are flicked on, and I moan as I roll onto my back. I just want to sleep for the next month with no one talking to me or in my space. At least out here I don't have to worry about interacting with other people. My antics have lessened over the last year since I'm too depressed to leave my fucking apartment most of the time, so why is my damn babysitter here?

"What the fuck, Ian?" I groan as I cover my eyes with my arm.

"Uh. I think there's been a mistake." *That's not Ian!*

I jerk upright, the world spinning for a minute as I stare at Asher fucking Vaughn. No. Absolutely not.

"What the fuck are you doing here?" I demand with as much indignation as I can muster.

"The same thing you are." He drops his bag on the seafoam green, velvet seashell chair on the other side of the bedroom, rubs a hand down the brown beard hiding his jawline, and crosses his arms, which only makes him look bigger and brings attention to the tribal tattoos on his skin. I'm minuscule next to him. He could snap me in half with two fingers. I hate it.

But I don't.

I want him wrapped around me, protecting me, so fucking bad it hurts.

His eyes drag over me, more assessing than sexual, and it makes me want to hide. Asher fucking Vaughn doesn't get to care about me anymore.

"Get out!" I yell, pointing toward the entryway. "This is my room! Find your own!"

"This is the one they gave me, wristband and all." He lifts his arm to show me. He's tired too. The deep, dark circles under his eyes and sag of his shoulders are dead giveaways. But he also has a split lip. What's that about?

I don't care.

Yes, you do.

I growl at myself and shove off the bed, marching past him toward the front door. The front door is next to a small kitchen-type area with white cabinets and a stone counter with a small sink. Across from the counter is a little table set up for dining and two chairs. The walls are a light blue, and the trim is a dark wood, which seems to follow through to the bedroom and bathroom. Not that I've looked around much.

I can't look at him anymore. Why can't I get away from him now? I didn't see him for six fucking years, and now I can't get away from him? This is fucked, and I can't do it.

Asher catches my arm before I can yank open the door.

"Eli." That name guts me. Forces me back to a time that hurts too much to remember.

"Don't call me that." My words tremble. Without looking at him, I pull my arm from his hand. "And don't touch me."

He leans a palm on the dark wood door next to my head to keep it closed and probably to bring our bodies closer together. I damn near vibrate with the need to lean back into him.

"Elliot, please." His breath fans over my neck, and I shiver. How can he sound so fucking broken? How dare he try to play into my sympathy!

Spinning around to face him, I find him closer to me than I expected.

"Get the hell away from me," I snap, and it carves another piece of my heart out. All I've ever wanted was to be loved by him, and I'm the one shoving him away. I can't trust him. Not again. "You left me! Ignored me!" I scream, getting closer and closer to hysterics with every word. My chest rises and falls too quickly with the air raging in and out of my lungs. "My brother was dead, and I was all alone!" I shove at his chest, hit and smack at his big body. Furious when he just stands there and lets me.

He's silent.

"Did you know he was dead when you threw me away? Huh?" I shove him again. "Was that your plan all summer? To fuck around with me, maybe convince me to let you fuck me, then walk away without a backward glance?"

Asher stares at me, absorbing everything I yell at him with tears once again streaming down my face. I fucking hate it.

"I'm sorry." He shoves his hands in his pockets but doesn't move back, just stands there and watches me.

"I'm so fucking tired of hearing you say that!" My nerves are shot, and my hands are trembling. I feel crazy. Why do I keep doing this? "Stay away from me. I may have needed you then, but I don't need you now."

I yank open the door, and this time he doesn't stop me. The pain in his eyes at my words is another slice to my soul. He ruined me, crippled my heart, and now what? He wants to watch me suffer? Fuck him.

Running down the wooden deck toward the resort check-in, I wipe my face and swallow back the tears. Somewhere I find a bank of inner strength I didn't know I had and square my shoulders before I step into the reception area. The gleaming floors and shining fixtures screaming privilege, paradise, and luxury.

I stomp my way to the front desk where a beautiful girl with perfectly applied makeup and styled hair smiles at me.

"Good evening, Mr. Cushings," she says sweetly. Does she know everyone's name or just mine? Was she here earlier and I just don't remember because it didn't matter?

"Yeah, hi. I was supposed to have my own villa, but someone else was also given the same one." I'm trying really hard not to snap at this girl, I doubt it's her fault, but I can't spend the next month with him.

"Oh, I'm so sorry about that." She starts clacking on her computer with her brow furrowed. "I've never seen this happen before, but we don't have any rooms available." Her face pales a little as her eyes meet mine.

"Then put him with someone else. I had that room first, and I'm not sharing it." Every muscle in my body is tense. I want to stomp my foot like a fucking toddler and yell that it's not fair. I want to destroy this stupid room and all its fancy, overpriced shit. My hands shake, so I clench them into fists and try to swallow back the wave of panic trying to take over at the very idea of spending time with him.

"Eli." My name is almost a bark, and I jump, but I don't turn to look at him.

"I told you not to call me that," I snap, too overwhelmed to fake nonchalance.

Asher takes a deep breath, and I can feel the frustration radiating from him, but I don't have the energy to care.

"Elliot." I flinch at my name. At him saying it. "We'll make it work. It's not this woman's fault."

I snap my head to the side and find him standing a few feet from me with his hands shoved in his pockets, attempting to look calm and unimposing. It's bullshit. All of this is bullshit.

The only response I can muster is the harsh rise and fall of my chest as I breathe ragged breaths. My teeth and jaw ache from the force I'm using to clench them shut. *Please don't make me do this.*

His shoulders droop for just a second before he straightens up and plasters on a charming smile for the woman behind the desk.

"Good evening. We understand there aren't any other rooms available. We can make it work for now, but can you let us know if another becomes available? Are there other options?" The bastard leans an arm on the granite slab of a counter.

I can't do this. I can't be trapped in a room with him. Sharing space like we're friends. Like he didn't break my heart.

"There's nothing else available at this time, I'm so sorry. It looks like both of you booked at the same time, and the system had some kind of a glitch. If another room opens up, we'll let you know immediately."

I don't want to be here. I want to hide from the horror of my life, but my fucking parents won't let me leave. They'll find a way to make sure I stay, threaten me with God only knows what, and make my life worse. I don't have a choice.

Closing my eyes, I force myself to take a shaky breath. *You're okay. You will survive this.* Avoid the room and pretend he isn't there when I go to sleep.

A big, warm hand presses into my lower back, and I jerk away from it with a hiss. "Don't touch me."

Crossing my arms in a lame attempt to hold myself

together, I stalk out of the room back to the pier that leads to the villas. Asher sighs behind me, following me into the fresh air that smells of sea and flowers.

I hate myself for acting like such a baby. *Just grow the fuck up and get over yourself,* but I can't. I'm not strong enough to be friends with him. Why does he have to be here? Why do I have to be tormented with what I wanted more than anything but can't fucking have? A knot forms in my throat, and tears threaten to fill my eyes, but with a deep breath, I force them back and disassociate from my feelings. They're fucking useless anyway.

Asher's steps are consistent behind me, and I force myself not to watch him, not to want him to fight for me and wrap his arms around me. My bottom lip trembles again, and I bite it to stop it. I can't have him see me this weak, but I'm so fucking tired of fighting my own head that I don't think I have the energy to fight him too.

It's a bit of a walk to the villa, but we make it without speaking. Stomping up the stairs, I put my wristband to the lock, but it won't open, so I have to stand there like an idiot trying over and over.

I'm about ready to fucking cry when Asher clears his throat. He puts his wristband to the lock, and it beeps open. He swings the door open and waits for me while I die of embarrassment. Asshole.

He keeps his face neutral as I rush past him, avoid the glass floor panel at the end of the bed that lets you see into the water under the villa, and shut myself in the bathroom. It's as big as the bedroom. Jesus.

Nine

ASHER

The bathroom door shuts as I enter the room. I'm exhausted and want to take a damn shower, but I guess that's out. Looking around the room, I take in the light airy feel of the space. It's all very expensive, minimalist boho chic. One wall is covered with curtains, and I head toward it to look out. The entire wall is window panels that look like they fold up like an accordion and gets rid of the wall. There's an outside space with a few different seating options and a private pool, outside showers, and I think the receptionist said there's some kind of hammock situation out there.

I can see myself eating breakfast out here, maybe convince Eli to join me.

It's beautiful, I have to admit. Everything about this tropical island screams money and extravagance. Clear turquoise water, white sandy beaches, palm trees. All the guests stay in villas over the water so the lapping of the waves can ease you to sleep. Hardwood, glass, and natural fabrics. It's gorgeous.

I push open the window panel that acts as a wall, and the soft crashing of the waves is calming. I drag in a deep breath of the salty sea air that has a sweet undertone, probably from all the flowers on the island.

Is Eli really going to stay in the bathroom all night? Sleep in the damn tub?

I head back inside to grab some clothes to change into and toss my dirty ones on the floor under the chair my bag is sitting on. The bedroom is made up of a king bed, two dressers that sit as bedside tables, and a small living room area with chairs that look like seashells and a TV.

Straightening my shoulders, I knock on the bathroom door. A little squeak comes from inside that has the corner of my lips lifting in a small smile.

"Come on, Eli—"

"Elliot!" His shout echoes in the space.

"You can't sleep in the damn bathroom," I say with more force than I should. I'm tired. Agitated. This day needs to fucking end, and if I have the opportunity to wrap myself around Eli, that's even better.

"Go away!"

I lean my forehead against the door. Exhaustion and frustration warring within me. As much as I want to argue with him, I don't have the patience, but every instinct I have says to not give up on him. It's Eli. My Eli. My boy.

"El—" I cut myself off and start again. "Elliot, you can't sleep in the bathroom."

"I sure as hell can. Go. Away," he yells back.

"What if I have to piss?"

"I suggest you find a nice plant to water."

Sassy little shit.

"Fine." I stomp my way to the bed, pull the plush blanket off the end of the bed and a pillow and put them next to the door. "You're acting like a child."

"Fuck off!"

With a huff, I slam my hand against the light switch to drown the room in darkness before ripping the blankets down on the bed and climbing in.

Even though I'm exhausted, I can't sleep. My hand aches, and my split lip pulls every time my mouth moves, but it's just a reminder of the situation I've gotten myself into. I stare at the ceiling until I can't stand myself anymore, then roll over and punch my pillow a few times. The bathroom door opens a sliver, and I lift my head. Light cuts through the room as Eli grabs the pillow and blanket I set on the floor, then douses me in darkness again when he closes it.

I huff and settle onto my stomach on the bed, irritated that he would rather sleep in a fucking bathroom than in here with me. Am I surprised? Not really, but that doesn't mean it doesn't hurt.

I've missed him. Sometimes I can bury myself in football and forget for a while, but it never lasts. His smile, scent, and the warm flush of his skin haunts me when I least expect it. When I'm trying to sleep or zone out during a meeting, he's there.

All night I toss and turn, waiting to hear the door open and finally have Eli come out. He's the only connection I have to Marcus. The only other person who knew him like I did. Since he died, I've had no one to talk to about him. Not really. No one to remember him with me.

When the sun rises in the sky, I stop pretending to sleep and get up. Nervous energy has me itching to move, so I grab both of our bags and unpack them into the dressers. I try my best not to look at what he brought with him, but it's damn hard not to picture him in the silk camisole or short skirts. My dick aches at the thought of being able to touch him while he wears it. Fucking him with a schoolgirl skirt on would be my fantasy come to life.

I set his toiletries next to the bathroom and stop in my tracks when I open a satin bag with a pearl necklace in it that I recognize. The urge to cry hits me like a punch to the chest as I run my fingers over the cool beads that once belonged to my mother. I knew she left a few things to him in her will, but I'd forgotten about this. Flashes of my mother baking chocolate chip cookies, laughing at our antics in the dining room, smiling at my father when he came home from work buzz in my head. My house was full of love and laughter once upon a time, but not in a long time. Swallowing past the lump in my throat, I put the necklace back in the bag and put it on his dresser before putting our empty bags to the side of the room. I assume there's a closet on the other side of the door with the bathroom since it's not in here.

My bladder is demanding I do something, so I get up and walk to the bathroom. Putting my ear to the door, I can hear Eli snoring softly. Carefully, I try to open the door, but it's locked. With a huff, I go out to the deck and find another way in. Opening the door slowly, I find him curled up in the bathtub with the pillow and blanket. Stubborn ass. His face is so peaceful and unguarded, it's hard to not kiss his forehead. Mom loved him and Marcus as if they were hers. They only got to know her for a few years, but it was enough to leave a lasting mark on them. Long enough to show them how fucked their own parents were. I hope Marcus and Mom are together, wherever you go after your heart stops beating. I hope she would be proud of me.

I'm sorry, Marcus. I'll do better for Eli. I promise.

Since my bladder is screaming at me, I sit to lessen the noise and take a piss. This space has to be the same size, if not bigger, than the bedroom with a huge, tiled shower, soaker tub, two vanities, and a closet. It's not until I flush and am washing my hands that he stirs.

I leave the bathroom before he's opened his eyes and get changed into my workout gear. There's not much for me to do here, and with training camp starting a few days after I get back, I need to make sure I'm in shape for it. The last thing I need is for the coaches to be pissed I've slacked off.

Picking up the phone next to the bed, I put in a breakfast order and ask the receptionist to set it up on the table on the deck. When I get back, I'm going to be starving, and I'm sure Eli hasn't been taking care of himself. He's so much thinner than I remember.

Ten

ELLIOTT

The door to the bathroom opens, and I jump when the light flicks on. "Elliot, get up. I need a shower."

I force my eyes open to find a shirtless, sweaty, flushed Asher towering over me. It's been the same every morning for the last three days. For a second, I forget that I hate him, and my eyes drag over his hard body. The black ink etched onto the arms that are now the size of my head and the light dusting of chest hair that looks so fucking soft I want to rub my face in it like a damn cat. *Holy fuck, the things I want that body to do to me.*

"If you're done eye-fucking me"—he smirks at me with a lifted eyebrow—"get out or take a shower with me. I don't care at this point." The tub is separate from the shower, but there's no way I'm going to lay in here and watch him bathe.

My face heats, and I grit my teeth. I hate how my stomach flutters at the idea of being naked with him. This is why I have spent the last few days avoiding him. Getting drunk on the beach all day, lounging at a pool, eating whatever sounded good, then finally stumbling back after dark to sleep in this damn tub.

"You wish." I force my stiff body to move. Every inch of me aches from laying in here all damn night, which is my own fault, but whatever. The bones of my hips grinding into the tub has been particularly joyous. I force my body to move and bite my lip to hold in a groan.

With his ass leaned against the sink, he watches me get up and limp from the room.

"Perhaps sleeping in the bathtub wasn't your best choice," he says in a deadpan tone.

"Still better than sharing a bed with you," I snap back and hobble away from the door so I don't have to look at him anymore. Though all the booze wasn't a good idea either.

I stretch and look around the room. Opening the dresser closest to me, my clothes are folded inside. Why did Asher unpack for me? I can't find anything.

My stomach growls when I see there's food on the table outside, so I step out onto the deck and inhale a deep breath of the sea breeze. The island has a ton of natural flowers and greenery, white beaches, and the clearest turquoise water I've ever seen. It looks fake, like a dream. On the table is a full breakfast spread with fresh fruit and drinks. There's way too much here for two people. It looks amazing, and it's still hot. The breeze is warm off the water, and the sun is high in the sky.

As I sit and pick at the food on the plate in front of me, I gaze at the water. My thoughts drift with the lapping of the waves, not really staying on any one thing for very long. I wish Marcus were here. I wish I knew what happened to him. Having Asher shoved in my face brings back all the pain of losing them both to the surface. I feel like I'm suffocating all over again. Lost in the unknowns with my soul ripped to shreds. The seventeen-year-old boy they left behind is so fucking desperate for love and affection while the twenty-three-year-old me is jaded and refuses to let Asher in to hurt me again. I hate him, but a part of me still loves him and is ecstatic he's here.

A door opening inside has me turning toward the room.

Asher is standing in the doorway to the deck freshly showered, hands shoved in his shorts pockets with no shirt on as he tries to read me. He probably can. I never was any good at keeping my thoughts from him. Somehow, he always could read me like a damn book while I was always left wondering.

"How are you feeling?" he asks, moving to the chair situated across from me.

"Fine," I mumble around a bite of mango.

"Feel any better?" He shoves a huge spoonful of egg into his mouth and locks his eyes on me. It's hard not to watch his throat work. The bobbing of his Adam's apple and the muscles of his neck flexing as he swallows.

I shrug and face the water again. "Stop pretending like you care."

Asher sits back in his chair and pins me with a look. "I do care. I've always cared."

"Right, that's why you vanished," I state, holding his stare with my own angry one. "Just gone." He doesn't flinch at my pain. "You made the worst night of my life worse. Did you know Marcus was dead when you left, or did you find out later and still not fucking call me?"

Emotion clogs my throat and flutters my heart until the

beat is erratic. I shove away from the table and walk away. I can't do this with him right now. Honestly, I can't know the answer to my question. Either answer hurts the same.

I find my phone and open my Kindle app to find something to disappear into as I settle into one of the chairs in the room. Asher comes in a few minutes later, and I force myself not to watch him. It's harder than it should be. I hate him but miss him. There are so many fucking questions I want to ask him, demand him to answer, but I don't. It will only lead to more hurt, more heartbreak, and I don't have the energy for any of it.

I settle on a book and flip through the pages, but it's not holding my attention, not really. More than anything, I want to listen to an audiobook so I can't hear him, but I didn't bring my headphones. Is there a store on this island where I can buy some?

The idea of playing a romance story at full volume from my phone almost makes me smile. Would he say anything about it or ignore it? Would the sex scenes read out loud *bother* him?

Once again, I'm flicking through books on my phone and jump when Asher shoves headphones on my head.

"What the fuck?" I jerk around to look at him.

"Listen to your music or book or whatever you do these days," he says with a lift of one shoulder. "I'm going to see what there is to do around here."

"I don't care."

He shakes his head and leaves the room that smells like his body wash. I scrub a hand down my face and bolt. I need space to breathe where I can't see him, or feel him, or smell him. Slipping on some shoes and grabbing the full-sized bottle of rum I find in a cabinet, I hustle down the deck to sink my toes in the sand.

There's a path from the pier toward the water, and it doesn't take me long to get to the sand. It's a beautiful little walk, though, and I push the headphones off to hang around my neck. The scent of his shampoo and cologne cling to the pads and tickles my nose with memories of him. The deep green leaves of the palms, the red, orange, and yellow flowers that smell so sweet, and the birds singing high in the trees mixes with the calming rush of the water, and it's perfect for my ragged heart. I could get lost here and never want to go home.

When my feet hit the sand, I kick off my shoes, open the bottle, and chug. It burns on the way down, and my face scrunches up because of it, but I lift the bottle to my lips again and take another drink. I tuck the bottle under my arm and keep walking along the surf. The water laps at my ankles, and the sand shifts under my feet as I walk. There's a soft breeze coming off the water that ruffles my hair. I'm sure it's a disaster after being slept on, but right now it's whatever.

Another shot of rum goes down, and the warmth starts to spread, dulling the pain from my heart. I don't know how far I've gone, but I want to sit and listen to my book in this beautiful place.

My phone has gone off with text message notifications, but they're probably Asher, and he can fuck off.

I find a shady spot and sit with my back against a coconut tree trunk. I open the bottle again and take two more mouthfuls. My book is loaded up, and I relax as the gruff voice of the narrator comes through the headphones.

"I need your knot, please." The narrator moans in my

ear, and my dick perks up a little too. My alcohol-addled brain gets lost in the possibility of fucking monsters and shifters. Of being so needed by my partner he can't stop himself from taking me.

A text message pops up on my phone from one of my semi-regular hookups back home. Phone sex isn't going to make me feel better right now since all I really want is to be cuddled, but I also want to be acknowledged.

> **ASTON**
>
> Hey, heard you were sent to rehab or whatever. Did you really, or do you want to meet up?

> **ELLIOT**
>
> I got sent to Black Diamond. You believe that shit?

> **ASTON**
>
> Holy fuck! Your parents weren't fucking around.

A picture pops up of Aston in an LA Chargers jersey and a jockstrap. Jesus. My audiobook has been forgotten even though the main character is still begging to be fucked by his werewolf mate. Blood surges to my dick just looking at Aston's picture. He's a muscular, take-charge top who is rarely not a good time. We've fucked a few times, but he wants to cuddle after, and as badly as I crave it, I avoid him most of the time. I want to be held but not by him. His body is a lot like Asher's, and it's just too close to who I really want.

Closing out of my messages, I open my camera app and lift my shirt up. Reaching into my shorts, I pull my dick out and stroke it a few times until it's hard, then snap a picture. I quickly get myself put away, then click back into my messages and send the picture.

Women's voices carry on the wind, laughing and chatting about sex. It's not long before the colorful women come into view with big cocktails in hand. They appear to be in their mid-forties, with tropical-print bathing suits and sheer wraps. When they see me, they wave with big smiles on their faces. I smile back and lift my hand to wave.

The pair sit in the shade not too far from me, and the blonde pulls out a paperback. The cover is familiar, but I can't remember if I've read it or not.

"Do you happen to be a reader?" she asks when she turns and sees me staring.

"I am!" I perk up, the rum now hitting my system full force and turning off the filter between my brain and mouth. "But it's usually about dicks and assholes."

They crack up and come sit next to me in the sand.

"Us too!" the brunette lady who is a little more sober than her blonde friend says. "What's the craziest thing you've ever read?"

"Oh my god, Chuck Tingle! His stuff is wild. Plus, basically all his dinosaurs come from outer space and like butt stuff. It's fucking great."

The ladies cackle, and my phone pings multiple times in close succession, but I ignore it. This is more fun than sexting with Aston.

"I'm Joy," the brunette says, pointing at herself. "And that's Marnie."

"We're both married to senators, but what the media doesn't know is that we're just a couple of dirty birds," Marnie pretends to whisper, then falls over laughing.

I smile widely at them. "It's so nice to meet you. I'm—"

"Elliot!" My name is barked angrily by fucking Asher.

"Yeah, that," I tell them before looking at the man who broke my heart all those years ago. "What do you want?"

"What the hell are you doing?" he demands, body tense and frustration rolling off him in waves. Hmm, what did I do to finally get under his skin?

"Uh-oh, someone's getting a spanking," Marnie giggles to Joy.

"Whatever the fuck I want," I throw back and roll my eyes.

"Is he bothering you?" Joy asks in a very serious tone.

I sigh heavily. "Yes, but he's not dangerous." Not physically, but he definitely isn't safe either.

"Are you drunk?" Asher comes toward me, lifting my face to his with his fingers under my chin.

God, I want to lean into his touch. Instead, I slap at his hand. "Don't touch me."

"Let's go." He turns his back to me like he expects me to follow.

"I'm not your damn dog," I yell after him.

"Oh, I don't know how long you've been here, but there's a bartender named Holden at Midnight Lounge that will sell weed to customers," Marnie tells me. "He's tall, slim—"

"Has a great ass," Joy throws in, and both ladies laugh.

"That he does," Marnie agrees with her friend. "Blond hair that needs a cut. Looks like a beach bum."

Asher has turned around, staring daggers at me. Is he going to make a scene? Spill secrets in front of these strangers that they can use against me? The bastard would do it, just to get me to do what he wants. I lift my lip and growl at him before relaxing again to say goodbye.

"Well, this has been a treat, ladies." I pat their knees and stand, brushing sand off my ass. "Read *Space Raptor Butt Invasion*. It's a trilogy, and you won't regret it."

They cackle, and Asher grabs my arm, pulling me away from them and down the beach. Once I'm away from the attention of the ladies, my fake persona drains away. In its wake is the angry, pain-filled, depressed Elliot that no one really wants to be around. Fun Elliot is exhausting, but everyone likes him more.

"What the fuck were you thinking?" he demands, spinning on me and getting into my face. "Why did you send me a dick pic?"

My head blanks at that question.

I did what?

"What are you talking about? I didn't send you a dick pic. I sent it to—" *Oops.*

Asher pulls out his phone as I start to tell him about my sexting with Aston, but stop when he shows me my own dick.

"That's not my best angle." I look at him over the top of the device, and I swear I can see Asher's desire to strangle me in this moment.

"Why are you sending pictures of your dick to anyone? Have you learned nothing from a viral sex video?" Asher starts patting my pockets and pulls out my phone.

"Hey!" I object and try to get it back, but much like when we were children, he holds it out of my reach. "Give that back!"

"Has this dude signed an NDA?" Asher asks as he reads

through my messages. Shame and embarrassment fight in my stomach and heat my face and neck. "And seriously, change your password. I got it on the first try."

"Give me my phone!" I yell, my fists clenched at my sides. "You have no right to go through my stuff!"

Asher faces me once again, our chests pressed together and our eyes locked. "Who was your first?"

"My first what?" I cock a hip and square my shoulders. "Blow job? To give or receive? Dick pic? To send to or to get from? First boyfriend? First public fuck? You're going to have to be more specific."

Anger and something I can't put my finger on flares in his eyes. For once, I'm getting under his skin. It doesn't feel as good as I had hoped, but it's better than the tears.

Asher leans in and speaks through gritted teeth. "Virginity. Who took your virginity?"

"Colin," I say with as much menace as I can manage. Asher hated Colin from the day I met him at fifteen. His lip lifts, and he bares his teeth.

"You let that self-absorbed asshole touch you?"

I lift onto my toes, loving the shift of power in this moment. For once, he's off-balance, not me.

"The video that went viral, Colin was the one fucking me." It's intoxicating watching the fury fill his eyes. *Now you know a tiny sliver of what I've been feeling for years, you son of a bitch.* I don't know if I should be satisfied or feel bad for his obvious distress, but I'm not dwelling on it. He deserves to hurt too. He did this to us.

Asher shoves my phone into his pocket and lifts me over his shoulder, carrying me like a sack of potatoes.

"What the fuck are you doing?!" I beat on his back, the

rum in my stomach threatening to make a reappearance. "What happened to my rum? I think I'm gonna be sick."

At the path to the pier, Asher drops me to my feet and shoves my stuff at me, then pushes me to walk in front of him. "Get your ass back to the villa, or so help me, Elliot, I'll tie you to the fucking bed."

I huff and slide my phone into my pocket before heading toward the pier. I can't get away from him, and I hate that I don't really want to.

Eleven

ASHER

The image of Eli's dick will be forever etched into my memory. I should delete the picture he clearly sent to me by accident, but I won't. For years I've wondered about him, what he smells like, how he tastes, how he sounds when he comes. I'll be jacking off to that picture later, I'm sure.

A big part of me hates that he was sending it to someone else. Some fucking hookup that probably doesn't give a shit about him past using him to come. Shit is about to change, and he may not know it yet, and he may not like it, but that boy is mine. He's always been mine, and he always fucking will be.

Even though he hates me.

I will find a way to make him see that me leaving was for the best. It hurt him, it was shitty, and I have a lot to make up for, but I can do it. I helped take care of him, held him when he had nightmares, when his parents' lack of attention crushed his young heart, and I'll help heal him now

"Elliot." Using his full name is such a foreign thing to me. The only time I've ever used it was when I was mad at him, and that didn't happen often. In the villa, he spins around on me, cocking a hip and folding his arms across his chest like a shield. "Are you sober enough to remember this conversation?"

"I can handle my alcohol," he bites out with more attitude than is necessary, using it as a weapon. Part of me has missed it. I loved the verbal sparring matches we used to get into. Watching his face heat with passion as we went back and forth in front of Marcus without him knowing what we were really doing set my blood on fire.

"I'm sorry." My words hang in the tense space between us. "For everything."

"Don't." His bottom lip trembles, and his eyes are too wide. My boy looks like he's on the verge of tears, and I want to kiss them away, but he won't let me. I'll let him keep the distance between us for now, but it won't be forever.

I take a tentative step toward him, and he tries to put more space between us but trips over a table. With quick reflexes, I grab his arms and pull him against me to keep him from crashing to the floor. His breathing is ragged, and his fingers are digging into my skin as he grips onto me. The alcohol on his breath and the faint remnants of his shampoo are intoxicating.

"You okay?" My eyes rake over his face, taking in the dark circles and exhaustion etched into the lines of his face. He's so far past tired it's not even funny, but it's not the kind that sleep fixes.

Eli closes his eyes and sucks in a shaky breath, then shudders. "Please don't touch me."

The pain in his voice is a knife to my heart. A boulder drops into my stomach as my hands fall from him, and I step back. I hate that I bring that kind of pain to him just by being here, and I know there's a ton I still need to tell him, but I can't tonight. He's not ready to hear it.

"You should drink some water, take some painkillers, and rest." I shove my hands in my pockets despite the clawing need to wrap my arms around him and breathe him in. "You've only gotten a few hours of shitty sleep. The tub could not have been comfortable the last few days."

"I don't want or need you to take care of me." Eli's words cut me to the core. "I've been doing just fine on my own for years." He turns his back to me and heads to the bathroom. I force myself to watch him go. Once the door is closed, I drop down onto the bed and drop my head back with a sigh. It's going to be a long month.

I haven't gotten any more sleep than Eli, but my head won't shut down. I turn the TV on and flip through the channels, stopping for a few minutes to catch the highlights from a game from last season.

My body wants to move, buzzes with the urge, so I change into gym shorts and strip off my shirt to start doing push-ups and sit-ups. Even though I worked out a few hours ago, I want to run, but frankly, I can't trust Eli to stay put. He's obviously not above getting drunk and doing stupid shit, so now I need to watch him. How quickly I fall back into taking care of him. It's so easy.

I've tried giving him space since we got here, but he obviously can't take care of himself. Not really.

On instinct, I call the front desk and request an older camera that uses film instead of digital for Eli and some paperback books. I'm sure he can read on his phone, but he used to love to read physical books. He said there was nothing like the smell and feel of the pages. Since I haven't been around in a while, I have to guess at what books to get him, but I pick a few that I know he used to read over and over.

It takes a while, but I manage to exhaust my mind and my body so I can sleep. I drop face down onto the bed and pass out, but my dreams are haunted by the ghost of my best friend.

A door latching closed wakes me. My eyes pop open, and I sit up automatically. It's been years since I've had to be responsible for anyone, but I guess some instincts never really go away. The toilet flushes and rustling around the room tells me he's getting dressed. I scrub a hand down my face and stand. I guess he came out here to grab clothes. The boxers I wear to sleep in ride low on my hips as I make my way to my dresser, then call down to the front desk for food.

Crepes, fresh fruit, eggs, bacon, ham, and sausages along with coffee, juice, and milk are set up on the table a few minutes later, thanks to a resort employee. I take a seat and shove some food into my mouth, listening for Eli. He doesn't take long to finish up, but when he takes too long to come out here to eat, I turn in my seat to find him looking unsure of himself in a white crop top T-shirt and baby blue shorts that stop at mid-thigh.

I drink him in, greedy for every drop of him I can get. His shoulders are rounded, his head bowed, and his fingers are picking at a nail. The poor boy is uncomfortable, but I'm not entirely sure why since I want to strip those clothes off and lose myself in him. Is he embarrassed by what he thinks I will think? That I'll think less of him for dressing less "masculine"?

"Hey." I nod toward his seat at the table. Forcing my eyes away from the bared skin of his abdomen is harder than I would like to admit. The urge to drag my lips along the skin right around his waistband is strong. Imagining the breathy moans as I nip and taste his flesh has my dick hard as a fucking rock.

Why didn't I put pants on?

"Come eat." I take a drink of my coffee to clear the food from my throat. "How are you feeling today?"

Eli takes his seat and looks over the spread that's been left for us, picking a few things to put on his plate.

"I'm fine," he mumbles but doesn't look at me, which bothers me. *Fucking look at me. Give me those eyes, baby.*

"What is your plan for the day?" I shove some perfectly ripe mango in my mouth, but Eli just shrugs at me. "Look, I know I'm probably the last person you want to spend time with. I have a lot of explaining to do, a lot to make up for. I know."

Eli's lip trembles as he pushes fruit around his plate, and he chews on his lip as he watches the water.

I get up and walk around the table, push his chair back, and hunker down between his feet. As badly as I want to touch him, I don't. I leave my hands on the arms of the chair.

"What are you doing?" His voice wavers.

"Eli, I'm so fucking sorry I hurt you." I close my eyes for a minute, sucking in a deep breath before I'm able to meet his eyes again. Tears are welling in his, and I want to cup his cheeks so fucking bad, but I don't think I can handle him telling me to not touch him right now, so I keep my hands to myself. "I knew Marcus was dead when I sent that text and walked away."

Eli crumbles before me, his body folding in half while tears stream down his cheeks before his hands cup his face. An agonizing cry leaves his mouth, a long, drawn-out sound that breaks my heart and makes me feel even worse. Guilt and shame eat at me like acid in my stomach.

"You knew, but you left me anyway?" He rocks in his chair. "I didn't know if you were alive or dead too. You were just gone! I searched the internet, called hospitals and morgues looking for you!" he screams at me through the anguish that's been crushing him since I left. He jerks up out of the chair, sending it crashing to the deck behind him. "You don't do that to people you love!"

I stand, and he shoves me, his hands pushing and slapping at me.

Tears clog my throat, making it hard to breathe as I watch this beautiful broken boy fall apart before me.

"I hate you!" He shoves me again, his face red and puffy, with tear tracks down his skin.

"I know." The words rip from my throat, tearing the scars open that night left me with. None of us were given a pass.

"Why?" Eli demands, getting into my space. "Why did you leave?"

"I had to go back to school." I struggle to find the words to explain my shitty reasoning to him. "I was the reason he died, and I couldn't face you."

He jerks back from me, eyes wide with fury and hurt,

covering his mouth with his hand. Before my eyes, I watch him steel his resolve. He wipes the tears from his face, straightens up, and faces me head-on. "Were you the one that called in his drowning?"

"Yes."

"How did it happen?" His voice is now devoid of emotion. I'm not sure if it's better or worse than the screams. He sounds empty, numb, and he's no life in his eyes anymore. They're blank.

"He saw us kiss when you left the cliff," I start, the memory playing like a recording in my mind. "We fought and he slipped, hit his head on a rock, and fell over."

I have to close my eyes and breathe through the memory that hits me like it was yesterday. My eyes are wet when they meet Eli's again. The pain of losing my best friend, of the terror that held me hostage for hours, trying so desperately to pull me back under.

"I jumped after him, but by the time I found him, he was gone." My voice breaks, and I let him see how much it hurt me. How fucking sorry I am for all of it. For the guilt that eats at me every fucking day because I couldn't save him. "I stayed with him for hours, tried to pull him to shore, but he was caught on something, and I couldn't get him free. I *tried*, Eli. You have to believe that. I tried so fucking hard to bring him back to you. Maybe I should have gone with him."

Once again there's tears streaming down Eli's face, but he's not alone in that. This time, I don't try to hold back. I go to him, cup his face in my hands, and press our foreheads together.

"I promised him I would come back when I was worthy

of you." My words hover between us. My need for him to understand them so fucking strong. "I wasn't then, and I'm not sure I am now, but I will do everything I can to be who you need me to be."

Eli, with cheeks still wet, shoves me away. "I needed you then, but I had to learn to live without you."

Twelve

ELLIOTT

I manage to hold it mostly together until I'm out of the villa and halfway to lost down some path through the trees. I stop in the middle of the dirt footpath, lean my hands on my knees, and sob. Finally letting out some of the pain that has etched itself into my existence, into my bones. This time, maybe I'll feel better when it's done instead of worse, but I'm so tired of crying. I just want to smile again.

Memories of Asher and Marcus drift through my head, back to a time when I knew there were people who loved me and cared about what happened to me. When I wasn't so fucking lost all the time. I want to forgive Asher. I do. Hating him hurts so fucking much. The tear in my heart keeps ripping, getting deeper. How much more can I take before it's ripped in half and no longer fixable? Is it even fixable at this point, or am I too damaged to recover?

I dig my phone from my pocket with shaky fingers and blurry eyes and find Jordan. I have no idea what time it is in

LA, and I don't care. I need her to talk me off this ledge. My phone wobbles as I lift it to my ear and listen to it ring a few times before she answers.

"Elliot," she says with relief. "Where are you? Are you okay?"

"He knew Marcus was dead when he left!" I sob, not entirely sure the words make sense to anyone but me.

"What? Who?" I can hear her scramble around wherever she is. "Where are you?"

"Asher. He knew." I weep a little quieter, rubbing the back of my hand against my face to wipe away some of the tears. How do I have any left? "He was there when Marcus died, called in the accident, and fucking left."

My knees give out, and I drop to my shins on the dirt. On this island paradise, my world cracks a little more, exposing truths I thought I wanted but can't move on now that I have them. I didn't know I could hurt so much more than I already did. Shoving a hand between my legs, I rub my fingers over the raised scars on my inner thigh until I find the newest one and pick at the scab. The sting of pain helps clear my head, but only a little.

"Oh, babe." Her sympathetic tone is almost a warm hug. "Are you at home? Can I come over? I don't want you to be alone."

"I'm at Black fucking Diamond," I grit out and wipe my face again, sniffling back the emotions that seem to barely be contained by sandbags during a hurricane.

"Seriously?" I can almost hear the wheels in her brain turning. "I can probably swing coming out there if you want company."

"Asher is here," I utter miserably. "I'm sharing a stupid villa with him. I've been sleeping in the damn bathtub to get away from him!"

There's silence after that revelation.

"Jordan?" I pull my phone from my ear to look at the screen to make sure the call wasn't dropped.

"No, I'm here." She clears her throat. "Why are you sharing a room with him?"

I cover my eyes with my free hand. "I don't know. Something about a mix-up and there not being any more rooms available."

"Right . . ." She's quiet for a few minutes, just letting me breathe and hold on to the only connection I have with someone who actually cares. "What do you need right now? Do you need to be angry? Sad? Do you need me tell you he's an asshole and you deserve better, or do you need me to walk you through it all logically?"

I bark a rough laugh at her questions. I love her. My lips tip up in a small smile knowing she has my back.

"Because it was an asshole move that he left knowing you lost your brother. You deserved better," she states very matter-of-factly.

"I hear a but coming . . ."

"But I can also see how he would have struggled to face you after the trauma of seeing his best friend die." She takes a deep breath. "I don't know him, and I don't know what happened, but I can't imagine facing the person I loved if I felt at all responsible, or was harboring survivor's guilt, after their loved one died while I was with them. It's a fucked-up situation all the way around."

Logically, I know that. "But how can I trust him not to disappear on me again?" I lean my head back and close my eyes, taking in a cleansing breath. "I don't know that I could survive it again."

"First of all, you have survived every bad day and fucked-up situation you've been in. Every single one. Did some of them leave a lasting impression? Yes, but you're still here. You would survive it because I wouldn't let you do anything less." Her adamance makes me smile and lifts some of the weight from my chest. "Second, you can't trust him. Not right now. Make him work for it. Make him earn it."

I nod, biting on my lip and wiping the tears from my face.

"So if you need to fall the fuck apart, rage, cry, and scream, do it. Get it out of your system because after that, we'll pull on our big boy panties and move on with life."

"*You're* going to wear big boy panties?" The giggle that escapes me is so unexpected I cover my mouth to hide the sound. The smile feels foreign on my lips. How sad is that?

"I'll wear whatever damn panties I want and dare you to argue with me." Her tone is playful, and I've missed it. I've missed the snark and love she shows me so unconditionally.

"Okay." I take a deep breath and release the pressure on my chest to the world.

"You can only control what you do, how you react. If he wants to work to get back into your life, let him try. I think both of you deserve that." She softens her tone and lets me hold on to that idea for a minute before continuing. "He fucked up, and it sounds like he knows it, but he wants to fix it."

I stand up and brush the dirt from my legs.

"I'm scared." I chew on the inside of my lip. "What if he makes me trust him, then walks away again? How much more of me is there left to break?" My words wobble.

"Love is fucked up that way. You have to have faith they won't break you or walk away and not let them get close. If you're willing to risk it, just be careful. I don't know him, but I get the feeling he won't do that to you. But if he breaks your heart, he'll have to deal with me. You know I'll mend your heart with coffee and junk food and movie marathons."

I take a deep breath and allow myself to take comfort in her being there. I can trust Jordan.

"Okay, thank you. I love you."

"I love you too, boo thang. Call me anytime, you know I'm here."

We hang up, and I make my way back to the villa slowly, enjoying the sounds and breeze and warm sun that hits my skin between the branches and leaves. I don't know how to let him in. How to face him after what he just told me. I don't know how to stop it from hurting.

As I head to the pier, the same receptionist as yesterday stops me.

"Mr. Cushings, your package has arrived." She smiles and hands me a box with my villa number on it.

Confusion has my eyebrows pulling together.

"Uh. I didn't order anything?" Did someone send me something? The only people who know I'm here are my parents, Aston, and now Jordan. I can't imagine anyone but Jordan sending me anything, but she wouldn't have had time.

"Then I assume Mr. Vaughn ordered it. A call was placed last night for it from your room." She holds out the box to me and smiles again.

"Oh, uh. Thank you." I give her a small, unsure smile and take the box. It's not very big, somewhere between a shoe and a boot box. It's heavier than I expected, but I get it to my room and find Asher sitting on the edge of the infinity pool outside.

"Did you order something?" I finally ask when he quirks a brow at the box.

"Yeah," he says. "Open it."

Nerves flutter in my stomach as I set it on a table and pull the tape off. I open the flaps of cardboard and freeze. What the fuck is this?

I snap my head in his direction, not sure if I'm touched or angry, but it's probably a mixture of both.

"What is this?" I demand with my arms crossed.

"What's it look like?" He gets to his feet and comes to stand behind me to peek into the box. The bastard smiles and lifts the black-and-silver camera out of the box, the neck strap a busy pattern of yellow, green, blue, and purple. "Looks a lot like your old one."

"It's very similar. This is a Pentax ME." I look at the camera in his huge hand and take it from him, turning it over in my hands. "I had a K1000."

I open the film compartment and pull out a roll from the box to load it. I get it set and close the door and turn it on. It whirs as it loads the film for use, and it makes me smile. I haven't held a camera in a long time, but damn does it feel good. The heavy weight of it, the sounds, the texture of the body, all bring back memories.

I'm lost in happier moments for a second. When I meet his eyes, embarrassment heats my cheeks for snapping at him and a shy smile takes over my face. The unsure lines of his face soften when he looks at me. His hand cups my cheek, and I close my eyes for just a second, absorbing his skin against mine, the comfort and compassion he always held, before pulling back.

"Thank you for this." I lift the camera like he would be confused by what I'm talking about. I swallow thickly and lower my gaze so I'm not looking at him anymore and set it down in the box. Carrying it inside, Asher follows me as I set it on the dresser.

He doesn't move away from me, and I didn't expect him to, but I really wish he would. It's hard to keep the wall up when he's so close.

I busy myself with emptying the box. There's more rolls of film and two paperback books, *The Song of Achilles* and *The Outsiders*. They were my comfort reads as a teenager. I don't know how many times I've read them. Sometimes I would pick one up and just skim to a scene that I needed to read that day, not sure what I needed when I picked it up, but I would always find it. In the pages of these books, I was comforted, shown love and family.

"You remembered these?" My voice is barely a whisper as I stare at the covers.

"I don't think it's possible for me to forget those two books." Asher shoves his hands in his pockets and heaves out a heavy exhale. "You always had one or both of them with you."

"Thank you." I finally look at him, and he's staring at the cover of *The Outsiders* with a sad smile.

"You're welcome." He kisses my temple, his beard tickling my skin, but the movement is so natural that I doubt he even thought about it. I'm choking back emotions when he walks away, back to the pool and his phone.

I stack my things on the dresser and throw away the box, then head to the bathroom for a shower. The blanket and pillow I used are folded over the side of the tub, either from Asher or from one of the cleaning staff. I strip off my clothes and turn the water on.

In the mirror, I take in my appearance. There's not much difference from my seventeen-year-old body and this one. In six years, I haven't gained any muscle mass; I probably lost some, actually. I'm only an inch or two taller, while he's gigantic. It feels like he's taller too, not just bulkier, but maybe that's because I feel so fucking small.

I want to take up space again.

Stepping into the shower, I let the hot water rain on my skin until the muscles underneath relax. Since I didn't remember to grab my shit, I use Asher's shampoo and body wash, but he doesn't have conditioner, which leaves me with only the resort stuff. It's not going to be enough to wrangle the curls, but it's all I have.

Asher's body wash on my skin and scenting the air makes my dick hard. I don't want to want him. I don't want to know what it feels like for him to fuck me, to love me, to use me. But my body does. Damn near desperately.

With conditioner still slicking my hand, I wrap it around my aching cock and stroke. My head drops back on my shoulders, and I moan as my eyes close. Instinct has my body doing what it wants without direction from me. It only takes a few strokes before my hips thrust into my fist, chasing the orgasm I know is waiting for me.

I use my free hand to press against my hole, teasing myself with the possibility of being filled, but in my head, it's Asher's fingers on my body. Asher playing me like an instrument, knowing just where and when to pluck my strings to get the sounds he wants while I'm helpless to stop him.

"Please, don't stop," tumbles from my lips.

My orgasm hits hard, damn near taking my knees out from under me as I ride through the pleasure pumping through my veins. Cum splatters the blue tile and my foot as my ragged breathing struggles to get enough oxygen in the humid air of the bathroom. My body is weak when I lean against the wall to regain my balance. Jesus.

I force my eyes to blink, trying to get my brain working again. I feel high as I shake my head, and make sure to wipe everything clean with a washcloth to get rid of any evidence.

Once the water is off and I'm drying my skin with a towel, I realize I didn't grab any clothes. Fuck. My face flushes in the mirror knowing I have to either put on my dirty clothes or go out there with only a towel on. Neither one is a good option.

Maybe Asher left.

I open the door to peek out and let out a breath when the room is empty. Dodged a bullet there. I already feel exposed to him, stripped emotionally bare. The last thing I want is for him to see me actually naked.

Opening the drawers, I look for clothes and grumble at what I brought. What the hell was I thinking? *You weren't.* Ugh.

I find some shorts that are long enough to cover the scars

on my inner thighs and a baggy T-shirt that may have belonged to Asher at one point. I can't keep track of who owned every piece of clothing I stole from Marcus's room after he died. Since he was the same size as Asher, they ended up with a mix in both closets.

Does he have any of Marcus's stuff left?

I look through the drawers for my toiletries but can't find them. Did I not pack them? In the bedroom, I grab my bag but it's empty.

Now I'm searching the room, opening every drawer I can find. Did they fall out somewhere? Did Asher hide my shit? The last place I have to check is the bathroom. I stand in the doorway and stare at the vanity drawers like they hold secrets. Did he put it away?

Slowly, as if approaching a scared animal, I step up to one of the sinks and reach for the drawer pull. Inside, my stuff is laid out neatly. Everything is out of the bags and organized, the way it's been for days.

Asher unpacked my luggage, probably folded my clothes since all I did was throw them in the bag from the hangers, organized my toiletries, and put them away.

Cold fear and shame hit me hard as I realize what I had in my bag. My knife kit. Fuck! I rummage through all the drawers in a frantic search for the black zipper bag. Everything is a mess when I slam the drawers and cabinet doors closed. My heart races as I try to think of where he would put it. It was with my bathroom shit, but what if he thought it was for protection? Where would he put it?

Hurrying to the bedside table, I yank it open and sag in relief when the familiar black canvas bag is there. With a shaking hand, I grab the bag and walk it into the bathroom to shove it into the back of a drawer.

Exhausted, I sit on the bed and flop back onto the plush bedding, dropping my arm over my eyes. I've been here for only a few days, but it feels like so much longer.

With that thought, I succumb to the blessed nothingness of sleep.

Thirteen

ASHER

I don't know what I'm doing, but listening to Eli jack off in the shower was the purest form of torture I have faced. Hearing his whimpers and moans when I couldn't touch him or even see him? It was too much. I bolted from our room without shoes on because if I didn't leave in that instant, I was going to fuck him in the shower.

Sweat beads on my forehead as I pace the deck area in front of our villa. There are people walking around, and if I really paid attention to any of them, I would probably recognize some, but that's not what I'm here for. I need to get my shit together.

Dropping down into a crouch, I grip my head in my hands. I have to work to focus on the air entering and exiting my lungs, slowing the thundering of my heart in my ears, and relaxing the muscles in my shoulders. Being around Eli is both amazing and horrifying. All my good intentions broke him. I did this to him. By trying to protect him, I hurt him so irrevocably I'm not sure he can be healed. Not really

The damage that was done will always haunt him. All I can hope for is that he can learn to put it in the past and find the joy in life again.

How do I fix him if he won't let me anywhere near him? And rightly so. How can I prove to him that he can trust me again? I've tried reaching out, waited with bated breath when I sent every text, but he never said anything. Ever.

That fucking dick pic is the first message I've gotten from him in six goddamn years.

Once some of the tension has left me, I stand and pace for a while longer. The slap of my bare feet on the wood planks a constant companion drumming with my heartbeat. I wait until there's no way he's still in the shower before I head back inside. My head is finally ready to sleep. Between jet lag and traveling, the hangover and busted knuckles and lip, I'm finally tired.

When I reach our door, I hesitate. If I open this door and he's naked, I'm going to lose it.

Holding my breath, I open the door, listening for running water or movement. When nothing moves, I push the door open and step in, letting the door close behind me with a soft snick.

The lights are on, and Eli appears to be passed out, sideways, on the bed with his arm over his eyes. His shirt makes me pause. The AC/DC concert tee was mine once upon a time. A lifetime ago. Does he know that?

It's faded, and the design is cracked and flaking off, the black fabric gray now, but I'm betting it is soft and comfortable. I didn't pay much attention to his clothes when I was putting them away. On autopilot, I just folded them and put them in the drawers without taking in any details.

Except skirts. I noticed the skirts. And the lack of underwear.

The slow rise and fall of his chest is calling to me. I desperately want him wrapped around me and to pass out. I want to be consumed by him.

Flicking off the lights, I carefully shuffle him under the blankets and run my hand over his curls, just once. The soft bouncy hair pulls at memories I can't think about right now. I've used football and being busy to bury the memories instead of processing them. But sometimes they come back out of nowhere and wake me in the dead of night, trembling and panicking. I can't jump off cliffs into the water anymore, and I struggle to be around if anyone else is doing it.

Eli rolls over, getting comfortable.

"Ash," he mumbles in his sleep as I make my way to the other side of the bed. "Hold me."

I freeze, halfway in the bed with one foot still on the floor. The words were so quiet, did I really hear them? Looking over at him, his face is pinched, but his eyes are closed. Laying down, I roll on my side to face him. His hand is between us reaching toward me, so I place my hand on top of it.

His face relaxes at the simple touch and settles back into a deep sleep. In sleep he's so innocent, there's no pain or hatred, just my Eli.

With my hand holding his, I close my eyes and fall asleep with my boy next to me.

At some point in the night, Eli wraps himself around me. His face in my neck, arm around my ribs, and leg over my thigh. It's the best feeling in the world. I pull him harder into me, chest to hip pressed together for the rest of the night.

I wake later in the night or early morning to find my thigh is between Eli's legs. He's whimpering as he thrusts against it. He's hard and his skin is flushed where his shirt has ridden up.

With lust humming in my blood, I slide one hand under his T-shirt, and the other goes to his ass, cupping the muscles and encouraging him to go faster. I need him to come. Fuck, I need to come too. Rolling him onto his back, I push my hips between his thighs and rut against him with my face buried in the crook of his neck. My body wash on his skin intoxicating. *He* is intoxicating. Everything about him calls to me, reels me in, and finally being able to take it is like coming home.

"Please," he whimpers in my ear, clinging to me.

The fabric of his shorts is too thick, I need to feel him, skin to skin. Lifting up to my knees, I rip the shorts down his legs without opening the button, taking whatever underwear he had on with them, then shove mine down to my thighs. When I lower back on top of him, we groan together. His skin just as hot as mine and his hands just as hurried.

I wrap my hand around both of us, and his back arches off the bed with a long moan.

"That's my boy," I say against his throat, and his dick throbs in my hand.

Eli is dripping precum, so much fucking precum, making a sticky mess before he's even come, but it makes the slide better when I thrust against him. I love it. The proof of how turned on he is, telling me I'm doing the right things, how close he is.

Eli digs his hand in my hair, gripping the strands in his fist and holding my face to his skin as he loses it. All my senses are filled with him. It slicks our skin, and his helpless sounds of release send me over. Our cum mixing between us and leaving us both panting in the dark. Nothing has ever felt as right as this. As touching him. He was the one I compared every girl I've ever touched to, and I was always left wanting.

"Fuck." Eli releases me to cover his face with his hands. His body trembles again, but it's not for the same reason as a minute ago. I lift onto my elbow to look down at him, and my heart sinks. His cum hasn't even cooled yet, and he already regrets it.

"Eli—"

"Don't."

My stomach clenches with guilt and rejection, dousing the post-orgasm high with ice.

"Elliot," I try again, a little more stern this time, and pull on one of his wrists. "Look at me."

"Get off me." Eli pushes at me, pulling his legs up in an attempt to get out from under me. *This is not how I wanted our first time to go.*

"No. Not until you talk to me."

"I can't do this with you." His face is back to being angry. Even in the dark I can read his expression. He's always been shit at hiding what he was thinking. Every emotion playing out across his features like a scrolling bar on a TV. It's both a blessing and a curse.

"Do what? Orgasm?" I scoff. "Pretty sure you're capable."

"I can't be." His hands move around in a weird pattern like he's not sure what to do with them. "Here. With you." Eli's eyes meet mine in the dark, and the pain is back. His eyebrows pull together, and the fight leaves his body as if he's resigned. "It hurts too much."

His words sting more than if he had swung at me. A bone-deep ache in my chest forms, and even with every molecule in my body telling me to keep him with me, I sit up and watch as he scrambles away into the bathroom.

I don't try to stop him, don't offer him comfort, or to help clean him up. Just sit and do nothing. Again.

When it's obvious Eli is hiding in the bathroom, I take my shirt off and wipe myself off, pull my shorts back on, and lay down. I stare at the ceiling. Sleep forgotten and guilt churning so damn hard in my gut, it's making me nauseated.

Eli used to come to me when he was hurting, when he needed comfort. Locking himself in the bathroom to get away from me is a slap in the face. One I guess I needed, but it hurts.

I rub at the pang in my chest and drag my eyes to the bathroom, wishing I could see inside.

Fuck it.

Tossing back the blankets, I get out of bed and stalk to the door. "Eli, open up."

The light under the door tells me he's probably still awake and pacing with the way the shadows are moving.

"Go away." Eli's voice is rough, like he's been crying, and it breaks my fucking heart.

"No. Open the door or I'm kicking it in." The shadows under the door stop moving like he's considering that possibility. "One." I take a step back, preparing to do exactly what I promised when there's scrambling inside, and the door opens.

"What the hell is wrong with you?" a red-faced Eli demands.

I move right into his space, my chest brushing his so he has to bend back a little to look at me. "Stop fucking hiding from me."

"Then get out of my room," he bites back with just as much frustration.

Taking him by surprise, I lift him under the arms and carry him across the room to set him on the counter, forcing my way between his thighs, and lean over him with my hand on the mirror behind him.

A blush rushes up his neck, and for a second he clings to me, like he's afraid I'll hurt him.

"Stop touching me!" He tries to put some distance between us, but I wrap my other arm around him and keep him pressed against me.

"Since when do you not want to be touched?" My voice dips low, seductive, as my hand traces over his spine. It's fucked up to play his body against him, but at this point, I'm fucking desperate.

"Since the only person I wanted to touch me left." He shudders as his words stab into my heart.

"Let me make it up to you." Leaning forward, I drag my beard across his neck, kissing the tender flesh. "You can trust me, I promise."

Eli's body doesn't relax, but he doesn't push me away either, and his fingers run through the hair on my chest. Holding on to that, I keep kissing his flesh, sucking his pulse on the side of his neck.

Finally, Eli grabs my face and brings my eyes to his. His

breathing is ragged, but determination is set in the lines of his features.

"No cuddling. If I let you touch me, it's to fuck, then you go away."

I hate it, but I can work with it. It's a start.

"Fine," I agree and lift him from the counter.

He slaps at me. "Hey! Put me down. You already got off. Leave me alone."

I lift an eyebrow at him while my hand is cupping his ass. "Are you saying you're done with one orgasm? I'm ready to go again, baby."

"Put. Me. Down," he demands. I slide him down my body until his feet touch the floor. "I'm not fucking you tonight."

He crosses his arms and cocks a hip. I smile despite myself. That bratty attitude is good. I hope he's able to keep it up because I can't wait to fuck it out of him.

Fourteen

ELLIOTT

Hold your ground. Don't back down.

Asher smiles at me like he's won. That makes me nervous. This is a horrible plan. I'm a fucking idiot.

Asher grips my jaw in his massive hand and crashes his lips to mine. Arousal shoots through my blood in a nanosecond as his tongue invades my mouth, dancing with mine and turning my knees to mush. My heart thunders in my ears, and I'm reaching for him when he pulls away. That knowing, smug smirk on his lips. The bastard.

"I'm going to get my workout done since I'm not sleeping any more tonight."

All I can do is stand there and stare as he disappears from the room. What a dick.

When the door closes behind him, I rub my hands over my face. What the hell was I thinking? God. Damn. It.

I'm such an idiot. This is going to break me even further.

Fuck.

With shaking hands, I find my phone and pull up Jordan's text thread.

ELLIOT
Are you awake?

JORDAN
About to crash, what's up?

ELLIOT
NVM good night.

I toss my phone on the bed and drop down onto it, holding my head in my hands. It rings a minute later, and I groan at Jordan's name.

When I answer it, I drop back onto my back and cover my eyes like that will make this better.

"Now I'm awake. What's going on?" I can hear the slap of her feet on the hardwood in her house as she paces.

"Somehow I told Asher we could fuck but not cuddle," I say miserably.

The pacing stops for a second before she says anything. "I see. What was the thought there?"

"He was kissing my neck!" Even to myself that's a shit excuse. "He plays dirty pool, the asshole."

"Ahhh, I see. And now you have regrets." Her pacing continues, and I groan.

"Of course, I do." I huff. "This is going to be awful. Nothing can come of it. I loved him so completely, Jordan. He's the only person I've ever really wanted to touch me. What the hell is going to happen when we leave here?" Emotions fill my eyes with tears once again, and I wipe them away roughly with a growl, irritated with myself. "Am I supposed to pretend like none of it happened?"

"You're really overthinking this," she says softly. "You are the master of casual sex. Enjoy the orgasms while you're there."

"I can't!" The urge to break down in fucking tears again is strong, but I'm tired of it. I won't allow myself to do it again. "It's not casual with him. Nothing ever is."

"Then tell him you changed your mind." It's so simple when she says it.

"Doesn't that make me an asshole?" My voice is small as I ask the question that shouldn't matter. I need to protect myself, but the need to be loved is too strong to ignore.

"Elliot, I don't give a fuck if it makes you an asshole. You need to set boundaries to protect yourself." Her mama bear tendencies make me feel better even though she's basically yelling at me. "Be friends with him, get to know him again if you can, but do not *ever* let someone touch you just because you're afraid to look like an asshole for saying no."

Why does it feel like she's given me permission? Why does it make me feel better?

"Okay." My voice is small but there.

"You are your first priority. Got it?" Her tone is hard, but I know it's out of love.

"Got it."

"Good, now go enjoy paradise."

I smile to myself as we say goodbye and hang up.

Be his friend. I think I can do that.

Light is starting to peek through the curtains, glinting off the camera he ordered for me. Sitting up, I stare at it for a minute. Friends. We can be friends, I think. Friends talk on the phone, text, cheer each other on. They can be long distance and not hurt.

I really want to play with that camera.

Grabbing a change of clothes, I take the camera and shove some extra rolls of film into my pockets, then leave the villa. There's a gym by reception that guests can use, and I find myself looking for it. I'm lying to myself when I say it's not to see how good Asher looks sweaty with straining muscles. Big. Fat. Lie.

Signs on the outside of reception direct me, and I find it without much trouble. From the window in the door, I can't see much, so I slowly push on it and hope it doesn't squeak. My heart pounds at the fear of getting caught sneaking a look at whoever is in here.

I can hear grunts and smell the rubber mats along with whatever they use to disinfect in here. It takes me a minute to find Asher at one of those machines that can do a million different workouts, like the Bowflex ones I've seen in home gyms.

He's facing away from me with his shirt off, pulling up on the handles that are coming from down low. The muscles in his arms and back flexing and bunching with each movement, making his tattoos dance on his skin. Without taking my eyes off his body, I uncap the lens and slide the cover into my pocket. Quickly, I adjust the settings to hopefully get a clear picture and raise the camera to look through the viewfinder. I snap a picture and manage to get his face in the mirror as well.

I freeze at the sound the camera makes and wait for him to notice me tucked in between the machines, but he doesn't. Keeping the camera raised, I wait for another shot and take another one, this time his eyes have just seen me and a smile is starting to form.

Fuck.

Anticipation tickles in my stomach as I wait for his reaction, but he doesn't stop. If anything, he pushes himself harder. Shit. With hot cheeks and my lip between my teeth, I back out of my hiding spot and flee the gym.

My face doesn't cool down until I'm on the beach and walking through the surf. The crystal-clear turquoise water laps at my feet and ankles, shifting the sand under me as I walk. I've always loved walking in the surf. The ground beneath my feet literally changes with every wave. In just a few steps, where you had been is different. The evidence of you is washed away to leave the sand untouched like you never existed.

I adjust my camera settings again and get some pictures of the water, birds, and flowers. It really is gorgeous here, and if I have to be trapped somewhere, there's definitely worse places. Since I'm supposed to be in therapy or rehab or whatever, Ian deleted all my social media apps off my phone, but I haven't had the desire to re-download them. It's freeing to not have them.

The news articles, comments, tags from everyone with an opinion on my life don't exist here. Most of the people on this island are hiding from something, so none of us exist. So far, no one has bothered me, asked any questions, or even acted like they knew who I was. Besides the resort receptionist who knew my name, but she wasn't weird about it.

Stopping in the surf, I close my eyes and lift my face to the sky. I drag in a deep breath of the salty air and let it take some of the stress and pressure with it when I let it out. The things I can control, I will. The things I can't, I have to let go.

I can't control Asher, only my reaction to him.

Since the island is small, it's easy to circle around and not realize that's what you've done until you recognize something. Somehow, I end up at the visitor section where there are flyers for all the things you can do here. Fishing, hiking, renting boats or Jet Skis, whale watching, swimming with dolphins. There's so much.

One flyer of a waterfall and beautiful pool below it catches my attention. It looks like it's only a mile hike or so from here. A secluded little spot in the forest that would be perfect for taking pictures or swimming. I wonder if you can jump from the top of the waterfall? It's been so long since I did anything like that.

The idea makes me smile. Marcus, Asher, and I spent so much time out at that stupid cliff, but we never went alone. Not until I was alone.

I've sat there over the years, wondering what happened, and just wanting to go back. To be surrounded by the escape we used to find there, but I never could. Now I know what happened, and it hurts to think of that spot even more. I can picture Asher scared of his best friend being angry with him, scared of losing the only connection he had. If Marcus cut Asher off, Asher would probably assume I would too. Thinking back, I'm not sure what I would have done. Marcus would have been so angry, betrayed by both of us, but would he have tried to force me to cut Asher off? Would I have allowed it for fear of him leaving me too?

I don't know.

Dragging my ass back to the room, I need a shower. I'm pretty sure I can still smell cum on my skin, and I'm sweaty from being in the sun. It's not until the lock beeps open that

I remember Asher caught me watching him working out. Fuck. I don't want to face him yet.

I freeze with my hand on the door handle, one foot in the doorway. Will he say anything? Probably. He's Asher. With a quick prayer to whoever might be listening, I push open the door, but it's blissfully empty. Thank fuck.

I get my stuff put away and dig in the drawers for something to wear. I have no shorts or pants left already. Shit. With shaking fingers, I grab a green-and-black pleated skirt that hangs down to mid-thigh, black shirt that barely comes down past my pecs, and a pair of gray hip briefs that cup my ass just right.

Normally, I love outfits like this. I feel sexy and powerful, but I don't want Asher to think I'm either weird for wearing a skirt, trying to seduce him, or both.

My shower is quick, and I hate that a part of me hates washing him off my skin. I can't let myself go there. Friends. I can be friends with him. Maybe. I have to talk to him and tell him sex is off the fucking table.

Once I'm dressed and deal with my curls correctly for the first time in months, I head out to find something to distract me for a while.

I find a bar that's over the water, like the villas we're all staying in, with a tufted roof and no walls. Everything here is airy, letting the breeze come through and not cutting off the views. It's set up with a round bar and stools around it with other small tables spread out on the decking. In the center of the space there's an opening where you can see the fish and sharks swimming below. It's beautiful and calming.

At the bar, the tall, blond-haired bartender with a nice

ass brings back the memory of Joy and Marnie on the beach the other day. *They said he sells weed, right?*

What was his name? Heath? Harry?

He turns around and his name tag says Holden. That's it!

He has an easy smile that turns flirty when he takes in what I'm wearing. The breeze coming off the water picks up the edges of my skirt to make it dance around my thighs. I hold my breath for just a second as he comes toward me, waiting for the reaction to me, but with every step he takes his demeanor becomes cockier. It would probably be a terrible idea to sleep with an employee on the island, but the vibe he's giving off says he's done it before and he'll do it again. The man is tall and definitely spends time on the beach if his light hair and tanned skin are anything to go by. He's not overly muscular but could probably throw me around a bit.

"Well, look at those legs in that skirt," he says, giving me another appreciative look.

His flirting is enticing. I feel confident in my outfit and love the attention he's giving me. It's been so long since I was in the headspace to tease that it feels like I'm rusty, but I do it anyway.

Leaning on the bartop, I order a drink. "I think I'll start with a sex on the beach."

His smile ratchets up, as does mine, before he winks and turns to make the drink. I sit on one of the stools and pick up a menu so I don't stare at him, and I'm suddenly starving. Reading through what they serve, everything sounds good, but the shrimp tacos sound amazing.

Holden the flirt slides my drink in front of me and watches as I take it.

It's sweet and tangy on my tongue, and I can't stop myself from licking my lips before I set it back on the bar.

"Delicious, thank you." I smile at him and enjoy the feeling of being wanted by a stranger. There's no history, no strings, just lust. Here I don't have to be Elliot Cushings. I'm no one. Anonymous.

He gives me a knowing smile, like he's got something else delicious I can put in my mouth. It's tempting. So very tempting.

"I think I'm also going to need the shrimp tacos." I drag my teeth over the corner of my lip, which does nothing to hide the smile.

He bites his lip and groans. "Oh yeah, those tacos are so *good,*" he says. "Gets a little messy, but I'm sure you can handle it."

Holden checks in on the other customers, and I assume places my food order on the computer. Forcing myself not to stare at his ass, I turn around and sip my drink while taking in the quiet. Even though I'm at a bar, there's no background noise. No TVs or music, there's no honking horns from traffic. A few people chat at a table on the other side of the deck, but they're far enough away from me that I don't hear them. It's just the water lapping against the pillars of the deck and some random boat engine as one passes.

"Hey, legs." Holden's voice has me turning around with a smile. "Enjoy your dinner. If you need anything else, just let me know."

"Thank you," I respond and pull my plate closer to me. Was that sultry? It felt sultry.

A throat clears to my right, and I about jump out of my

skin when I see Asher glaring. How the hell did he find me out here? How did I not notice him approaching?

My heart thunders, and embarrassment turns my stomach. I place a hand on my chest like that can slow my erratic heart rate.

"Jesus, you scared the shit out of me."

"Yeah, I noticed," he scorns and sits down next to me. "You done eye-fucking the bartender?"

I pull back and glower at him. "Excuse me, I can flirt with whoever the fuck I want."

Asher grabs my knee and turns me to face him, his eyes dropping to my leg when his hand meets bare skin. The tension in his body changes from frustration to arousal when he sees the skirt. He runs his hand up the top of my thigh until the tips of his fingers are under the fabric. I try to clench my thighs together, but his knees are keeping them apart, so I shove one of my hands between them so he can't see or feel the scars. Why did I wear a skirt?

My breathing shudders at his soft touch, and I scan the area around us, looking for anyone who might see him touching me like this. He has to protect his reputation. The last thing he needs is a gay lover scandal.

"Flirt, fine, I'll deal with it, but no touching." His head is still lowered over my legs, but his eyes shoot to mine. "No one touches you but me."

My dick twitches at the growl in his tone, in the possession of his touch. I crave it. To be owned by him, only ever by him, but I can't let myself have it.

"Ash." His name is barely more than a breath. "People can see."

He leans in until his mouth is pressed to the sensitive

spot behind my ear. The musky scent of his cologne and body wash filling my head as he speaks against my skin. "You're going to ride me in this skirt and get your cum all over it."

Goose bumps break out across my skin, and my dick is achingly hard. Jesus fuck.

"Asher," I attempt again, and this time my words are steadier. "Friends. We can be friends." My hand grips the bartop so tightly my fingertips turn white.

He sits up enough to see my face, and he stares hard into my eyes. "You want to be friends? Fine. We can be friends, after I fill you with cum."

His words set fire to my blood. It's a terrible idea, but at this particular moment I can't remember why.

Asher's fingers trail up my leg while his eyes are locked on mine, until he gets to the edge of my underwear. He slides his finger along the slick fabric, barely caressing my dick and balls before removing his hand with a knowing smirk.

"Eat. We have to keep your energy up." Asher picks up a taco and brings it to my mouth. He watches as I take a bite and sets it down before pulling me closer to lick a drop of sauce off my lip.

"Jesus Christ, Asher." I grip onto his knee and close my eyes, willing my body to relax.

"What?" he says with mock innocence. "Just making sure my boy eats."

My boy.

Two simple words have this illusion crashing down around me. Damn it. I *want* to be his. I *want* this to be normal for us. But it can't. Not as long as he's playing football. I shouldn't have to hide that long. Being referred to as his fucking roommate or best friend's little brother will kill me.

Sitting up, I remove my hand from his leg and pick at my food.

"What just happened?" Asher's eyes are on my face, scanning every muscle twitch for information. "What did I say?"

I shake my head and chew on the inside of my lip to hold myself in check. After a deep breath, I force a smile on my lips and shake my head. "Nothing."

He knows I'm full of shit but isn't calling me on it. Yet. I'm sure the second we're alone he'll be all over it, but for this moment, he relents. "You need to eat." He nods to my plate, and I pick up the taco. It really is delicious, and I end up eating all three of them. It's the most I've eaten in months.

Holden appears again and takes my plate with a wink that makes Asher growl. I snort, trying to keep my chuckle in, but Asher catches it and pulls my stool between his legs so I'm basically sitting in his lap.

Once again, I scan the area.

"You have to be careful," I chastise him, getting off the stool and paying for my food and drink. "People can see you."

"Everyone signs an NDA when they get here. No one will say shit," he scoffs like he doesn't remember how back-handed and fucked up the elite are.

"All it will take is a hint for the media to blow it up. I'm sure some of these people can find a way to mention something without really saying it that people will figure out. You want a scandal right now?"

I chug the rest of my drink and step away from the bar.

"Have a good day, legs!" Holden calls as I walk away, and Asher growls before grabbing my hand.

"Seriously. Do you not listen to anything I say?" I jerk my hand back and cross my arms. *Please stop touching me. I can't take the teasing of you claiming me in public when I know the second we leave you won't. Leaving here is already going to hurt so fucking bad. Don't make it worse. Please.*

It's not fair. None of this.

Asher spins around and backs me into the railing of the deck, pushing his chest against my crossed arms.

"You're giving me mixed goddamn signals here. First you sleep in the fucking bathtub to stay away from me. Then you cling to me at night, come on me, tell me I can fuck you, now I can't touch you at all. What the fuck do you want from me?"

"I want to not get hurt. Again." I push back against his chest so I can fucking breathe. "I don't know how to be friends with you or to be okay with you touching me." Apparently, the drink is loosening my tongue, and that's not going to end well for me, but fuck it. I've come this far.

I turn away from him to look out over the water that's so beautiful it looks fake. "You're the only person I want to touch me, but I don't know how I'll survive afterward. You have a career to get back to, I understand, but you aren't out." A tear slides down my cheek and cools in the sea breeze. "If all you want is a quick fuck, to know what it's like because we never got to, fine. But stop touching me the rest of the time. I can't start to rely on you, just for you to leave again."

Asher's hand grips my hips, and he presses his chest against my back. I close my eyes and try to steady my breathing.

"I want so much more than a quick fuck." He stops for a minute, maybe looking for words, I don't know. "It was recently brought to my attention that every person I've hooked up with looked like you."

That was not what I was expecting him to say. What the fuck?

"It really had nothing to do with how they look, but it was as close to you as I could get. I wanted you. Only ever you." He sags and presses his forehead to the back of my head. Why is this so hard? "Come on, let's go back to the room, watch a stupid movie or something. Just relax."

With a jerky nod, I let him turn me and cup my face. Asher leans his forehead against mine and slides his thumb over my bottom lip. Our eyes meet, and he lowers his lips to mine, giving me plenty of time to turn or pull away. More tears fall as his mouth takes mine. It's a soft pressure, but it's everything. It's all I've wanted for years. To be the center of his attention, to matter, to be worth it.

He slants his mouth over mine and encourages me to open for him, which I do with no hesitation. I love the feel of him against me, even knowing it's going to hurt later. I can't keep myself from him. Not when I'm forced to share space with him. Not when he's offering me what I've always wanted. Him. Even if it is for a limited time.

What's the saying, it's better to have loved and lost than to never have loved at all? I guess I'm about to find out.

Fifteen

ASHER

L ifting Eli off his feet, he wraps his arms and legs around me so I can carry him to the room. I have to hold his skirt down so the wind doesn't show his delectable ass to anyone walking past. His face is pressed into my neck, and I can feel his chest expand when he takes a deep inhale. He's breathing me in and melting against me.

It's not far from the bar's pier to our room, and with the wristband as entry, I don't even have to let him go to get inside. The door closes behind us with a snick, and I head straight for the bed, crawling into the center to lay down on top of him.

"Movie or . . ." I trail off, but he knows what I mean.

Eli uses his legs wrapped around my hips and grinds against me. I groan and thrust out of instinct, our cocks lined up perfectly. I guess he's made his choice.

I grip his thigh and roll us so he's on top. I need to see that fucking skirt. He smiles so fucking big above me, leaning onto my chest for leverage as he drags that bubble butt against my dick.

"Are you trying to kill me?" I grab his throat and pull him down for a kiss. I don't want to think of anything but him. With my mouth ravaging his, Eli gets my pants open with jerky movements. I let go of him long enough to shove them down my legs. The slick material of his underwear slides across my hot skin, and I grab for his hips to hold on to while I thrust against him. He sits up and drops his head back, moaning as he rocks his hips in time with my thrusts.

"Lube," I demand. "Get that hole ready."

Eli scrambles off the bed but freezes. His cheeks flush, and his shoulders hunch a little like he's nervous or embarrassed.

"Bedside table," I tell him in a calm tone.

Eli looks up at me with a raised eyebrow, the question in his gaze so loud in the room.

"I had some in my bag since sometimes I hook up on the road during away games," I answer the unspoken question.

He moves to the drawer and pulls out the bottle of lube and a condom.

Eli shimmies out of his underwear but leaves everything else on. It's sexy as fuck to know he's bare under that damn skirt. The urge to wreck him is fucking strong. I pull my clothes off and shift on the bed until I'm sitting with my back against the headboard when he climbs back over me. In this position he's taller than me, and I love looking up into his baby face. He's dirty innocence, and I love it.

The soft features with a knowing glint in his eye that tells me he knows exactly what he's doing. It's my undoing. With my hands on his lower back, I run my palms up the bare skin of his back and under his shirt, loving the way he arches into me.

"Get your hole ready for me," I tell him before ducking my head under his shirt to lick and suck on his nipple. He shudders and moans, cupping my head to his chest. The lube bottle clicks open, and he adjusts on my lap to get his fingers to his hole. I bite at the flat nipple and slide my hands under his skirt to cup his ass cheeks, spreading him open. His hand is moving quickly, thrusting his fingers in and out as he rides them.

I smack one delicious cheek and love the feel of it bouncing in my hand. Pulling my head out from under his shirt, I watch him take his pleasure. The flush of his skin, the long tender column of his throat with his head dropped back.

He's a mess of moans and whimpers, and it's exactly how I want him. Crazed.

Finding the lube, I slick up a few of my fingers and slide them along the crack of his ass to his opening. While he abuses his hole, I push one of my thick fingers inside too. He gasps, holding on to my shoulder for support, and pushes back onto it. I let him get used to it, fucking himself on our digits before adding a second.

"Such a good boy," I say against his throat. "How many fingers are there, baby?"

"Four," he whines as he sinks back onto my hand. "Fuck, please."

"You take those fingers so well." I nip at his throat, and he shivers. "Is your dick wet? Are you leaking for me?"

Eli nods quickly, his face creased with concentration as his body stretches. His skin is hot against mine where he's bare. I love the tease of his clothes. The skirt fanned out to cover our laps, hiding the obscenity I know is lurking.

"Give me a taste." I want all of him. To know what every inch of him tastes like and smells like, but I can't have it all tonight. Eli's thrusts stop so he can sit back enough to reach his dick. I keep my eyes on his as he swipes his finger over his tip, then drags it over my bottom lip. I quickly lick it off and growl at the bitter bite of him. "Ride me, Eli. Show me how well you can take it."

He slams his lips to mine in a hot quick kiss, both of our fingers leaving his body, then he finds the condom and slides it over me. Eli adds more lube, then lifts and adjusts until my dick disappears under his skirt and presses against his puckered hole. His face slackens as he sinks onto me. He bears down, and the perfect squeeze of his ass around me almost makes me close my eyes, but the need to watch him is stronger.

I slide my hand under his shirt again and play with his nipple as he bobs on my cock a few times. He works his way to sitting on my lap and stays there for a moment. His eyes are glassy as he starts to move—up, down, grind, repeat. Oh fuck, I'm not going to last long.

"Look at me," I demand, and his eyes snap to mine. It's fucking perfect. So much more than I thought possible. I've had anal sex before, with women, but that's not this. They weren't Eli. This is more than our bodies working together for pleasure.

I won't be complete without him. Not after this. He's utterly wrecked me for anyone else.

Eli rocks against me, bouncing on my cock until I'm damn near seeing stars, panting and trying to hold back my impending orgasm. I've waited too fucking long to rush this.

"Are you a slutty boy for me?" He tenses a little, dragging his lip between his teeth. "Or my good boy?"

The flush creeps up his neck, and I feel his dick throb between us. A smirk lifts my lips as I get my answer.

"You're my good boy, aren't you? Only mine." I suck on his skin, leaving red marks everywhere I can reach. "Fuck me, baby. You can do it."

He whines, embarrassment clear on his face, but he does what I've said.

"Such a good job, baby." I plant my feet and thrust up as much as I can in this position. It forces Eli to put both hands on the headboard and drag his dick against me with every movement. His whimpers turning desperate as the angle changes.

"You take it so well." This time I bite at his neck, leaving teeth marks on his skin.

"Fuck," he groans, wrapping his arms around my neck and gripping my hair to claim my lips. "I need to come."

"Hold it," I say against his mouth and slap around for the lube bottle again. I find it quickly and put more on my fingers. Sliding my hand under his skirt again, I trace down his crack to where my dick is penetrating his stretched hole. Watching his face carefully, I push a finger in. He whimpers and clenches around me, slowing down for a second.

"Such a good boy," I praise him again, impressed he let me do it in the first place. "You want another?"

"Yes, please." He shudders against me, his precum dripping onto my pubic hair and making a mess. Slowly, I add a second finger, and this time he gasps a needy sound, gripping my hair so hard it burns my scalp, but I don't complain. "Holy fuck."

"Come for me. Show me how much you like being stretched."

Eli damn near sobs as he starts moving again, pushing back on me hard, taking me as deep and frantic as he can, and trembles a few seconds later as he comes, flooding my lower stomach with warmth as his cum hits my skin.

Watching him get off because of me slams my orgasm into me at high speed, taking me by surprise as I fill the condom and shiver in his hold. My eyes cross, and my pulse races in my ears as I pant. His forehead drops to mine, and his hand in my hair loosens.

"I . . . fuck," he says, and if I had the energy, I would laugh. My entire body sags against the headboard.

"I'll help you clean up once I can feel my legs again," I mumble to him, but he shakes his head.

"I'll take a shower. It'll be easier." He's stiffened up again. Opening my eyes I watch him, but he won't look at me as he climbs off and hustles to the bathroom. What the fuck was that?

I pull the condom off and follow him, annoyed when the door is locked.

"Eli?"

There's a sob, and I try the door again.

"Elliot, open this door." I don't know if I'm more pissed at being shut out or scared I hurt him. Equally both? "I will break this fucking door down."

My shoulders tense, hands clenching and unclenching as I wait.

"What do you want?" Eli calls from inside, but it sounds like he's crying.

"Open. The. Door," I demand.

"I just need a damn minute!" he snaps. That doesn't work for me. I just got him. I can't lose him already. The worst-case scenarios run through my head. Eli ending whatever this is, sleeping in that fucking tub again, or sneaking back home to hide for the rest of the time he's supposed to be in treatment. Leaving me alone once again after I know what it's like to have him will kill me.

I pound on the door, but he opens it this time, a towel wrapped around his waist and a watery glare on his face.

I enter and don't hesitate to get into his space.

"Did I hurt you?"

He looks away, sucking that lip between his teeth, and tapping his thumb against his thigh.

"Elliot." I cup his face and turn his head to look at me.

"I just need a minute." A tear streaks down his cheek, and I wipe it away with my thumb. "That was . . . intense."

His gaze pleads with me for something, but I can't tell what. To hold him closer? To leave him to his thoughts? I don't know, and I hate it. He's been alone for so fucking long and honestly, so have I.

I kiss his forehead, needing the connection, but he pushes back away from me.

"No cuddling," he grumbles.

I lift an eyebrow at him but take a step back. "Caveat: after intense sex, cuddling is sometimes necessary, and I will make you do it if I think you're making poor choices."

He rolls his eyes at me and crosses his arms. "Fine."

I grab a washcloth and clean up our sex mess from my

body, then leave him to shower. Stubborn little shit. He closes the door, and I get dressed. The bed isn't too bad, most of Eli's cum landed on me, so I pull back the blankets and find something on TV to watch for a while.

The shower turns on, and I sigh. I don't know what to do with him. He's got trust issues when it comes to me, I get it, but he's mine. For as long as I can keep him, I'm not sharing him with anyone, and this was not a one-time thing. I need him, and this time, I'm not walking away without a fight.

Once we leave this island, I don't know how it will all work, but I'll figure it out. He's not going back to pretending I don't exist.

Sixteen

ELLIOTT

What the actual fuck am I doing?

Sitting on the floor of the rainfall shower, I let the hot water pound my skin while my mind replays every touch, every word Asher just said. I feel like I look like a kicked puppy that's desperate for attention. This situation isn't going to end well.

This is going to hurt so fucking bad.

I don't want to hurt anymore. I'm tired of hurting. When is it my turn for happiness? Am I capable of accepting whatever this is while we're here, then walking away unscathed when we leave? No. Not a fucking chance. I'm already too emotionally attached to him, and we've only had sex once.

My ass clenches at the thought. Fuck, that was amazing. I've never been stretched, used, like that. Never been called a good boy. My dick twitches at the reminder. Why was that so fucking hot? Normally, my hookups are into degradation, calling me a whore or a slut. It's whatever. But praise? Jesus, that does it for me, and by the way he kept doing it, Asher fucking noticed. I came without touching my dick. My body is going to crave him even more now.

With my knees drawn up, I drop my head to my arms. I should stop this now while I still can. No more touching. Period. Friends. That's it. Nothing more.

By the time I get out of the shower, my skin is pruney and the mirror is fogged up. Once again, I forgot to grab clothes, so I wrap a towel around me and peek out into the room. Asher is passed out on the bed. Thank fuck.

I dig through my pile of dirty clothes and find some shorts, then in the drawers for everything else.

I'm dressed quickly, grab my camera, phone, and wristband, then head out. We need space from each other. At least, I do. I can't remember why being close to him is a bad idea when he's in my face.

I find the poster about the waterfall and read the directions on how to get there. There's a trail marker off the east side of the building that will point me in the right direction. Perfect. I grab a water bottle from the fridge in the lobby and one of those drawstring backpacks with the resort's logo on it, then head out.

I feel like an asshole for running from Asher, again, but at this point I have to do what I have to in order to survive. I can't deal with him right now; I need to clear the fog from my brain.

An idea hits me when I see the pier with the bar on it, and I head that way instead. It's starting to get busy out here, so I won't keep Holden long, but I do have a question for him.

"Hey, legs." He smirks at me with a head nod when he sees me.

"Hey." I flush, remembering Asher's reaction to the skirt I was wearing when I met Holden. I lean onto the bar so I can talk quietly, and he does the same. "A little drunk bird told me you sell weed."

A conspiratorial look enters his eye, and he wags his eyebrow at me. "It's true."

"Any chance you make *special* desserts to sell as well?" I ask in mock innocence.

He winks at me. "I may have some brownies on hand."

I gasp. "That sounds amazing."

He looks around quickly, then digs in a bag behind the counter. I pay the man and shove the brownie in the backpack with the water and film. I thank him and head back to the trail.

It's truly like being in a different world. It's so lush and green. The sounds of the water and birds the only noises here. The lack of traffic, honking, and buses is so foreign, like being on a different planet. Everything here is so peaceful. Why do I live in a big city again? This is much better.

I snap a few pictures along the hike to the waterfall. Glimpses of the ocean through the trees or a beautiful flower. I get a few birds, but I'm not sure what they are since they aren't my thing. As I go, I find the little river that must be coming from the waterfall, the trickling water mixing with the waves and birds.

The last six years, I've felt completely alone, but it was dark and miserable. Jordan had to force me out of my apartment sometimes just so the sun would touch my skin. But right now, I'm so distracted by what's around me that I'm not lonely. It's an experience, and even though all of my problems are still waiting in my room and I will have to face a pissed-off Asher when I get back, I'm enjoying this. When was the last time I enjoyed anything? Really enjoyed it, not just tolerated it to get a basic need met. I don't know. How sad is that?

I pull my phone from my pocket and take a selfie to send to Jordan.

ELLIOT

#boyinnature #exercise #lookatmenow

JORDAN

I love your face.

I smile and put the phone back in my pocket.

The hike isn't too hard; it's mostly uphill but not steep. I'm sweaty and breathing hard by the time I reach the clearing with the pool. I sit by the edge and kick off my shoes to put my feet in the water while I drink from the water bottle. This waterfall isn't a defined cliff you can jump from, but there's some boulders you can jump from into the water.

After a few minutes. I grab my camera and take a few pictures of the waterfall from a few different angles. I strip off my shirt and wade into the water and climb on some boulders to get better shots.

Once I've filled the roll, I put the camera in my bag and climb back onto a big boulder. The rough texture of the rock scratches at the soft parts of my feet. I stare at the water for a few minutes, both wanting to jump and afraid to. Back when I was growing up, we made a pact to never jump if there were less than three of us. If someone needed help, one would stay with them and one would call an adult or 911.

Out here, I'm alone, and I have no idea how long it would be until someone came across me. I could break a leg and be out here for hours. Maybe days.

How long before Asher would come looking for me? I'm almost positive he already is.

Sucking in a deep breath, I take a few steps back, then run. As I'm about to launch from the stone, someone yells, and I stumble. I scrape my arm on something in the water as I plunge under the surface. I'm still under the water when someone crashes into the water not far from me. They're yelling something, but I can't hear through the water in my ears. Kicking hard for the surface, my head is barely in the air when I'm grabbed and suffocated against Asher's trembling body.

"Marcus!" he yells, anguish dripping from the name as he holds me so tight it's hard to breathe. "I'm so fucking sorry." He's dragging me toward the shore before I can wrap my head around what is happening.

"Asher." I try to get his attention, but he doesn't stop pulling me toward the shallow end of the pool. "Asher, stop, I'm fine."

Asher breaks, falling to his knees and taking me with him. I end up on his lap with my arms around his shoulders as he cries, sobbing into my neck. "I should have told you about Eli. I'm so sorry. Come back, please."

A knot forms in my throat as the words ramble from him and realization sinks into me. These words are not meant for me but for my brother who never got to hear them. His body shakes, and he's rocking us back and forth, desperate and full of grief which he obviously hasn't dealt with.

"Don't leave him. He needs you. Please, Marcus, I'm sorry."

I don't know what to do. His tears hit my cool skin, hot drops of sorrow and fear searing his pain into me. More weight to carry on my weary shoulders.

"I know I'm not enough for Eli, but I'll learn how to be, and I'll come back for him. I promise I'll come back for him." His voice is a mess of tears. "I should have told you when I kissed him and that I was falling in love with him. I should have told you I left to play football because I feel invisible in my own house since my mom died and my dad is working himself to death and there's nothing I can do about it."

My own tears rain down my cheeks as Asher relives this horrific memory. One that probably haunts him. It's clearly etched into his being, and as much as I'm angry at him for leaving the way he did, I wouldn't wish this kind of suffering on him. On anyone. No one deserves this. How many times has he relived this, said those same words? Once was too many.

So I hold him while he once again loses his best friend and try to block out his words so they don't torment me later.

Running my hand up and down his back, I talk softly to him. Something will sink in at some point, right?

"You're okay, Asher," and "I'm here." Over and over for what feels like hours. The shaking and rocking slow. All of a sudden, his body feels heavy around me. His arms fall to my hips instead of being steel bands around my ribs.

"Asher?" I try to sit up, to see his face, but his arms tighten around me again.

"Asher?" I murmur into his hair. My heart breaking and

the dim light I found snuffed out, once again leaving me in the dark. It's so fucking unfair how quickly it sucks you back in. I'm already exhausted, and it just started again. Why does it have to take everything from me?

He tenses, spine straightening, and muscles bunching under my hands. His face leaves the crook of my neck, and he looks around for a minute in silence. Part of me aches for him to be wrapped around me, protecting me from my own thoughts, but the other part is terrified and wants him off of me.

"Eli?" His voice is rough from crying.

"Yeah." I release a breath of relief that he's back with me and not trapped in his memory anymore. I can't imagine reliving that memory. I already live in the past, my pain wrapped around me like a suffocating blanket to keep the present from seeping in. Like the only way to keep their memory alive is to constantly grieve.

"Did I jump in the water?" His eyes finally meet mine, and for the first time in a very long time, he looks lost. I haven't seen that expression since his mom died, and it guts me. How do I handle someone else's guilt when I can barely breathe through my own? Am I being punished? Is this what I get for being happy for a few minutes? I'm forced to relive this with him when I wasn't there the first time?

"Yeah." My throat tightens around the word.

"Right." Asher looks around again and swallows hard. "Let's head back, yeah?"

"Okay, just let me grab my things." His arms fall from me, and I climb off his lap, searching for my stuff. I get my shoes on and my shirt pulled over my head. My arm smarts as the sleeve rubs over the abrasion and I hiss but ignore it.

Is he shutting down, or am I? I'm numb but aching. Is that possible? I wish I were empty. I was content for a second, enjoying the moment, and now I'm forced back into this hell, and it's so much worse. It was a tease of what could be.

"This yours?" Asher asks, lifting the backpack.

"Yup." I pick up the camera and hang it around my neck, then take the backpack and swing it on. He grabs my hand and just about drags me down the path. I guess he doesn't like it here.

Stumbling after him, I trip and fall into his back. Why does he keep touching me? I need him to stop fucking touching me. I came out here to get the hell away from him. Why did he follow me?

You knew he would.

"Asher, stop." Panting, I'm frustrated at this stupid walk and myself. "I can walk just fine on my own."

He stiffens and grumbles something but drops my hand, and I drag in a deep breath while leaning on a tree for a second. With him ahead of me on the trail, I remove the used roll of film and refill it, then take some pictures of him. I'm not technically allowed to take pictures of other guests here, but I doubt he'll care. Though everything will be developed and checked by security before we leave so he'll know I took them. That's future Elliot's damn problem.

I meander down the path after him with him stopping every few minutes to wait for me. His long, football-trained legs eating up the distance much faster than me, but since he's hurrying me along, the walk is much quicker than it was getting up there. I wish he would just fuck off, but I also don't want him alone. I've never experienced anything like what he just did, and I don't know what happens next, but he's edgy or irritated. He's off.

By the time we get back, I'm sweaty and stuck in my head. Everything is too much but not enough. It hurts, and I'm spiraling. I just need it all to stop.

Seventeen

ASHER

I crashed for about half an hour and woke up to find Eli gone. When he didn't answer the text I sent him, I went looking. Noticing his camera was gone, I figured the bar was out. I ran along the beach, but he wasn't there. Fear clawing at my insides, I asked the woman at the reception desk for places people go for pictures. She rattled off a few things, but when she said waterfall, I knew.

The entire way up there, anxiety ate at me. What if he was hurt? I can't lose him too. I just got him back, and I'm keeping him this time. That boy is mine.

I'm not sure what happened at the falls, but it wasn't good. He's being weird, so I can only imagine what I said, but he's shutting me out. I can feel it, and I don't know how to stop it.

Back at the villa, I grab him, and he doesn't say shit. No argument. Nothing.

I start stripping him out of his clothes. When I reach for his pants, he shoves at my hands.

"I can do it myself," he bites out but won't meet my eyes.

"Fine, get out of the wet clothes yourself then. I'm taking a shower, and, Eli?" I wait until he looks in my direction again. "Don't leave this room, do you understand?"

He clenches his jaw and rolls his eyes. It's as much of an agreement as I'm going to get. I make quick work of my wet clothes and take a quick shower, finally rinsing the dried cum from my body that I missed with the washcloth. Part of me doesn't want to. It's proof he liked it too.

When I get out of the shower in loose shorts and no shirt, he's curled up on the edge of the bed, staring at the wall in a baggy shirt he must have dug out of the laundry. I climb into bed and pull him against me, needing to touch him.

He doesn't react, doesn't stiffen or acknowledge me at all. Wrapping my arms around his slender body, I pull his back against my chest and bury my nose in his hair. Eli shudders, and I slide my hand under his T-shirt to stroke his skin.

I get one pass of my palm against his body before he reaches for my wrist and pulls my hand from his shirt and drops it on my own side. My hand clenches into a fist, and I tap it against my thigh.

"Eli," I start, but he's back to limp and not there. "I'm sorry."

I kiss his neck, and this time he shivers, his breathing hitching at the touch, but he lifts his shoulder to get me off him again.

I'm desperate for a connection. I need him to touch me or at least let me touch him. I need to know we're okay. The horrors of my past are raw-dogging me, and I need a fucking anchor in the here and now.

"Eli." This time, his name is harsher, more of a command. "I need to touch you."

"Fine," I hear his barely-there whisper, but it's all I need. I shove his shirt up to expose his torso and shove my hand into his purple underwear. He's half hard, which stings, but I stroke him until he's thrusting into my hand. I'm grinding my dick against his ass and sucking on his neck until he's just as lost as I am. His skin heats as I play with him, and I growl into his skin.

I try to force his legs open, but he stiffens and just says, "No."

I freeze and lean up on my elbow to look down at him, but he's looking at anything but me. Embarrassment or nervousness making him jumpy, and I have no idea why.

"No what?" I demand. Frantic energy trying to take over every thought and action I'm capable of.

"If you want to fuck me, fine, but leave my legs alone." Eli is almost angry. "Don't touch my inner thighs."

My brain pauses for just a second, attempting to understand or process what he just said. Fuck it. I can work with that.

I pull on his underwear until it's at his knees and roll us so he's under me. I reach for the lube on the bedside table and hesitate.

"No condom."

Eli whimpers, flicking his gaze over his shoulder, and gives me a nod with his lip caught between his teeth. Thank fuck.

I straddle his thighs and drag a lubed finger through his crack.

"Spread your cheeks, show me your hole."

With shaking hands, Eli complies, burying his face in the pillow and groaning when I breach him.

"You want to stretch on my dick or fingers?" I slide a second finger in, crooking them along his insides to find that magic spot. His body shivers after a minute and he groans, "Oh god," when I find it.

"Your ass looks so good stretching around my fingers."

After lubing up my cock, I shuffle forward and push my head against his hole.

The pitiful whimper that leaves his mouth spurs me on. I don't give him time to adjust, just start thrusting, taking my pleasure while he struggles to stretch. If this is what it takes to get a fucking reaction out of him, so be it.

"Just like that. You're doing so good for me," I groan as I grip his shoulders to hold him still. The snap of my hips is punishing, unyielding, but he's pushing back into me now and arching his hips.

"You like being used, Eli?"

His fingers dig into the muscles of his ass as he struggles to hold them open.

"You're mine."

A desperate moan drags from his throat, long and loud as he takes the pounding.

"That's it, moan for me again."

I'm riding him hard, and I know I should be careful, be softer with him, but I can't. Not right now. I have to bury the memories so they don't haunt me anymore. Comfort myself the only way I wanted when it happened—with Eli.

"Please," he begs into the pillow.

"Please what? Fill your ass with cum? Stretch you wider? Use you for my own relief?"

"Yes. More. Please." His back arches, changing the angle, and he gasps.

I grab the lube and slick up my fingers before sliding one in, and I thrust a few times before adding a second one.

Eli shudders, his ass clenching almost painfully around me as he comes. I chuckle darkly and keep up my pace as he makes a mess on the sheets. My dirty boy. He's panting and goes limp, his hands falling to the bed. He's wrung out. I lean over him and moan in his ear.

"Your hole is loose and sloppy now, stretched out and so easy to fuck." Sliding my hands under his body, I grip his shoulders again and use them for leverage as I chase my release.

"Dirty boy, laying in your own cum while you get used." My balls are heavy with the need to come, to fill him. I close my eyes and bury my face in his neck as I let it crash over me, my hips jerking against his ass as cum erupts from me.

All my muscles give out, and I'm left struggling to breathe on top of him. I know I'm heavy as fuck, but I can't make myself move.

My skin is still hot and slick with sweat when I regain the ability to move, but we don't go far. I roll us back to our sides, keeping my dick inside of Eli and settling into the bed. Grabbing the corner of the sheet, I clean him off the best I can, and we wrangle the shirt off his body, then I pass out.

The waves are crashing into me, throwing my body against the rocks as I struggle to hold on to Marcus. Wait. Eli?

Eli is gone? No.

Tears are hot on my face, my throat sore from screaming for help.

"I'm sorry. Please don't leave me. I can't lose you too," I sob

into the curly hair that is Marcus's but sometimes Eli's. I don't understand. "I'll do better. I promise."

I smack into the rock again, hitting my head, and I gasp awake.

My heart is pounding in my chest, my breathing erratic, and my body jerks upright.

Quickly looking around the room, I recognize the décor and scrub a hand over my sweaty face.

Just a dream.

Fuck. Looking down at the bed, there's no Eli. Where the fuck is he?

"Eli?" No answer.

I scramble from the bed to search for him. If he went to the fucking waterfall again, I'm going to beat his ass. What the fuck was he thinking going out there alone? Doesn't he realize how dangerous it is? I can't lose him.

I'm pulling a shirt over my head when light under the bathroom door catches my attention. Striding over, I open the door and freeze. Eli is sitting on the floor with his back to the tub, legs spread, and a knife blade pressed to his inner thigh. He jumps and drops the knife, slapping a hand over the wound he caused.

"Asher!" he yells with wide eyes as his face pales. Blood trickles through his fingers and down his leg to pool on the white tile floor.

"What the fuck are you doing?" I demand, grabbing a towel from the counter and rushing to him. There are tears running down his face, sobs shaking his slim body, and his lip trembles as he looks up at me with scared, shame-filled eyes.

"I'm sorry," he manages to say as I pull his hand off the cut and push the towel against it.

"What were you thinking?" My eyes meet his. Fear still riding me from the dream and seeing him jump off that fucking boulder to finding him cutting his fucking leg open. "Do you do this a lot? When did you start cutting?"

Logically, I know I need to be nice, to be careful, but I'm not capable of that right now. I'm demanding and harsh, and that's just the way it fucking is right now. I'm pissed.

Eli recoils from me, trying to take the towel from me and push me away.

"I'm fine. Go away." His voice shakes a little, but it's stronger than it was a second ago. Good. Maybe getting him angry will get some of his fight back.

"No. What the hell were you thinking?" I demand again, shoving his hands away. "You could have hit something major and bled out."

I jerk on his leg, pulling him closer to me so I can get a better angle in the light. The bleeding has slowed but is still beading up at the edges of the cut. There's blood splattered on the floor and the wall, probably from dropping the knife.

The knife. Fuck.

I search the floor and recognize the blade I gave him for his birthday. All I can do is stare at it for a minute. The black coating on the blade is scratched up, but it looks like it's been used and probably sharpened a few times. I gave that to him for protection, not for him to carve himself up.

When my eyes finally drag back to Eli, he's sobbing into his hands.

There's a lump in my throat, and it hurts to swallow.

"Eli." My voice cracks this time. His pain echoing off the

walls of the luxury bathroom. It just goes to show you that demons don't care how much money you have. They'll haunt anyone, drag you down into hell where your money is no good for anything except a fire starter.

I drop to my ass on the tile and bring him into my lap, still holding pressure to the wound. I don't think he'll need stitches, but it'll definitely be sore tomorrow.

Eighteen

ELLIOTT

I don't know how long I sit in Asher's lap, his arm rubbing circles over my back as I drown in the darkness that's kept a hold on my ankle for six years. Hell, probably before that. I just wasn't consumed by it before then. I had someone to pull me out of the quicksand, to shine a flashlight in the inky nothingness that was my head.

I just needed to feel something, to have a way to get the overwhelming numbness to escape. Sometimes, bleeding is the only way to make it stop. The bite of the blade, the burn of the cut slicing through the paralyzed emotions. It lets me breathe without the weight on my chest. Allows me to purge, leaving me a trembling shell of pain, but it's better than numb.

Asher's fingers trace the scars on my other thigh. I think he's counting them. Part of me wants to know what he's thinking, but the other part knows. Now he knows I'm weak. This is the physical proof of not being able to handle my life.

There's no way he can see me as anything other than broken and fragile.

He pulls the towel back to check the wound again and seems happy with it. I can't look at it. Shame tells me I'm useless and disgusting. Unlovable.

Look at yourself, a fucking disgrace.

I suck in a shuddering, hiccupping breath, and wipe at my face.

"I need to clean this." Asher's sudden voice makes me jump.

"No, I'm fine. I'll do it," I tell him and stand on shaking legs. I'm kind of surprised he let me get up, but I glance at myself in the mirror, and I'm horrified. My eyes are a mess, bloodshot, puffy, and with dark circles under them. I'm pale and look ridiculous in Asher's shirt that I stole when I got out of bed.

I tried to sleep, but I couldn't make my head be quiet. After two orgasms today, I should be passed out cold, but I can't seem to get there. My body is exhausted, but my head won't stop.

Asher stands next to me, leaning on the counter and watching me in the mirror. I grab a clean washcloth and get the water running so I can clean up the mess I made.

"No." He takes the towel from me and spins me around, stepping into my space. "I'm going to clean you up and get you tucked back into bed. You're going to sleep."

"I can't," I growl. My breathing picks up at the idea of him taking care of me. Jordan is the only one I let take care of me sometimes. No one does it anymore, not really. I can't depend on it, only for it to be taken away. Again.

"Can't what?" Asher grips my chin and turns my face up

to him. Why does he have to be so damn tall? So big. It's rude.

"Can't sleep." I cross my arms to put something between his chest and mine. "Can't depend on you."

His jaw clenches, and I flick my gaze to the floor, away from him. I hate myself for saying it, for lashing out, but I need space.

Asher pushes his face into mine, digging his fingers into the skin of my jaw. "Listen very fucking carefully." I swallow and carefully watch him. "You are mine. You've always been mine, and I'm done sharing."

I jerk my face out of his grasp. As badly as I want to believe that, I don't. There's no way this will work when we leave the island, and I refuse to be a dirty little secret.

"I will not be your dirty little secret that you hide away in your house, telling anyone who sees me that I'm *just your roommate*. I won't." I shove against his chest, but he doesn't budge, the big bastard. "Just get away from me. I can't do this with you. Don't you see that being around you fucking hurts? You're going to walk away again and leave me even more broken!"

He grows so still I swear he stopped breathing. Fuck. I didn't really mean to say that. It was fucked up. It's true, but it wasn't fair.

"I left because I couldn't bring my shit to you, knowing I was the reason you were hurting. Me. I'm the reason Marcus was dead, and I couldn't face you." His voice is quiet but powerful. "I needed you. Craved you with every fiber of my being, but I didn't deserve to feel comforted by the person I had gutted." His hand is once again on my face, keeping my gaze locked on his. "In my fucked-up head, you were better off without me, and not having you was my punishment."

"I won't survive you walking away again." A tear slips down my face as I stare at him. "Being with you is everything I ever wanted, and giving it to me now only to turn your back on me again will ruin what little scraps of myself I still have left." It's his turn for tears to well up in his eyes. "Please, I am begging you not to take the fragile pieces I'm barely holding together, because I'm not capable of keeping them from you. If you don't stop, it will destroy the broken shell of a person I already am."

For a few frozen moments, there's nothing between us but our pain as our breaths mingle.

"You haven't figured it out yet," he starts, desperation seeping in. "I can't." Asher lets out a shaky breath and cups my face in his palms while a tear slowly trails down his stubbled cheek. "I loved you more than I have words to explain. I couldn't move on. I can't let you go."

His lips press to mine, soft but sure. The kiss is salty and full of the agony we know is waiting on the other side of this. Is it worse to know he'll be broken by us too, or better to know I won't be alone?

"Let me take care of you," he says against my mouth. "Please, I need to."

I nod, too close to another breakdown for words.

He gets the washcloth wet and cleans my skin, careful of the scab that's formed. It's really close to my groin, too fucking close to important shit that could have really hurt me. It was stupid, but I didn't want him to see the mark. Old scars I can brush off, but a new one would be easy to spot and hard to explain.

"Stay right there. I have a first aid kit in my bag." Asher gives me a stern look, and I watch him exit the bathroom and hear him rummage around in his suitcase. Do NFL players keep bandage supplies with them? Don't they have a team doctor for that kind of shit? He comes back with a red shaving kit bag and sets it on the counter to dig through it. He finds some ointment and big bandages to cover the wound. It's going to hurt like a bitch to get the adhesive out of my leg hair, but oh well, I guess.

Asher leans down and kisses the pad of the Band-Aid, then puts his supplies away. I slide off the counter and wash my hands that are now crusty with dried blood. He comes back in and picks up the knife, holding it in his hand. I'm sure he remembers it.

"When I unpacked your stuff, I thought you kept this with you because it made you feel safe. For protection." He runs the blade under the water, dries it, then picks up my kit and puts the knife back in the case. "I'm not giving this back."

Feeling minuscule, I nod as I dry my hands and leave the bathroom. The room is dark, bed is a mess, clothes every-where. I'm fucking tired.

Crawling back onto the bed, I curl up on my side into a ball and hug a pillow to my chest. Asher shuts off the bath-room light and joins me on the bed. The clock says three a.m. on the side table, and I just stare at it until my eyes burn. Asher doesn't try to touch me for a while. Long enough that I think he's fallen asleep, but when I sit up, he *tsks* me.

"Lay down." His words make me jump.

"I can't sleep. I'm not just laying here to stare at the wall," I tell him.

He rolls toward me, grips the back of my shirt, and pulls me back onto the mattress. Taken by surprise, I don't fight him, and I find myself enveloped by him. My face in his neck, leg over his hip, and his arms banded around me. He pushes a thick thigh between mine and slides his hand into my underwear to hold my ass cheek in his hand, then settles solidly against me. The pressure of his body on mine, surrounding me, is what I needed. Finally, I'm able to relax, and my head quiets.

Two days later, while Asher is in the gym, I find the laundry bag the resort offers and stuff all of our dirty clothes into it. Since we're here for an extended stay, I told the front desk to have the maids come in twice a week to straighten up, but that we definitely didn't need them every day.

I don't know how to feel about Asher, how to process what's happened. With anxiety making me edgy, I clean up the room. Organize the bathroom supplies, find a silicone mouth sex toy that Asher must have left in the shower, stack the books neatly on the dresser, and empty the backpack from the hike the other day. The brownie I bought from Holden calls to me, offering peace. After tossing the backpack in the closet, I rip open the packaging and break off a piece of the thick, chewy brownie. The sweet fudge flavor hits my tongue, overpowering the weed taste, and I'm a goner.

I quickly straighten out the blankets on the bed and sit crisscross in the middle with the sugary treat and a paperback. It's rich and heavy so I can't eat much before my stomach complains, but hopefully it's enough weed for the high to slow the anxiety. I'm flipping through the pages about half an hour later when the high starts. My head quiets, and I can breathe. The tension in my shoulders leaves, and I fall back on the bed with a sigh.

My skin is tingling as I run my fingertips over my stomach and thighs. Closing my eyes, I think of Asher, and my dick hardens. He's so much better than I could have imagined. Controlling my body with a few soft words. He tells me I'm good and I'm his. It's all I have ever wanted.

My fingers are dragging along the ridge of my dick through my underwear when I remember the sex toy I found in the bathroom when I was cleaning up. I jump up and grab the silicone mouth, pour some lube into it, and lie back down on the bed when the door opens.

"Eli—" I force my eyes open when he stops short. He's sweaty from his workout but so fucking sexy. The bulging arm muscles decorated with tattoos, the soft chest hair that I love to rub my face against, all on clear display since he took his shirt off to dry his face with.

"What are you doing, baby?" He leans against the wall and watches me with that smile that's all sex.

"Thinking of you," I whisper. My eyes are locked on his face while my hips arch and roll as I slide the snug toy down my cock.

He raises an eyebrow and watches my hand between my thighs.

"What about me?"

"How you fuck me." I pull my lip between my teeth, run my fingers down my dick still confined in my underwear, and arch my back. My thighs fall open as precum wets the fabric. The high lets me forget to be embarrassed over shit Asher doesn't care about. It's so freeing.

"Show me." His voice is rough, body tense as he watches. He wants to touch me, I can see it, but he's holding back.

Shimmying my underwear down, I drop them to the side and wrap my hand around my straining cock and groan. My head is sticky with precum, and I drag it down the underside of my shaft.

"Asher," I moan as I force the toy to swallow my cock. It feels good, tight and wet, but I want his hands on me. Finally leaving the wall, he drops to his knees at the end of the bed and grabs my hips to pull me to him. I let out a surprised squeak that quickly turns to a moan when his tongue slides over my hole.

"Oh fuck," I gasp as he holds my cheeks open and buries his face in my ass, sucking and licking the flesh. My hand stills for a minute, distracted by the sensations.

"Fuck yourself with my toy and come for me, Eli. Show me what a good boy you are."

Electricity shoots up my spine, hardens my nipples, and tightens my nuts as my hand gets back to work. I've never had anyone talk to me like that during sex, and I fucking love it. I want to be his good boy.

His finger pushes into my ass, and he nuzzles my sack as the obscene sounds of sex fill the room. The sucking and wetness of the lube in the toy are a soundtrack to my pleasure.

"I love the way your body takes me."

"Please fuck me," I beg the man driving me fucking crazy. "I need it."

"No, you're going to come like this, then I'm going to use your mouth." The words are firm, no nonsense, like he's telling me about the fucking weather.

My back arches, and I'm done. Exploding over my chest and inside the toy. It lands on his shirt that I stole last night, and I cry out in a pitiful whimper of release. Breathing hard and weak, my hand loosens on the toy.

"*Tsk, tsk*, such a messy boy," Asher scolds, picking up my hand and licking my cum from my skin. I watch his tongue dance over my hand, cleaning me, while the haze of the high tries to drag me to sleep. Once my hand is cleaned off, he removes the toy from me, picks up my dick, and gives my tip a hard suck. I'm so damn sensitive after I come I hiss at the contact, but he's already letting me go.

"Come here," he orders, standing up and dropping his clothes to the floor. His dick is thick and veined, standing straight out, full and hard. My mouth waters for a taste.

I struggle to sit up, and he grabs my hand to pull me toward him, then helps me out of the cum-stained shirt before stepping back enough for me to drop to my knees on the floor.

"Tongue out, eyes on me."

I stick my tongue out as far as I can and drop my head back to watch him. His hand buries in my messy curls, and he uses my mouth like a fuck toy. I'm good at sucking dick when I'm in control of it, but like this I gag when he goes too far. He doesn't slow and stop, just keeps fucking his cock with my mouth. I fucking love how he uses me.

"Such a sweet mouth," he groans, thrusting to meet my

mouth, fucking my damn throat while saliva and tears run down my face. I wrap my arms around his powerful thighs and watch as the arousal claims him. A shudder rolls across his body in a wave as he comes down my throat.

His eyes close and he pants, his dick throbbing on my tongue as he empties himself into me. At this point, I've got more of his cum than food in my body when I swallow.

"Suck."

I close my mouth around him and do what he said, sucking the last few drops of cum from his dick as he pulls out. With a hand on the back of my neck, he lifts me from the floor and kisses me hard, in a claiming kiss I feel down to my toes. It turns me on that he can taste himself on my tongue and doesn't care.

"Get dressed for the beach."

I nod quickly, licking his taste from my lips.

"I'm going to shower, then we'll go sit in the sand for a while."

Asher kisses my forehead and heads to the bathroom. I watch his sexy ass walk across the room, then dig in my drawers for a bathing suit. I think I shoved something in here.

After five solid minutes of searching, the only thing I can find is a yellow goddamn speedo. I slap my hand over my eyes and try not to scream. Why am I like this?

Begrudgingly, I change into the damn thing, all the while singing "Itsy Bitsy Teenie Weenie Yellow Polka Dot Bikini" in my head. Looking in the mirror, I can see the edges of my scars and the bandage from the other night. Unease quivers in my stomach at the idea of someone seeing it. It's bad enough that Asher knows, but I don't want whispers or stares. Shit.

I dig through some of the complimentary shit the resort gave us and find sunblock. We will need more, but it's a start. My pale ass will burn to a crisp if I'm not careful.

Grabbing the backpack I tossed in the closet, I wrap the brownie back up after shoving another huge bite in my mouth and put it inside—being high as fuck on the beach sounds magical—along with a book, my camera, film, and some snacks. I'm going to need the high in order to wear this outside. Why do I even own it? I have no damn idea.

Asher opens the door to the bathroom and stops when he sees me.

"Absolutely not."

I turn around to face him with my hands on my hips. "Excuse me?"

"You're not wearing that in public." With only a towel wrapped around his hips, he stalks toward me. "Not only does that show off what is mine, but I'll have a constant hard-on. Find something else."

"I don't want to go to the beach." The words tumble from my lips without my brain okaying it. I can't look at him as embarrassment floods my system. Will he ignore the request and drag me along anyway? Usually, I just go with whatever others want to do, not making my needs or wants known.

He growls and drags his eyes over my body, stopping at my thighs. His body language goes from agitated to understanding. My shoulders lower, curving in around me, and I pick at my fingers. Asher comes to me, cupping my face in his palms.

"There's one of those net hammock things out back. We

can lay out there instead. Sand in your ass crack is the worst anyway." He shrugs and strides for his dresser for shorts.

Now I feel like shit. Did he really want to go to the beach? Am I keeping him from what he wants from his time here?

"No." I rush forward. "You can still go. It's fine. I'll just lay on the deck and read or something."

My chest is tight as I try to backpedal. I should have just kept my mouth shut. Ideas race through my head as I try to find a solution. I can change into a dirty pair of shorts that cover the scars or wear something wrapped around my waist.

I'm rocking back and forth, not really seeing the room or Asher anymore until he grabs my face and turns it up to his.

"Hey." He pulls me against him. "I want to spend time with you. The where doesn't matter. Plus, out here, I can touch you without worrying who will see."

On the back deck is one of those nets hung in a frame that you can lay on over the water. The breeze is amazing, and at this time of the day, it's covered in shade, so we don't need to worry too much about sunblock.

With my book and brownie, I sit on the edge of the deck with my feet in between the squares of the net, waiting for Asher.

He found the liquor bottles in the cabinet and the small fridge of mixers, so he's making something for us to drink. It's probably not my best plan to get drunk while also getting high, but I'm past the point of caring, and honestly, it's not the first time. My head needs a break from all the thinking and feeling.

I open the brownie and pop a piece in my mouth—the

damn thing is huge, like the size of my palm—and open my book. Skimming the pages, trying to find something that grabs my attention, when Asher comes out with a bottle of what looks like vodka held against his chest and a stack of shot glasses.

"Change of plans."

I lift an eyebrow as he stops at one of the tables on the deck with a big tic-tac-toe board. He clears off the pieces and sets up the shot glasses, one in each square, then starts filling them.

"Are we getting wasted?" I eye him warily.

"Yup. Go grab some chasers from the fridge."

I huff but pick up my brownie and book to sit on the chair and head to grab some sodas, an orange juice, and a cranberry juice.

Sometimes I need the chaser, but I might power through it this time just because. I've spent a lot of the last six years in a bottle and can drink people twice my size under the table.

I'm halfway to the table when I notice Asher has my brownie.

"Dude, this is delicious, where did you get it?" He's eaten half the damn thing. Oops.

"Uh, from the bartender at Midnight Lounge." I set the drinks down on the table and snatch the treat from him, quickly shoving it into my mouth. I'm going to be so high in an hour. Oh well.

"Has kind of a weird aftertaste." He grabs a Mountain Dew and takes a swig.

I roll my lips between my teeth but don't say anything. Maybe he'll learn to stay out of my shit. I doubt it, but it's worth a shot, right?

"Okay, take a shot to claim your square," Asher tells me, waving a wand over the board. "X or O?"

"I'll be O." I grab a corner glass and swallow the vodka in one go with barely a hiss. Both of Asher's eyebrows shoot up, but he doesn't say anything. I set the glass in front of him and wait for him to take the middle spot, because he always does. His face scrunches up, and he quickly takes a drink of his soda, which makes me laugh.

I grab the opposite corner and toss it back. It's smooth as fuck, barely burns.

"Seriously? No chaser?"

"Nope." I pop the P and wait for him to go.

Asher shakes his head and snags a corner shot, leaving just one and playing right into what I want him to do.

He swallows it and coughs, chugging Mountain Dew after it while I laugh at him.

I pick the last corner which leaves me with two ways to win and no way to block me. Keeping my eyes on him, I drink the vodka and set the glass down.

"That's sexier than it should be," he tells me, licking his lip.

The internal monologue in my head quiets as the high from the brownie sweeps in. My shoulders relax, and I lean back against the white cushion of the chair as all the stress leaves my body. There's a slight buzz that calms my frayed nerves, and I close my eyes to enjoy the relief.

"That's even sexier." Asher's gruff voice is closer to me than it was when I closed my eyes. "All relaxed and recently fucked."

I bite my lip as tingles start in my belly.

Asher nips at my inner thighs, kneeling on the wood

deck between my legs, licking the scars that mark my pain with physical proof on my skin. I run my hand through his hair, enjoying the soft strands on my palm.

"Let's lay in the hammock," he says with his lips against my lower stomach. He sucks on my skin, licking at me.

"Mmmm," is all I can muster, so he stands and lifts me in his arms. He finds the rectangular net that's secured in a frame over the water and sets me down. The rope digs a little into me, but the breeze off the water is perfect. Asher settles next to me, so I roll into him. When my eyes meet his, I can see the glaze of the high has taken him over too.

His fingertips barely brush along the center of my body until he gets to the stupid swimsuit. Gripping one leg, he pulls it over his to open me to him.

He locks his gaze with me as he palms my dick over the thin fabric.

"I can't get enough of you." Asher watches my mouth when it falls open on a moan. The way he plays my fucking body is criminal. "I crave you. I'm desperate, all the fucking time."

His hand slides inside my suit and cups my balls, one finger sliding between my cheeks. His lips crash into mine, and I whimper as he fucks my mouth with his tongue.

I'm hard, aching already. Lust mixing with the high to shut down any and all inhibitions. This is Asher. My Asher. I love him even when it hurts. I can't tell him no. Nothing matters but him, this moment, when he touches me.

Wrapping my arms around his neck, I pull him on top of me, my thighs spread wide to accommodate his hips. He wraps a hand around me, stroking me quickly, and even though just I came an hour ago, I'm riding that edge in a matter of seconds. He does this to me. Only him.

"I'm going to use your cum as lube," Asher growls in my ear. Heat floods my body, arching my back, and cum shoots from me on a ragged cry. He chuckles, the vibration of it humming along my chest.

"There's my good boy." He nips at my neck and sits up, pulling my swimsuit off and tossing it on the deck. He swipes his fingers through the cum on my chest while I try to remember what planet I'm on and swirls it around my hole. Coating his fingers in my cum, he pushes two inside at the same time. The stretch is perfect, and I grip the ropes of the net for something to hold on to.

In and out, his fingers keep a steady rhythm, scissoring them, then adding a third.

"Fuck," I moan, my spent dick twitching. "Fuck me, own me, please." I bury my face in my arm as I let him take anything he wants from me.

"I already own you." Asher collects more cum, and his fingers leave my body. I lift my arm to peek at him, seeing him coating himself in me, and I bite my lower lip as my skin flushes. "Up on the deck," he instructs, and I scramble to get up on the solid surface despite feeling like I'm floating.

He climbs up after me and positions me so my head is hanging over the edge of the hammock with my legs shamelessly spread in invitation. He kneels in between my thighs, sliding his dick between my cheeks and watching my face as he pushes inside. He leans over me, wrapping a hand around my throat as he thrusts mercilessly.

"I. Own. You." He punctuates every word with a hard, deep thrust. "Always. Mine."

He fucks me harder than he has before, almost brutal, like he has to leave proof on my body. Doesn't he know he's etched into every cell of me?

Wrapping my arms around him, I dig my nails into the skin of his back, raking long lines into his flesh. My proof that he's mine.

He draws out his orgasm, using my body to edge himself, and it's the hottest thing I've ever experienced. When he gets close, the ruthless beast slows, kissing and sucking on my skin with sweet, slow thrusts just to turn around and pound into me savagely. It's intoxicating, and I don't want it to ever fucking end.

All the praise he freely gives me works my body better than any touch ever has.

Asher cups the back of my head and lifts it up.

"Watch how beautifully you take me." He grips my dick in his hand and strokes me in time to the rough thrusts. Watching his body roll against mine, the muscles flexing and dancing while he disappears into my now gaping hole, is overwhelming.

My heart jackknifes, and my body tightens so hard it's almost painful as my orgasm climbs higher than I've ever experienced.

"Tell me what a good boy you are while you come. Tell me," he demands. His breathing is just as ragged as mine.

"Oh god." My eyes start to roll into the back of my head as tingles explode over my skin.

"Tell me!" he roars.

"Fucking good boy." The words tumble from my lips as I'm taken over by the intense release. It steals my breath and thinking ability. Every muscle in my body is tight enough to snap as hot jizz coats my stomach once again. Asher pounds into me unyieldingly, growling as he finds his own release and fills my sloppy hole with cum.

Both of us are sweaty, weak, and covered in cum when he drops onto me. He's heavy, but I love the pressure of him on me. Dropping my head back, I pass out on the deck.

Nineteen

ASHER

Over the next five days, we fall into an easy routine. Morning sex, I work out, shower, breakfast, find something to do and have lunch, fuck in a new place, then dinner and more sex. It's paradise. I don't know how, but I can't let this end when we leave the island. I need him.

Tonight, we're going to a bonfire the resort is having on the beach. We haven't interacted with others much while we've been here, mostly just kept to ourselves, away from anyone who might see us together. I have a lot on the line if the media finds out I'm with a man. Am I really willing to sacrifice my career? The longer I'm here, the more it's a possibility, the more I wonder. I love Eli with every fiber of my being, nothing will ever change that, but I'm scared.

Eli comes out of the bathroom scrunching his blond curls, looking sexy as fuck in a velvet purple skirt that swishes as he moves and a baby pink, silk sleeveless tank that molds to his tight body perfectly.

"Is that my mom's necklace?" Around his neck hanging to just below his collarbone is a soft pink pearl necklace.

Eli smiles shyly at me, running his fingers over the beads with nervous energy humming around him.

"Are you sure about this?" His free hand picks at the edge of the skirt as he shifts on his feet.

"Baby, you look fucking amazing." My open white, short-sleeved, button-down shirt swirls around me as I walk toward him. His eyes are huge as he looks up at me, chewing on the inside of his lip. "If anyone so much as looks at you funny, I'll rearrange their face."

I lift the necklace from his skin and run the beads between my fingers before letting it fall back in place.

"It's beautiful on you," I murmur in the quiet of our room. It's not until this moment that I realize his color is better, the dark circles under his eyes are gone, there's a lightness in his eyes again, and a tan on his skin. He looks healthy, happy. Sliding my hands behind his neck, I pull his lips up to mine for a soft, lingering kiss.

Eli holds on to my wrists as he relaxes into my kiss.

"You look amazing," I tell him with my lips still pressed to his. "How am I supposed to keep my hands to myself with you dressed like this?"

He lifts his mouth in a devious little grin and widens his eyes in mock innocence.

"I guess you'll just have to try harder." Taking a step back, he grabs his camera, and we head out toward the beach. The sun is sinking, but it's still light enough to see everything clearly. There's a big bonfire on the beach with some pop-up stands, looks like food and drinks, along one side. There are chairs and tables, benches around the fire, and lots of space for blankets and towels.

Music starts playing from speakers that are set around the outside of the designated area, giving it a real beach party vibe.

"Let's get drinks." I nudge Eli, and he nods, watching everyone around us. It's not very often that he leaves the safety of his house dressed like this, too scared of being attacked by a homophobe, but I won't let that happen.

"Do you want to sit, and I'll get you a drink?"

Eli shakes his head, still watching those around us. From what I've seen, no one has even looked in our direction.

"Eli."

"Hmm?" He doesn't look at me, just pops his knuckles with his head on a swivel.

"Elliot." This time his head snaps to me, eyes wide.

"What?"

"You're safe. Take a deep breath and relax. I won't let anything happen to you." I shove my hands in my pockets so I don't touch him. The crowd is growing here. Soon we'll be able to disappear into it, but it's not there yet. I hate that we have to be careful, that people are such judgmental assholes, but that's the reality of our world. People talk. The elite world is small, drama and rumors spread like wildfire, even with the NDAs we all signed. People talk quietly in the dark corners, using code names in case they're overheard. Word would get out, and I would catch the brunt force of the backlash.

At the small bar, I get a beer, and Eli gets a sex on the beach. I hand him the highball glass, and we walk toward a bench. He takes a drink of it, and I mutter, "I'll give you sex on the beach," with my beer bottle to my lips.

He chokes on a laugh, coughing into his arm. I pat his back a few times, and he glares at me.

"What?" I smile, but he turns away from me to eye the crowd again. "If you're that uncomfortable, we can go back so you can change."

"No, I don't want to change."

My phone rings in my pocket, so I pull it out and answer it.

"Hello?"

"Good evening, Mr. Vaughn," a cheerful female voice says. "This is Kelsey from Black Diamond Resort."

"Oh, hi." I stand and walk away from the crowd so I can hear her better. "Is there a problem?"

"No problem at all. I was calling to let you know there's another villa that has become available, and we can have your luggage moved over first thing tomorrow."

A buzzing fills my head. I don't want to leave him. I can't.

My heart rate jacks up in my chest, pounding in my ears at the idea of him not being with me every second of the time I have with him here. I don't even know how I'm going to get on that fucking boat to leave the island without him. Just thinking about it makes me itchy, makes the panic start clawing at the back of my throat.

"That's okay. We've worked it out, and I'll stay where I'm at. Thank you." The words rush out so fast I'm not sure she even understood them.

There's a long pause before she says, "Are—are you sure?"

"I am, thank you." I hang up the phone and turn around

to find that damn bartender sitting on the bench facing Eli, dragging the back of his fingertips down Eli's arm. Abso-fucking-lutely not.

Eli has a blush on his cheeks and a cocky smile. He's flirting with this asshole! What the fuck?

Stalking over to them, I grab the guy's arm and shove him off the bench.

"You're in my spot," I snap at him, dropping down onto the wood.

"I'll see you around, legs." The man winks at Eli, and I jolt to my feet. Eli grabs my hand and pulls on me.

"Asher, stop it. You're making a scene," he says sharply under his breath so only I can hear him.

I spin on him, my chest tight as I fight with myself for control. I fucking hate that I can't touch him, can't claim him right here in front of everyone.

He looks up at me with sadness in his eyes that hurts on a bone-deep level. Sadness I can't fix. Not here and not now.

"Don't worry about Holden." Eli's voice is soft, probably so no one will overhear. "But honestly, it's probably better if everyone sees us with other people. It's suspicious that you're staying in the same villa as me while I'm dressed like this. We're always together unless you're in the gym. You aren't acting straight. People will talk unless we give them a reason not to."

Eli stands and folds his arms around his stomach. It's an old, self-soothing motion that I haven't seen in a long time.

"If people want to talk because I'm spending time with a man I grew up with, that's on them. That's not suspicious." I lift my bottle to my lips and take a long pull to give myself something to do.

very out gay man, and no one has seen you with a chick since you got here. You're possessive and have touched me in public in ways that say it's suspicious. At the bar on the pier? You were wrapped around me while I was wearing a skirt." Reaching for his glass, he swirls the thin straw around. "You need to find a . . . woman to be seen with."

"No." The word is out before I've even thought it through. Is he playing it smart? Yes. Do I like it? Not at fucking all.

He sighs heavily, not looking at me. "You have to think logically. When we leave here and go back to the real world, you don't want rumors of this to follow you."

"Excuse me," a feminine voice says behind me. Spinning around, I'm met with a sexy redhead in a white bikini and sheer blue cover-up that actually covers nothing. Even if I wasn't here with Eli, I wouldn't be interested.

"Yes?" I force my shoulders to relax and force a smile to my face.

"Do you play football?" Her expression turns sultry. Seduction is her game, but I'm not interested. Movement behind me catches my attention. Turning my head, I watch Eli walk away from me toward that damn bartender again. Fine. If this is how he wants to play it, I guess we will.

Twenty

ELLIOTT

I'm trying to hold back tears as I walk away from Asher, away from the redhead with a barely-there bikini, showing all her secrets to anyone who will look. It hurts.

Everything fucking hurts.

Again.

I don't even notice I'm heading toward Holden until he whistles at me. He's sitting with a group of people I assume are his coworkers. They don't exude entitlement anyway.

"What do you need?" He steps closer, making sure our bodies are flush, and starts swaying to the music. My body follows his on instinct, the roll of his hips against mine is sensual and promising.

"I need to be seen." My words are small, but there are so many meanings to that one sentence.

"Hey there." His smile is laced with sexual intentions and mischief.

"Hi." I take a big gulp of my drink, making a plan in my head. "Can I talk to you for a second?"

Can I trust him? Can I trust that he'll follow the NDA I'm sure all the employees have to sign? Does he have connections to the rich and famous, or do most of the people who come here blow him off as *the help*? Am I willing to risk it?

I guess I am.

Holden stands and I step away toward the fire, where there are more people to see me with him. In the crowd, I'm less likely to be heard over everyone's conversations, the crackle of the fire, and the music.

When I stop and turn back to him, someone bumps into me, forcing me closer to the tall man. He wraps an arm around my waist to steady me and leaves his hand on my lower back as he watches me.

"You good, legs?" He lifts an eyebrow, studying me.

"Yes, but I need a little help." I swallow thickly and look around quickly. So many things are in play here, my own safety being part of my anxiety right now. If someone attacked me, would Holden be attacked too? I'm not sure I could manage the guilt from getting an innocent bystander hurt. "My name is Elliot, by the way."

"I prefer legs. What do you need?" He steps closer, once again leading my body to sway to the music.

He flicks his eyes to something behind me, and I assume it's Asher, but I force myself not to turn and look. Watching him flirt with that woman won't do me any favors.

"Trying to make the boyfriend jealous?" Holden smiles down at me, mischief dancing in his eyes.

"Not my boyfriend." I shake my head vehemently. I hate that he thinks it, but he has every right to. I'm sure he saw

Asher with his hand on my legs the other day at the bar, pressed against me just a few minutes later. "He *was* my brother's best friend. He's just a nice guy looking out for me."

Holden looks like he doesn't believe me but doesn't argue. "Right."

The song changes to something with a sultry beat, and I wrap my arms around his neck, careful not to spill my drink on him. Holden shifts our position until one of his thighs is between mine, and one hand splays on my back, while the other trails my outer thigh. We move to the song, getting lost in the music for a few seconds, and letting our bodies just move.

A hand cups my ass, but I don't react to it. I hate that I need it to happen, and I wish more than anything that I was high right now. Some cocaine would make this a lot fucking easier, but instead, all I have is alcohol.

Holden spins me, pulling my ass against his crotch, and nuzzles at my neck. My eyes close as I take a long drink from my glass and let it happen. I need to be seen like this. Up to my normal shit so people ignore Asher.

"You're being watched," he says against my skin, his hand sliding down my torso toward the waistband of my skirt.

My eyes pop open, and through the flickering light of the fire, I meet Asher's furious gaze. His arm is around the woman's shoulders, and she's pressed against his chest. I want to rip her fucking hand off for touching him. Shove her away from him and scream at her to get away from what's mine.

I fucking hate this.

Swallowing the last of my drink, Holden takes the glass from me and sets it on a table not far from us and comes right back, pulling my body against his. I lift an arm to hook around the back of his neck and lean into our dance. Thrusting back against him, letting my body enjoy his touch. My heart hates it, but my body craves touch.

It's kind of sexy, though, to be watched by someone who wants me, working him up, and knowing he can't do anything about it. If I make it a game, will that make it easier? See how far I can push him before he snaps? I feel almost powerful. It's not a feeling I'm familiar with. It's heady and slightly terrifying at the same time.

I've gotten really good at making a scene for attention, but this is different. The men I usually fuck don't want any more from me than a warm hole. Asher wants more. Will I have to break his heart this time? Will he ask me to come with him, and I'll have to say no, walk away, and disappear?

I can't do this with him. Let him fuck me into oblivion in the safety of his house, only to be relegated to the roommate in public. It's not fair of him to ask that of me. I hope he understands that and doesn't push it.

Closing my eyes, I lean my head back against Holden's shoulder and try to force the spiraling thoughts from my head.

"Do you want another drink?" he asks against my ear.

"Good idea." I nod, and he grabs my hand, leading me through the crowd of dancing people to the bar. The line isn't too long, so we don't have to wait more than a few minutes.

"Hey, Holden, getting into trouble already?" The man behind the bar laughs. Holden wags his eyebrows and looks at me with a big smile on his face.

"Only the best kind."

The bartender smirks at Holden, then looks to me. "What can I get you?"

"Two shots of vodka, please," I tell him.

Two shot glasses are set in front of me, and he fills them. I toss back both quickly with barely more than a hiss after the second one.

"That was sexy as fuck," Holden says, leaning on the bar. I laugh and pay for my drinks with my wristband, and we wander away.

As we find something to do, Holden keeps glancing over my shoulder.

"You think if I kissed you, he'd deck me?"

"One hundred percent." Shit. I should have denied that. Goddamn it.

On the outside of the crowd, Holden grabs my hand and spins me. A laugh builds up in my chest and a smile splits my face at the motion. We dance around, laughing and just moving, nothing sexual or heavy, just letting the energy of the night surround us. We get more drinks, letting the alcohol blur the complications until I just don't care anymore.

I trip, stumbling over my own feet, and fall into Holden's chest, laughing. He catches me, but before I can look up at him, I'm jerked away from him with a harsh grip on my arm.

"Get the fuck away from him." That low, possessive tone has a shiver racing up my spine. Asher.

For a second, I let myself lean into him. I allow myself to be comforted by his presence. Asher wraps an arm around my body, his skin hot against the thin fabric of my shirt.

Holden looks between us, watching carefully. "Legs, you good?"

"Mmhmm," I mumble. I inhale Asher's sensual cologne and try not to nuzzle his neck.

Holden holds up his hands and backs away.

"You're driving me fucking crazy," Asher bites out and grabs my hand, pulling me away from the beach and toward the trees. "Letting that fucker touch you? I should break his fucking hands."

"You had that woman's tits on you!" I yell back, allowing my frustration at the situation to bleed through. "You aren't being careful, so I have to!" I jerk my hand out of his grasp and stop. "You're forcing my hand to fucking protect you."

"Who asked you to?" He spins around, crowding me against the side of a building hidden in the trees. "I didn't."

"You have no idea what this could do to you, to your career! Your life as you know it will be over!" I shout, shoving at his chest and getting even more frustrated when he doesn't budge. "I might not be a famous *sports ball* player, but I've been out, publicly, for years. Every time a mic is shoved in my face, I'm asked about my sex life. How my parents feel about it. Were they accepting? Do you have a boyfriend? Do you top or bottom? Is it true all gay men love sucking dick? Do you dress like a girl because you wish you were one, or do you just want to be treated like one?" I'm yelling by the end, panting as my anger takes over. It hums into my body until I want to cause damage. I want to hurt someone. I want him to bleed inside just as much as I have.

"Have you ever had men look at you sideways, shifting uncomfortably because they think you're checking them out? Had them not want to sit next to you or share a bathroom with you? Or sneer at you, calling you horrendous names?" I shove at him again. "I have. Every single one of those things. It hurts every goddamn time!"

Asher drops his forehead to mine, sharing my air as I vibrate with fury.

"Now imagine it's your teammates. Guys you think of as your friends now don't want to share a locker room or a shower with you. Won't sit next to you on the bus or plane."

"Stop," Asher says, pulling me against him.

"It only takes one bad, convincing person to turn a room."

He slams his lips over mine, forcing me to stop talking by shoving his tongue into my mouth.

With a hand on my throat, he releases my mouth.

"You don't want me to come out? Fine. I'll make sure you don't leave that fucking villa without me dripping from your stretched-out hole."

I shudder, sucking in a gasp at the image. Arousal sparks to life, and I reach for his belt, flipping it open. He growls, sucking on my lip and pulling it between his teeth.

"You want to be used, Eli?"

No. I want you to love me.

"Yes." I rip his pants open and reach in to grab his dick, shoving his underwear down to get it out of the way. His cock is gloriously hard and jutting out from his body.

I stroke him a few times before he spins me around and lifts my skirt, tucking the edge into my waistband to hold it up. With no finesse, he shoves my underwear down and kicks my feet apart. I'm aching for him. For the words I know he'll give me. I need them.

Asher smacks my ass cheek hard enough to make the

skin heat and sting. I hiss at the burn, but it lights me up inside.

"Your skin is so fucking pretty with my handprint on it." Asher rips open some kind of package and slick fingers slide between my cheeks. I moan as his finger pushes into me, thrusts a few times before a second one is added, then a third.

My eyes roll back as he stretches me, making my hole sloppy with lube before he fucks me.

"Please," I beg, forcing myself back onto him.

"Don't worry, baby, I'll have you coming on my dick in no time." His hand grips my hip hard, making me arch my back for better access. The hard, hot tip of his cock drags through my cheeks until he finds my stretched hole, and he slides inside in one thrust. My body being forced to stretch where his fingers didn't reach, so fucking deep.

Asher's free hand grabs my jaw and pulls my face from the wall, bending me back.

"Look at you taking my dick like such a good boy," he groans in my ear. "Does it feel good to be used?"

"Yesss," I hiss as he thrusts into me with slow, hard, deep strokes. He has full control over my body, my head, and I'm addicted to it. Finally, the doubts are quiet, and I can just let him take what he needs from me. There's no future, no past, no worries. Just this.

"You think you can walk away from me? Walk away from us?" His fingers dig into my flesh, leaving bruises on my skin. "You're mine, only mine." His snarl has goose bumps erupting over my body. "I don't fucking share."

My breathing hiccups in my chest as my brain is over-whelmed with stimulation. His rough hands on my skin, his words and growls in my ear, the drag of his dick inside of me. I can't process it all.

"Are you going to come? Spray the wall with it, show everyone how much my sweet boy loves to be used."

Wrapping a hand around myself, my dick is sticky with the precum running down my shaft. I jerk myself hard, in quick strokes, needing the high of the orgasm his body is promising mine. His words echoing between my ears.

"That's it, squeeze my cock, take it. Make me fill you up so you'll feel me for the rest of the night."

I'm done. With a gasp, my body shudders so hard the only thing keeping me upright is Asher's hold. A loud, long, ragged moan rips from my throat, and I don't give a shit who hears me. My cum hits the wall I'm pushed against, and I don't care about that either.

Asher grunts and picks up speed, slapping against me in a vulgar mix of flesh meeting flesh and his sounds of pleasure. Heat spreads in my gut, and he trembles against me as he comes. His grip on me loosens, and I'm forced to stand on my own. The hand on my hip slides around my waist to hold me against him, and he turns my chin to kiss my cheek. We're both panting, shivering in the cool breeze as it hits our sweaty, overheated skin.

"I love you, Eli."

My stomach tightens, and my heart hurts at the words I've waited my whole life to hear because I can't keep him. He has to go back to his life, and I have to let him go.

Placing my hands on the wall, I push against it, needing space. Tears are welling up in my eyes already. I need to get out of here.

"Eli?" Asher takes a step back, but he pulls me with him, keeping himself buried in my body.

"I heard you." My throat is tight around the knot of emotion I'm trying to hold back. "I can't."

I reach for my underwear and pull them up. Asher finally releases me, slipping from my body with a hiss. With shaking hands, I adjust my clothes.

I hate myself for not saying it back to Asher. He deserves to hear the words because they're true, and I know he's probably just as alone as I am. After his mom died, his dad disappeared into work, and I doubt that's changed. Every fiber of me hopes he has friends, a found family with his team to help him pick up the pieces. Maybe he can't tell them about me, but they'll know he's broken and support him while he heals.

"I'm sorry," I whisper to him as I straighten my spine and walk back toward the bonfire.

"Eli!" He quickly catches up to me, but I stop dead in my tracks when I'm suddenly face to face with my parents. My heart drops into my stomach, but I wrap my arms around my waist and force myself not to look back at him. I can feel him like a shadow behind me, fully aware he's not done with that conversation, but I can't do it right now.

Guilt and shame color my face, and I drop my gaze to my feet.

"Elliot Martin." My mother's disappointed tone cuts through me like a hot knife through butter. "Why do you leave a trail of destruction everywhere you go?"

I close my eyes and swallow back the tears.

"Mr. and Mrs. Cushings." Asher steps up next to me, offering his hand to shake, but they don't even look at it.

"Get out of here, son," my father says to him while my mother's glare continues to hold me captive. I can feel her taking in my clothes, how disheveled I am, probably smelling of sex, and her disapproval smacks me in the face. "You damn near lost your career before it started because of him, don't let him take it from you now."

"What the hell are you talking about?" My words are watery with tears.

"You think we didn't know about you two when Marcus died? We paid a hell of a lot of money to keep that detail out of the report so no one would find it later!" my father shouts at me before turning back to Asher. "Don't let him ruin your life. We all make mistakes."

Every word is another knife in the back.

"Sir," Asher starts. "Eli is not a mistake."

"Just go," I all but shout at him. God. Doesn't he realize how much worse this will be if he argues? We're all trying to save him, and he won't take the fucking lifeline we're throwing him. I am a fucking mistake. Already, I'm the dirty secret he can't ever tell anyone about. Why can't he get that?

"Eli . . ." Asher reaches for my hand, but I jerk out of his grasp.

"It's better this way." My words are soft but hurt so fucking badly.

"This is what you want?" He turns to face me. "Look at me and tell me this is what you want."

Pulling on every molecule of self-control I have, I force the knot down and look at him.

"Go back to your life." A tear falls down my cheek, but I don't brush it away. For a split second, there's so much agony in his dark eyes that I almost drown in it, but I stand strong despite the need to dissolve. Is this what he felt like when he walked away? He thought it was in my best interest even though it gutted him to do it?

I guess I get it now.

"I forgive you." The words are quiet, and by the way his jaw clenches, I'm sure he knows what I mean.

For a split second, I can see the pain on Asher's face before he buries it behind the mask that fools everyone but me. With his shoulders squared and head held high, he walks away from me, but this time, I'm the one who pushed him. He quickly makes it back to the crowd and is swallowed by the mass so I can't track his movements anymore.

With my heart in his hand, I face my parents and prepare for the mental war I'm about to lose.

"Why do you have to drag down everyone around you? You're risking his career. Are you really that selfish?" My mother's words rip apart every insecurity I have. It's no wonder where I get them from, I know. "He's done nothing but be your friend since you were a child, and this is how you repay him?"

Like I picked this? He chose this. I told him it would be a bad idea, but he wouldn't listen.

"You finally did something right in your life by telling him to leave," Father tosses out.

I hate them. But I hate myself more for believing the lie I told myself.

"And you look ridiculous. What were you thinking leaving your room like that?" Mother scoffs, and once again I drop my head so I don't have to look at her. I've always felt so fucking small next to her. Not once has she encouraged me to be who I am, just picked me apart until I have no thoughts or opinions. What's the point when I'm always wrong?

"You're an embarrassment to your brother's memory." She shakes her head as my tears drip onto the sand. "Why would you humiliate Asher like this, being out in public dressed like *this*?" She points to my clothes, disgust clear on her face. "Why are you so selfish, Elliot? Isn't it exhausting being this self-centered all the time?"

"I'm sorry," I mumble as my lip trembles in the shadows where she can't see. That makes me weak too.

"Go pack. The plane is waiting. You obviously can't be trusted here either. You're going home."

I nod without argument and head toward the pier. Before I know it, I'm running as fast as I can toward the villa. The tears fall so fast the wind can't dry them, and I'm sobbing by the time I get to the door. I can't go in there. Everything in there is etched with my time with Asher. How did I get this deep in such a short amount of time? I'm once again cut open, hemorrhaging at his loss. How do I have anything left to lose?

I collapse on the deck and cry into my hands, sobs racking my body while I rock on my knees.

Nothing is fair in war when love is a battleground. Shrapnel rips through you, leaving scars you carry for the rest of your life. Trauma festers until there's nothing left but the monsters in the dark. Light is snuffed out before hope can grow, leaving you an empty shell of who you used to be.

Twenty-One

ASHER

With every shot of tequila, Eli's words dim just a little more. Eventually, I won't hear them, right? Or they won't hurt so much?

How did we get here? We still have a little over two weeks left to figure it out. Wasn't that the plan? To find a way to make this work once we left here? Was it just me?

Was he planning to go back to his life in LA, back to ignoring my existence?

As I rub at the pang in my chest, the redhead from earlier comes over and tries to sit in my lap.

"Nope," I say too loudly, but I don't care.

"Are you sure? I promise I'm a good time." She puts her hand on my knee and starts sliding it up my thigh, but I shove it off. My dick tries to retreat into my body at the thought of her touching me.

"Not interested." The world is starting to spin, and my lips are numb, but Eli's face is still clear as fuck. That goddamn tear on his cheek. He told me to go. Last time, I didn't give him an option, yet we have the same outcome.

Stumbling to my feet, the world tilts and shifts under me, but I find a quiet spot and lay down, just until the spinning stops, but the world goes black.

My head is pounding, and my mouth tastes like shit. When did this bed get so hard and lumpy? And why is it so fucking bright?

I lift a hand to cover my eyes, but something scratches my arm. Jerking my eyes open, I'm looking at the underside of a bush. What the fuck? Looking around, I'm definitely on the beach, and I'm not sure why. What is happening?

Forcing my body to move, and with a lot of cursing, I roll out from under the bush and sit up. My stomach turns, and I lean over to puke stomach acid onto the sand. Oops. Now my mouth really tastes like shit, but the pressure in my head is a little better. Where is Eli?

Once my body settles, I struggle to my feet and search my memory for how I ended up here.

I head toward one of the piers and hope it's the right one.

Eli and I went to the bonfire, he was super antsy. A redheaded woman who I can't remember if she told me her name since I wasn't paying attention, and Eli danced with that fucking bartender. We fucked against a building, I have no idea which one, and . . . oh fuck. His parents.

His dad told me to leave this *mistake* behind.

Eli told me to go.

Running now, powered by the fear of losing him again, I find our villa quickly.

"Eli!" I yell as I open the door. The dining area is empty,

so I hurry to the bedroom, but he's not there, and the bed is made.

"Eli!" I tear into the bathroom, but he's not there either. Shoving the back door open, I yell his name again outside, searching everywhere, but he's gone.

Panic is taking over, making my hands shake, and my stomach recoils. On his side of the bed, I jerk open the drawers, only to find them empty.

"Fuck!" I scream into the empty space, dropping to my knees and pulling my hair. "Elliot!"

I can't lose him again. How am I supposed to function without him when he's the air I need to live? I just got him back.

Digging into my sandy pocket, I pull my phone out and find his number. It goes straight to voicemail.

"Fuck!" I pace the bedroom, slapping the phone against my palm. I go onto Instagram and find Jordan's message thread.

ASHER

Where is he?

The three dots dance on the screen for a second, disappear, then come back. I hold my breath as I wait for her answer.

JORDAN

Even if I knew, I wouldn't tell you. If he wants to talk to you, he will.

ASHER

His parents are feeding him poison and trying to pass it for truth. I need him.

JORDAN

I'm sorry.

Gripping the device in my hand, I throw it as hard as I can. It crashes into the TV, fucking up the screen, but I don't give a shit. I flip the bed and the chairs, taking my anger out on the furniture since I don't have anything else. Finally, something on the outside matches my insides. Storming to the closet, I find my bag, rip clothes off hangers, and shove my stuff in it. I don't even know if everything I toss in here is mine, the resort's, or left from Eli, and it doesn't matter.

The memories of Eli in this place are choking me. I can't stay here any longer. Let Coach and Franklin yell at me, I don't give a fuck anymore. I will burn this world to the fucking ground to get him back.

I storm my way to reception, wearing my hurt like a shield, protected by my anger.

"Oh, good afternoon, Mr. Vaughn, is there a problem?" the woman behind the desk asks, but I haven't even taken the time to learn her fucking name.

"Yes, but it's not your problem. I'm checking out and need the ferry back so I can catch a plane."

"Of course," she says, clicking away on the computer. "Okay, you're all settled. Is the card on file the one you want charged?"

"Yes, for damages too. The TV was my fault."

She pauses for a second but doesn't ask, just adds it to the notes and prints me off a paid invoice. "The ferry will be back in about an hour. You're welcome to wait on the dock."

The only thought I have in my head is *get him back*. This can't be the end for us. It can't be. I can't go back to my useless existence. I was able to bury myself in football once, workouts and games keeping me busy and exhausted, but there's no way I can do that this time.

I've been standing in a rainstorm for years, the waters rising around me with no one noticing I can't swim. Barely keeping my head above the water on my tiptoes, but a tidal wave is coming, and I can't get out of the way. I don't know if I should be scared or relieved of drowning.

BY THE TIME my feet land in San Diego, I'm itchy, irritated, and pissed off. I have no phone since I left mine buried in the TV, I've only had airport food, and can't call my own ride home.

As I step out onto the arrivals curb, looking for a taxi, a black BMW X5 pulls up in front of me and stops. Franklin, my agent, stands and waves me over.

"How did you know I was here?" I ask as I toss my bag in the back seat and climb in the front.

"If you think for one second the resort didn't have orders to call me if you left, you're an idiot," he says without looking at me and pulls out into traffic. "You know you're about two weeks early, right?"

"I don't fucking care." I close my eyes and lean against the headrest.

"You had better have your head on straight. Stay out of the news, you hear me?" he demands in that tone he gets when I've pushed him to the edge.

"Yeah, *Dad*, I fucking hear you." I turn away from him

and look out the window before remembering something he should probably know. "If I'm piss tested, I'll pop for THC. I ate a weed brownie, not realizing what it was."

Franklin huffs, swearing under his breath, but doesn't say anything.

He drops me off, gives an update on the schedule for the team, and as he climbs back in the car, I stop him.

"Hey, I need a new phone. Mine broke."

He sighs and nods. "I'll have one dropped off in a few hours."

Then he's gone. Just that quickly, I'm alone again, and no one cares that I'm suffocating.

Twenty-Two

ELLIOTT

It's been a week since my parents convinced me to leave the island and dragged me back to the house I grew up in. This place is tainted with memories. Rooms that hold emotions that linger from the past. I haven't been here since my eighteenth birthday.

I wander the halls or hide in Marcus's room. His room has been cleaned, but nothing else has been touched. It's musty and no longer smells like teenage boys, but it's still his, while my room has zero trace I ever existed.

Laying on his bed, I stare out the window at the pool. We spent so much time out there, our skin always tanned and glowing, laughing and fucking around. Even when we would fight, it never went past an hour or two of not talking to each other. Asher would always pop over, ask to play something or shove food into our mouths, and we would get over it. All my memories include Asher and Marcus.

How do you move on when everything you know is infused with people you can't have?

At least I'm mostly numb now, the gushing of my heart being ripped from my chest has slowed to a trickle. Shouldn't there be a physical mark on my skin from it? The pain is so sharp it feels like you should be able to see it.

"Goddamn it, Elliot," Mother snaps in irritation. "Stop tainting your brother's memory with your bullshit."

With a heavy sigh, I force my body to move and leave the only room with any amount of comfort left. My room isn't mine anymore. I hate everything in here. The seafoam color on the walls, the white bed set and violet décor. It's impersonal. No part of my life is here. There's no proof of a kid growing up between these walls. No story to be told. I've been erased.

I shouldn't be surprised since I was the disappointment from the beginning.

Flopping onto my back, I stare at the ceiling. I wish I could not feel anything. My fucking emotions are so goddamn strong they're suffocating me. Numb is so much easier.

My head spins memories of Asher, wrapped in his warmth. For those few days, I was safe. I knew this was coming, but I tried so hard to just let it be what it was. Now my phone is dead, I don't know where my computer is, and I don't have the brain power to care either. Once again, I'm back in survival mode where the only thing I feel is anger. Why can't I just go home? Why do I have to suffer here in this fucking house where memories strangle me?

Sitting up, fury like I've never felt wells up in my body until my hands clench and my vision blurs. Grabbing the lamp on the bedside table, I rip the cord from the wall and throw it as hard as I can across the room. It dents the wall with a satisfying thunk, the bulb shattering onto the floor. Reaching for a framed drawing of fucking flowers, I throw that too, screaming as I do. The only sound in my ears is my own heartbeat.

Hurt and angry, and with no way to get it out, I destroy this room. Everything not nailed down I use as a weapon to purge the pain boiling inside of me.

The door opens, and I spin around, one of the lamps still in my hand like a bat. Panting with tears streaming down my face, I stare at my mother. She surveys the damage and opens her mouth, but I cut her off.

"Shut up!" I scream at her. "I hate you. I hate this place. I don't deserve this!"

I swing the lamp at the mirror above the dresser next, and the glass shatters.

"You don't love me; you never have. I deserve so much better than you!" Flinging the lamp across the room, I take a step toward her. "You never wanted us. We were a prop in this bullshit story you call a life. After Marcus died, you pretended like I didn't exist. You put him up on this fucking pedestal that I can't ever live up to, and I'm done trying! Why did you even have me?"

I shove past her, running through the hall and down the stairs. Past my father who's reading a damn newspaper in the living room and barely glances up as I storm from the house. On the wide brick steps, I put my hands on my knees and suck in deep breaths.

What the hell did you just do?

I have no shoes on, no phone, nothing on me, in the same pajamas I've been wearing since we got here. Fuck it.

I rush down the steps and across the driveway to the

sidewalk in front of the house. I'm done. With anger burning through me, I walk out of the neighborhood and find a restaurant. With zero shame, I walk to the hostess stand of the Mexican restaurant. She eyes me before forcing a smile to her beautiful face.

"Just one?"

"Can I use the phone? Mine died." I'm not actually sure where my phone is but she doesn't need to know that.

"Oh sure." She nods and has me step down a hallway and offers me a landline. For once my anxiety is paying off because I have Jordan's phone number memorized for exactly this situation.

"Hello?" she says after three rings.

"Jordan, it's Elliot. I need a ride."

She doesn't ask any questions besides the address, and I thank the hostess on my way out to wait for her.

Jordan's little blue Maserati Quattroporte pulls up, and I hurry to get in.

"Where the hell have you been?" she demands as she exits the parking lot.

"My parents' house." I sink into the seat and close my eyes. The rage of a few minutes ago gone, leaving me weak and tired. "Do you still have a key to my apartment?"

She scoffs, merging into the freeway. "Of course I do."

The motor purrs as she handles the car, getting to the lane she wants and setting a course to my place.

"Where's your key? And your phone?" She eyes me for a second while I stare out the passenger window.

"Still at my parents', I think."

"Right. Why are you back so early, and why is Asher

blowing up my phone?" The exit we need is coming up, so she moves through the traffic again and pulls off.

The empty space where my heart used to live aches at the mention of his name. I can't be his secret. A knot forms in my throat, but I force the tears back and take a deep breath.

"Probably because my phone's been off since I got on the plane." The words are soft, but she hears them. "I doubt they turned it back on when we landed."

"I've noticed that. You didn't even tell me you were coming back early." Pulling up to the underground garage, she punches in the number, and the gate lifts. She finds a spot, but we sit for a few more minutes.

"My parents basically forced me off, telling me that I was ruining Asher's life and to stop being selfish." I chew on my inner lip and drop my gaze to my hands, shrugging when she turns in her seat to look at me.

"You know that's bullshit, right?"

"It's not, though. He has a lot to lose, and I'm . . . I'm not worth it." This time I can't hold the tears in, and they fall onto my hand.

"I am judging your parents very harshly right now." Jordan reaches for my hand, and I let her take it. "Fuck your parents. You are worth *everything* to me, and more importantly, to the right person."

"I just want to go to bed." I wipe at my face and open the door. I know she means well and truly believes what she's saying, but it makes me feel worse. Once upon a time, I thought Asher was it for me. My be-all and end-all. Now I understand why he walked away better than I ever could have dreamed, and I think it's a deeper wound knowing he would burn his life to the ground for me, but I can't let him. I'm the one who isn't deserving of it, and it has nothing to do with him. That's a bitter pill to swallow.

I'm protecting him from himself. Asher deserves the life he's worked so hard for.

Jordan gets us in the elevator and in my apartment that has been cleaned since I left. I look around the space, with boring colors that were picked by my mother. There's no part of me in here. I guess I let her erase my existence a long time ago and never noticed. I'm twenty-three and don't even know who I am. My entire life I was *that Cushings kid,* never given my own identity, except to Marcus and Asher. When people look at me, they see dollar signs or a way to my parents. Once they find out my parents don't give a shit, they bounce.

Jordan's hand rubs my back, and I walk deeper into my apartment. I'm betting it won't be much longer that my parents pay for it. I'll have to move out and get a job. Oh well. I guess it's time to grow up, right?

What the hell would I even do? Do I even have any marketable skills? No.

With a sigh, I head to my bedroom and drop down onto my bed. I should shower. I haven't since I got back. When we got back to LA, the numbness had taken over, and doing what they wanted was easier than fighting, so I took the damn shower that Mother demanded, but I haven't taken one since. Jordan comes to stand in front of me, wrapping her arms around me until my face is pressed against her chest. I can count on one hand the number of times I've hugged her in the five years I've known her, not because she doesn't offer them, but because I don't allow them. It hurts to be touched when you've been starved of human contact for so long.

"I don't know how to help you, but I'm here to sit in this dark place with you for as long as you need."

My arms wrap around her waist, and I let out a sob. "I don't want to be in the dark anymore, but I don't know how to get out of it."

She cups my head with one hand, rubbing my back with the other in big, comforting circles while I pour out all of the sadness and frustration and hopelessness of the last week. Until my throat is sore and my voice is hoarse. My eyes are swollen, and I'm empty. I have nothing left. What's the point?

When I drain the last of my soul from my body, Jordan pulls the blankets back and I lay down. She pulls her boots off and climbs in with me, even though it's noon and I know she's not tired, she pulls me against her, and I fall asleep.

Twenty-Three

ASHER

For a few days, I was told not to step foot outside of my house since I'm supposed to still be in treatment. For a week I've done nothing but pace and workout to the point of exhaustion. I'm not eating like I should be, drinking way more than I should, and passing out in the living room instead of going to bed.

Minicamp starts in a week for the team, so I need to get my shit together, but without Eli, I just don't care. Nothing matters. The team wants to fire me? Fine. Go ahead. At least then, I'll be able to go find him. Does he think this is better? That I'm better off without him? He's wrong. His parents are wrong. I can't breathe without him.

While I'm dripping in sweat in the gym with the news on silent and music blasting in my AirPods, Franklin shows up. I finish my set with the leg press before I pull my earbud out and chug water.

"What?" I holler at the impeccably dressed man watching me from the doorway.

"Are you ready for camp? The team is waiting on you."
He slides his hands in his pockets, not taking his eyes from
me like he's waiting for me to attack.

"I'm ready." I squirt more water into my mouth and wipe
my face off with a towel.

"You look more pissed off now than when you left." He
shakes his head. "Are you sure you can handle this?"

"What the fuck do you want? Ask whatever it is you want
to know, then get out of my face." I'm done dancing around
shit.

He holds my gaze, challenging me. "No more shit this
year or the team is done with you. Are we clear?"

"Crystal." I sit on the chest press machine and put my
water bottle down. Franklin watches me for a minute before
turning around and heading out. Images of the days I had
with Eli spinning in my head until I want to scream. I need
him back.

Letting the machine fall with a loud clang, Franklin
jumps and turns to look over his shoulder.

"Hey." I stand and wait for him to turn all the way
around. "I'm in love with a man."

Franklin raises an eyebrow but otherwise doesn't react.
He sits with the information for a minute, probably figuring
out the best way to handle it.

"Not what I was expecting, but okay." He just accepts it.
The stuffed shirt doesn't question it at all. "Are you dating
him?"

"Not exactly." I let out a breath, my shoulders dropping
some. "He's afraid it'll fuck up my career if I come out as bi."

"Ruin it? No. You may end up bounced around a few times,

but that's probably more for your attitude than who you're dating." He taps his thumb against his thigh. It's the only tell I've been able to figure out. He's processing, running scenarios through his head, and making a plan. "Can I ask who it is?"

"Elliot Cushings."

His hand stops moving, and that damn eyebrow rises again. "You're fucking with me, right?"

Clenching my jaw for a second, I force myself to take a deep breath and relax.

"No, I'm not. I've known him since I was ten. Been in love with him for years."

"He just had a sex tape go viral!" he shouts before pinching the bridge of his nose. "Okay, do you have plans to make this public anytime soon, or can we at least get through camp?"

"I don't have any set plans."

He nods. "Anyone in the locker room you think will be a problem?"

A few faces come to mind, but it won't be anything I can't handle, so I shake my head.

"Good. As long as you play your best year, it'll be fine."

No pressure then.

ONCE I'M DONE PUNISHING myself with my workout, I head to my bedroom to shower. It's mechanical, wash the sweat off, get out. Nothing extra, no relaxing in the hot water. My bag from Black Diamond still sits in my closet, packed and haunting me. I barely remember what's in it, but I stare at it every time I come in here for clothes.

Fuck it. Rip the Band-Aid off.

Dropping down to a crouch with a towel around my waist, I quickly unzip the bag and upend it on the floor. Clothes, toiletries, and random shit tumbles out. There's just a slight scent of Eli that tickles my senses, and I lift the clothes to my nose to inhale.

It's there, somewhere. With frenzied hands, I pull everything apart and lift everything to smell it. Finally, I find a shirt Eli had worn. The memory of him in it, curled up with me in bed, arms and legs wrapped around me, and his curls tickling my skin flashes over me like a physical weight.

It hits me like a boot to the chest, stealing my breath as I bury my face in the fabric. My knees hit the carpet, and I curl around the stupid shirt. My hand trembles when I find the satin bag. Lifting it from the floor, I don't have to open it to know my mother's necklace is inside. The weight of it heavier on my heart than in my hand. He loved my mother so much. Did he leave this on purpose, to show just how done with me he is? I need him so fucking badly. I feel half crazed in my desperation to get him back into my life. What do I have to do?

I don't know how long I sit on the floor, misery soaking into the cotton as hopelessness eats through my stomach lining.

Shifting on the floor, I clutch the shirt to my chest and dig through the rest of the stuff that was in the bag but freeze when I find the black canvas zipper bag. Fuck. Eli's knife.

With shaking hands, I unzip it and find the blade I gave him when he was a teenager. I cleaned it before I put it away on the island. Finding him cutting himself, blood all over the place, was terrifying.

I have to check on him. Climbing to my feet, I find my phone and check for messages. He hasn't even opened the thread. I try calling him for the hundredth time, but it goes straight to voicemail. Did he change his number?

I find Jordan on IG and send her a message.

ASHER
Please make sure Eli is safe.

JORDAN
What?

ASHER
He hurts himself sometimes.

The three dots pop up and disappear a few times before she finally sends something.

JORDAN
Okay, thank you.

Tossing the phone on the bed, I pull the shirt on that smells like Eli and find underwear. I've barely pulled them on when my phone rings. Racing for it, hope blossoming in my chest that it could be Eli, I answer it.

"Hello?"

"Hi, I'm looking for Asher Vaughn," a male voice I don't recognize says.

"That's me."

"My name is Stephen, and I'm a nurse in the Mercy Hospital emergency room. Your father is here, and we need you to come in."

My heart sinks into my stomach. Fuck. What happened

to my dad? Fear trickles through my body, frigid and unstoppable.

"What happened?" I rush for the closet to finish getting dressed.

"I'm sorry, sir, I can't give details over the phone." The man pauses, and I swear my heart stops.

All the blood drains from my body in a second, leaving me cold and so fucking alone. Dad is the only family I have left; our relationship sucks, but it's there. This can only be really bad, right?

"Okay, I'm coming from San Diego, so I'll be there as soon as I can."

"Thank you. When you get here, just tell the nurse at the desk that you got a call about Mathew Vaughn, and she'll get you where you need to go." The line disconnects, and I quickly scroll through my contacts until I find my teammate Aaron's number. I hit call as I pace the entryway of my house while it rings.

"Asher, my ma—"

"My father's in the hospital. I need a ride to LA," I cut him off. "I'm sorry. I don't have anyone else to call." That truth is a punch in the gut. I don't have many friends. We're friendly, sure, get along all right, but I'm not really close to anyone.

"I'm on my way. Call Coach." The line goes dead, and I swipe through my contacts until I find the head coach's number, relieved that he's willing to help.

"Vaughn, please tell me you haven't been arrested."

"My father is in the ER. I'm not sure why, but the hospital just called me. I'm going to LA to see him. I'll be back before camp starts." I run my hand through my hair, pulling on the strands as my mind races. What if he dies? That's what he's been trying to do for years. Part of me understands now, how desperate he is to be back with Mom, because I feel it myself for Eli. I have no one to handle the estate, if he even left it to me. I have contracts to uphold, and unfortunately, the NFL doesn't care about your personal problems. During the season, you play unless you're hurt. Period.

"How are you getting there?" Immediately, he switches into problem-solver mode, and since a lot of the guys are young, the coaches end up stepping into a father role a lot. "Do you have a place to stay arranged already?"

"Aaron Thomlyn is driving me, and yeah, I can stay at my dad's house." I find some shoes to slip on and step outside, locking the door behind me, and hurry to the elevator when I get the text from Aaron saying he's here. "We're leaving now."

"All right, keep me updated."

"Will do. Thanks, Coach."

I end the call and buckle my seat belt as Aaron gets us back on the street.

"Thanks, I really appreciate it."

"Of course, man." He fist-bumps me quickly and finds the I-15 entrance.

My knee is bouncing as I watch out the window. Aaron lets it be quiet, not needing to fill the silence with meaningless chatter. I'm too lost in my head, in the fear and guilt and sadness eating at my insides. Tapping my phone against my thigh, I let myself imagine meeting Eli at the hospital. Being able to count on someone having my back, holding my fucking hand as I deal with whatever is going on with Dad, knowing I can lean on him would be everything. When I lost

Mom, I had Eli and Marcus to keep me together. I knew if I strayed too far into the endless depths of grief that they would find me and pull me back to the land of the living.

Who will pull me back now?

Even though I don't talk to Dad often, I knew he was there. I wasn't really alone. If he dies, I'll have no family left. No one.

The knot of emotion burns my throat as I try to keep a lid on it. I don't know what happened; for all I know, he just fell and broke his leg or something. Maybe he just needs surgery.

"You want to talk about what you're thinking?" Aaron finally asks after an hour of silence.

"I'm fine." Fucking liar.

"You can just say no. Don't lie to me, man." He taps out a beat on the steering wheel that only he knows.

I pinch the bridge of my nose and force myself to breathe.

"There's nothing to talk about. I have no idea what's going on besides he's in the ER."

It's quiet for a minute.

"Sure that's the only thing going on with you?" He gives me the side-eye. "You assaulted some dude in a bar and disappeared for *anger management,* then suddenly reappeared and didn't speak to anyone. What the fuck, man?"

I can't talk about Eli or Black Diamond without spilling all of my secrets. I'm tired of hiding, and God, I just want to be able to tell someone about him, but he walked away. What's the point of rehashing it all when it won't change the outcome? Eli left me and won't respond. He's gone.

Twenty-Four

ASHER

Standing on the front steps of my childhood home is strange. I'm numb but screaming inside at the same time. It's a weird combination. Like directly under my skin is the need to destroy the world if only I would give in to it, but if I don't, I'm empty. It's all or nothing.

My father is dead. I'm twenty-six years old and have no family left. Completely alone.

Using my key, I get the door open and disarm the alarm system, then just stand there in the foyer. Nothing has changed since Mom died. He never redecorated, only replaced furniture when it was necessary and found something as close to what she'd picked as was possible.

Ghosts of my childhood linger in the echoing space around me. Each one picking at a sore in my soul. The hopelessness taking over until my body trembles with the sobs tearing from the core of who I am. I will forever be changed by yet another death.

What did I do to deserve everyone I've loved to leave? How much more am I supposed to take? I have no one left.

"Come on, man." Aaron wraps an arm around my shoulder and leads me toward the navy-blue couch with big pink flowers on it. Mom loved this damn thing. My teammate didn't leave when we got to the hospital, despite me telling him it was fine and he could go back home. He told me to fuck off and followed me into the ER, not leaving my side when they pulled me into a stupid room to tell me my father was dead. He finally had the major heart attack he was working so hard for.

A tear falls down my cheek, and I swipe it away quickly.

"Where's the liquor in this place?" Aaron asks as I sit on the couch. He looks around the room, taking in my childhood home with interest.

"Probably in the office down the hall on the right." I drop my head back and close my eyes. "That's where the good shit will be anyway." I hear him walk in that direction, and I let out a breath.

I'm alone.

Truly, wholly alone.

Dad is with Mom and finally at peace.

The stabbing pain in my chest at not being enough for him has me rubbing at it.

"Time to get fucked up and maybe break some shit. Who knows?" He comes back carrying a bottle of Balvenie Port-Wood 21.

"You found his cheap shit," I tell him. That's bottom rung for the old man at two-fifty a bottle.

"I know nothing about scotch. If you want something else, you'll have to go get it yourself." He sets the bottle and glasses on the coffee table and pours a healthy amount in each. He hands me one and clinks our glasses together before taking a swig. I watch him and huff a small laugh at his face when he hisses.

"That's great." His voice is strained from coughing.

"You definitely look like you're enjoying that." I shake my head, lifting my tumbler to my lips. It's smooth alcohol, with notes of honey and raisins with a slightly nutty aftertaste. It's one of the first I tried when I started drinking scotch since I recognized it.

We don't say anything as we drink, just let the heaviness of the situation sit in the air. By the time my glass is empty, I'm buzzing and pour myself another glass.

"Have you eaten anything?" Aaron eyes me as I take another drink.

"I don't know," I mumble with the edge of the tumbler to my lips.

Every second of the last few hours, only one thought has been repeated—I need Eli. I've tried to call, text, I even texted Jordan again, but nothing. I'm sure the news of my father's death will hit news outlets soon. Will he care? Will he stay away?

"Is there anyone I can call for you?" Aaron asks again.

"Nope, there's no one left." My gut clenches at the reality of the statement. I guess it doesn't matter what I do anymore. There's no one to care. I can't disappoint or embarrass anyone if they're dead.

"Are you sure, man? A close friend, aunt, grandparent?"

"The only time I met any of my extended family was at my mother's funeral. I don't even have contact numbers for them." I clasp my hands together and release them, then get off the couch to stand in front of the pictures on the wall. There's nothing here more recent than when Mom was sick. That was what, almost fifteen years ago? I can probably count on my fingers the instances when I actually spent time with Dad after that. Sure, he came to my high school graduation and called when I got picked up in the draft, but he's never come to a game that I'm aware of. Since I started playing, I think we had dinner once.

Aaron steps up behind me, a smile tugging at his lips as he looks at the happier times of my life.

"That your mom?" He points to a picture of Mom and me with Mickey Mouse ears on at Disneyland when I was about five.

"Yeah." I smile at the dim memory I have of that trip. "She was amazing."

"What happened to her?" He's standing shoulder to shoulder with me now.

"Cancer."

Aaron wraps his arm around my shoulder again, offering me support and comfort.

"I'm sorry, man."

I brush it off like it doesn't matter, but it shaped who I am today. Who I've allowed into my life and how I love. The conversation we had on the bus a few weeks ago circles through my head, and it makes me sick.

"Hey, you remember the blond at that food drive thing?"

"Yeah, El, right?" He lifts his glass and takes another drink.

"Elliot." I suck in a deep breath when he tenses. "His name is Elliot."

"So not a chick then."

"Not a chick."

I turn my head just enough to get a look at his face, waiting for his reaction. Will he be okay with this or punch me in the face? At this point, I wouldn't pass on a good fight, though Coach would be pissed.

I can see him working through the information in his head, maybe replaying what he saw with a new light on it.

"You can't have him, so you find someone else close enough when you're desperate." The words tumble from his lips like he's telling me about the forecast, when in fact he's shining a spotlight on my darkest secret.

"I didn't realize it until you mentioned it on the bus," I mumble.

"I'm sorry you can't have the person you love." Aaron pulls me into him and gives me a tight hug. I'm so caught off guard that for a second I get my hand with the cup trapped between us and my other hand just hangs limply at my side. "If football is why you think you can't have him, you're wrong."

I wrap my arms around him, dropping the cup, and accept the physical comfort he's offering me. The pressure in my chest builds until I explode and scream into his shoulder. A loud, earth-shattering, tormented scream. He just holds me tighter, lets me yell and fall apart. My arms tighten around his ribs past the point of pain, my fingers gripping his shirt in a fist until they ache, and my throat burns. He holds me up when my knees threaten to give out.

He doesn't say much. "Let it out" or "You're gonna be okay" as I lose my shit all over him. I haven't felt this kind of acceptance since Marcus died. It hurts but soothes a ragged part of me I haven't let myself explore. Just shoved it behind a door with my attraction to Eli to fester and die. Only it didn't die, just got worse. Now it's infected and pissed off, demanding I acknowledge it.

I don't know how long I rage against him, my only friend, but he takes all of it without a blink of an eye. By the time I calm back down, his shirt is wet with tears and saliva and scotch.

All of the muscles in my body going weak at the same time as the energy evaporates.

With a rattling breath, I let go of him and step back, wiping at my face.

"We should probably eat," he says when I open my mouth to apologize.

"There should be meals in the fridge and freezer we can make quickly." We head for the kitchen, and I stumble as the alcohol takes full control of my brain.

Aaron laughs when I lean against the wall but steers me toward a chair.

"Sit your ass down before you break something."

He rummages through the kitchen for food and comes back with a few helpings of fettuccine Alfredo with grilled chicken.

"I don't think there's any vegetables in this place," he grumbles as he finds a pan to heat the food in. "Guess I'm going grocery shopping tomorrow."

We all take our diets seriously, but especially right before the season and during the season when we're pushing our bodies to their limits. We all know the importance of fueling our bodies correctly to get the best performance possible. This is definitely not on our menus this time of the year and especially with no vegetables.

"Is there more to the story with Elliot than being a football player?" he asks as he brings over the plates of food.

"Lotta history," I mumble, shoveling food into my face. I'm starving all of a sudden. I don't think I've eaten at all today.

We're quiet as we eat, though Aaron grumbles every few bites about the food. I clean my plate, too drunk to give a shit about my diet, while he picks at it.

Now that my stomach is full, my body is heavy with exhaustion. I just want to sleep until the season starts, then I'll be too busy to think about anything else.

"Sleeeeep," I mumble, laying my head on the table.

"Hey!" Aaron shouts. Coming around the table, he forces me to my feet despite my protest, and we stumble up the stairs. "Which way?" he asks when we get to the top.

I point down the hall to where my room is and stop in front of my old bedroom. Has he changed it? Probably not.

"'Tis me." I open the door, and he stumbles in with me, making sure I make it to the bed. I crash-land face first and immediately pass out.

Twenty-Five

ELLIOTT

Jordan convinces me to shower, but what I really do is stand in the water that's so hot it physically hurts. But it's something. I hate being numb but don't want to feel anything either. All of it is exhausting.

I manage to wash my hair, face, and the important parts before getting out. In the closet, I pull on some underwear and sit on the floor, running my fingers over the scars. I've thought about adding another one a lot over the last few days. I need some control over my life, and right now I feel like I have none. But I don't have the knife I've always used.

My parents are going to kick me out of the apartment, I can feel it. Take away my trust fund and leave me scrambling to figure my life out. I hate how dependent on them I've allowed myself to be.

Getting up, I find my jewelry drawer and realize my favorite pearl necklace is missing. My heart breaks knowing I left it at my parents' house. Fuck. Now I have to go back.

Grabbing some clothes, I get dressed and go looking for

my best friend. I find her on the couch, eyes glued to her phone.

"Hey, can you—"

Her head shoots up, expression carefully blank, and I stop talking.

"What?"

"Mathew Vaughn is dead." There is no inflection in her voice as she delivers the news.

Asher's dad is dead.

He's alone.

I need to call him.

Tearing through my apartment, I search all my normal spots for my phone before I realize it, too, is at my fucking parents' house with my damn keys.

"Jordan!" I shout, rushing down the hall toward the door. "I need a ride!"

I rip open the front door with her hot on my heels as we run for the stairs, too impatient to wait for the elevator. I don't even have shoes on, but I don't care. I have to find him. All I can picture is the angry, hurt boy Asher was after his mom died. He has no one to give him a hug. No one to care for him. I can't not go to him.

We hit the parking garage in a rush and climb into her car.

She gives me her phone to plug in my parents' address while she gets us onto the street. It's only a twenty-minute drive, luckily, and the traffic isn't bad, so we make good time. We get through the gate, and Jordan pulls right up to the front of the house. I'm out before she gets it in park, and I shove the front door open without knocking.

The phone is in the spare room that was once mine.

"Elliot!" Mother's shrill, surprised yell follows me up the stairs. "What the hell do you think you're doing? Barging into my house that way!"

"I'm getting my shit, then I'll be gone!" I yell back. Jordan's boots pound on the hardwood stairs behind me, then follow me down the hallway.

"Wow, your mom is a bitch," she says as I open the bedroom door and stop. It hasn't been cleaned. There's broken glass all over the floor, and I am barefoot.

"Oh shit." Jordan stops short, barely bumping into me. "What are we looking for, and where should it be?"

"My phone should be by the bed." I point to the side I slept on and the overturned nightstand. She squeezes past me and squats next to the bed to look under it.

"Found it." She reaches under and pulls out my phone that I'm sure is dead. "Anything else?"

"Is there luggage in the closet?" She pockets the phone and opens the closet door to find it empty. "Fuck!"

I need that necklace and my knife back. It would kill me to lose the camera too.

Jordan comes out of the room as Mom is storming around the corner.

"You have a lot of nerve—" she spits.

"Where's my bag?" I demand, cutting her off. "I want my stuff."

"I don't care what you want. Nothing in here is yours. I paid for all of it, so I'm keeping it." She folds her arms over her chest and squares her shoulders.

"No, you didn't!" I yell back. "There were things in that bag that were given to me, and I want them back! Now!"

She steps forward and cracks me across the cheek with

her hand. The sound reverberating in the hallway as the sting steals my breath. My skin hot and sensitive when I put a protective hand over the abused flesh.

"Don't you fucking dare." Jordan steps in front of me and shoves Mom back. "Don't lay a hand on him again, or I'll show you exactly what kind of person I was raised to be." Every muscle of Jordan's body is tense, and Mom withers under her stare.

"Where's my stuff?" I demand again.

When she doesn't answer, I go around her toward her room. Glancing around, I don't see it laying around, so I check her closet. Shoved in a back corner is my suitcase. I pull it out and unzip it, digging through it, but I don't find the knife or the necklace.

"Elliot Martin!" Mom shrieks. "Get out of my room! Get out of my house!"

She's coming into the closet now with clenched fists and Jordan right behind her.

Standing up, I face her with my own anger.

"Where's the necklace?" I demand, finding my keys and shoving them in my pocket.

"What are you talking about? I haven't even opened that suitcase."

"There was a pearl necklace in a satin bag. I want it back."

She looks legitimately confused, and the fear of losing the necklace has me starting to pant. I can't have lost it. I can't. I have to find it.

Rushing toward her jewelry, I pull open all the drawers, but can't find it.

There's a band around my ribs tightening until I can't

breathe. What little air I can manage comes in gasps between despair and guilt. Jordan wraps her arms around me, and for once, I collapse into her comfort, too weak to resist.

"Get out of my house!" Mother demands again, and I recoil like she hit me. She doesn't care. She has never cared about anything that didn't revolve around her.

Jordan moves us to the suitcase and shoves my stuff back inside that spilled out in my frenzied search. Tears are running down my face, and I can barely see through them. Jordan grabs the handle of my bag and wraps an arm around my waist before stopping in front of the woman who gave birth to me.

"You are the worst kind of mother. You pretend to care about your children, but you use them to get sympathy to try to get ahead. To the world, you put on this mask and let everyone think you're this caring, sweet human when really, you're a selfish, coldhearted bitch who uses the bodies of people under you to lift yourself higher, sacrificing your children for your own fame." Jordan shakes her head like she's disappointed but walks us past her down the hall and toward the front door.

With the door open, we stop when Mom speaks again.

"I highly suggest you find yourself a job and a new apartment." With those final, biting words, I walk out of my childhood home for the last time, somehow feeling like less than when I entered. I thought I was past the point of being hurt by her, but I guess not.

We get in the car, and Jordan plugs my phone into her car charger, then pulls away from the house and down the street. The screen lights up, and once it loads my lock screen, the notifications go crazy. Missed calls, voicemails, text messages, mostly from Asher.

I let out a sob and lift it to unlock the screen. I don't open the messages, just find his number and call him back. With every ring, doubt creeps in. Am I doing the right thing, or am I just making everything worse? Cutting off contact all at once is easier, right? Will I just cause him more pain by coming back, just to walk away again?

My eyes shut when his voicemail picks up. I don't leave a message, just hang up. And sink into the seat. I guess that's my answer.

How much pain can one person suffer and not die? I guess I'm going to find out. I thought Asher had taken my heart, ripped it right out of my fucking chest while it still beat, yet it aches. Every bone in my body thrumming with the sorrow of being rejected. Again.

Jordan doesn't say anything, just reaches for my hand and holds it while we drive back to my apartment.

"You should come stay with me until you get on your feet," she says as she parks in the underground garage for my building.

"I don't know," I mumble and slink from the car, too defeated to care about anything else. I just want to sleep for the next week, or month maybe. What was the point of all of this? Why give me a peek into what real happiness could be like if it was just going to be taken away from me again? How is that fair?

A single tear slips down my cheek, and this time, I don't wipe it away. Jordan wraps an arm around my waist again and pulls me against her as we ride the elevator up to my floor.

"Were all those notifications from him?" she asks once we've gotten inside.

I just nod and drop down onto the couch, pulling a blanket from the back to wrap around myself.

"And you called and he didn't answer?" She sits next to me and lifts my head so I can use her thigh as a pillow.

I nod again, closing my eyes when she runs her fingers through my hair.

"I'm betting there's a lot going on right now for him. He might not have heard the phone or was on the other line with someone else to make arrangements." What she says makes sense, and a tiny spark of hope appears in my chest, but I'm terrified of it. Having hope leads to disappointment, which leaves more pain.

But what if he's done with me? I didn't answer his messages, so he's finally stopped trying. Given up. I don't know where he is, so it's not like I can show up and check on him or send Jordan to do it. I know she would if I asked her to.

Jordan turns on the TV and starts up *Archer* with the volume down. I watch a few episodes before my eyes get heavy, but before I can fall asleep, a thought hits me. Asher would be at his dad's house, right?

Sitting up, I look at Jordan with my thoughts going in a million different directions.

"Are you up for a drive?"

Twenty-Six

ASHER

I passed out when my face hit the bed, but I've been half awake for a while. Dozing in and out of consciousness for hours or minutes, I don't know. I'm cold and exhausted and alone in my old bedroom. I didn't think I would ever sleep in here again.

My head is still buzzing with the scotch, and I'm floating. My eyes aren't open, and it almost feels like I'm sleeping, but I have a train of thought, though it's slow. I don't know how long I was asleep, but since I can think, it must have been for a few hours, not that it really matters. Thinking and sobriety is overrated anyway. Maybe I should get another drink.

Something is pulling me toward consciousness. I shift and shove the pillow under my head.

"Asher!" a panicked yell echoes in the empty house. *Why is Eli yelling?*

Eli?

My eyes spring open, and I jerk upright as he appears in

the doorway, and my heart just about leaps from my chest. My boy.

"Asher," he breathes, halfway to hysterical. He launches himself at me and straddles my lap. My arms automatically pull him tighter into me, and I breathe in the scent of his skin as he wraps his body around mine. Relief eases the pressure in my chest just enough to calm the urge to burn the world to the ground.

"Eli." I splay my hands over his back, touching as much of him as I possibly can. "Please tell me I'm not dreaming." My body shudders at the heat of him seeping into my skin. He's my goddamn air.

"I'm sorry," Eli mumbles against my hair. "What can I do?"

"Just don't leave." My voice breaks on the last word as a knot forms in my throat and tears fill my eyes.

"I'm right here." He runs his fingers through my hair, massaging my scalp like I used to do for him when he was upset and needed to sleep. "I'm so sorry."

I shiver at his words and the cool nip in the air. Dad always liked having the air on until Mom needed a sweater. Goose bumps cover my skin, and Eli rubs at my arms.

"It's the middle of the night. Let's get some sleep." I pull back enough to look up at him in the darkness of the room. I'm exhausted, but I'm afraid to sleep. What if I wake up again and he's gone again? I don't think I would be able to keep my shit together.

"You can't leave again," I tell him with his eyes locked on mine, his blue eyes dimmed by sadness. "I woke up and you were gone. I won't live through it a second time."

He chews on his lip for a second, searching my face for

something. Fear, pain, and sadness flash across his features, but I'm sure it's a mirror of my own.

"You're mine, and I will find a fucking way to keep you. Just give me some time to get it sorted." I sound desperate and pathetic, but with nothing but raw vulnerability left, I don't have a choice. There's nothing left inside of me. No mask. No shield.

"Sleep," he says, trying to slide off my lap, but I don't let him move. I roll us and settle on top of Eli. I need to know he'll be here when I wake up, that he can't or won't slip away again.

With my face in his neck, I close my eyes, breathing in the only safety net I have. It's frayed and barely hanging on, but it's keeping me tethered to the shore. The floodwaters are rising, but with him, I'm not afraid.

Eli plays with my hair, relaxing into the mattress and pillows like he's been waiting for this too, and I quickly fall asleep.

WHEN I WAKE AGAIN, the room is full of light, and Eli is squirming under me.

"Stop moving," I grumble, wrapping my arm under him to palm his ass.

"I have to pee. Get off!" He shoves at my shoulder, and I reluctantly roll off of him.

He races from the bed to the bathroom, and I sit up when I hear him flush and wash his hands. My stomach clenches with anxiety at the thought that he's going to run off again.

In the morning light, the tragedy of my life is just as ugly, but I can't lose him. He's the only bright spot in my world. He's all I have. My anchor when the storm rages.

He stops in the doorway when he sees me sitting up.

"Are you hungry?" he asks, shuffling his feet and chewing on his lip. I don't respond, just look at him. Really *look* at him. There are dark circles under his eyes. The glow is gone, and it looks like he's been wearing that old T-shirt and sleep shorts for days, yet he doesn't look or smell like he hasn't bathed.

I get off the bed and stalk toward him with long strides. Reaching for the back of his neck, I pull his face up to mine and take his lips. He gasps against my mouth, opening so perfectly for me. My tongue tangles with his, needing every connection to him I can get. He won't promise not to leave, or he would have already, but I'll take anything else I can get from him.

When I release his lips, he's flushed and panting, gripping my shirt in his hands for balance.

"Shower with me," I say as I push on his hip to back him into the bathroom. He goes willingly, watching me as he steps backward until he hits the sink. I spin him to look in the mirror and strip him bare. His cock is half hard in the reflection, so I reach around his body to stroke him. He sucks in a breath when I pump him quickly. His chest blossoms in a beautiful shade of red, and his hands clench at his sides.

"Asher," he starts, turning to look up at me.

"Watch." I keep my eyes on his face in the mirror as I

drag my other hand up his body to pinch at his nipples. His moan echoes in the room as I pick up the speed of my strokes. I want him desperate, needy, aching to come.

Eli's breathing picks up, his hips thrusting against my hand until he's throbbing. He's sticky with precum that I itch to taste. My poor boy is so close already.

His breath hitches as his body tightens, his orgasm so fucking close to the surface when I let go of him, and he sinks against the counter with a heartbreaking whimper.

"What the fuck?" Eli sobs and drops his head to hang from his shoulders as he trembles. I wrap my arm around him, my hand flat against his lower stomach and my mouth on his neck. I can feel his muscles twitch and clench under my palm.

"I'll make up for it, I promise."

Once he's steady on his feet, I strip my clothes off and turn the water on. Reaching for his hand, I thread our fingers and pull him in with me. I step under the spray and pull him against my back. His arms wrap around me, our fingers still intertwined. I lift our conjoined hand to my lips and kiss the back of his hand.

He kisses along my spine, my ribs, everything he can reach from this position.

With the heat of the water on my chest and Eli wrapped around me, I can pretend for just a minute that everything is normal. That I'm not completely alone. That I don't have the weight of my father's estate looming over me while I'm trying to keep my performance up on the field. Who needs rest?

Do I sell the house or use it as an investment property? I can't imagine ever wanting to live here again. Does that make me a bad person? For not wanting to hold on to the few memories I have of my parents that aren't tainted with sorrow?

"What do you need right now?" Eli asks with his lips pressed to my skin.

"A distraction." The words are out of my mouth before I think about it. I should allow myself to feel whatever it is I need to, but I don't want to ruin this time I have with Eli. I know I'm going to turn around at some point and he'll be gone. I need to use every second he gives me.

Moving around me, Eli looks at me like I looked at him earlier. Looking past the mask into my soul.

"How about I feed you, then we can figure out what needs to be done today?" He's trying to take care of me like I've done for him. I hate it.

Grabbing his throat, I push him against the tiled wall and press my body into him. "Why don't you shut up and let me lose myself in you?"

Eli's body shudders against me, his dick hard between us, and he moans when I rock into him. The way his skin heats for me, melts for me, is addicting. Every part of him has always called to me, and I finally feel like I can answer that call.

"I need you," I groan into his ear when he wraps a hand around my cock and strokes. "I need to fuck you like I hate you."

Eli moans again, his throat bobbing against my palm, and his body shudders.

"You can take it, can't you?" I bite at his neck and lift one of his legs by the back of the knee. "Your hole will look so pretty stretched out and abused."

"Asher," he whines, and I smirk, knowing I won. I find the oil I left in here for jacking off and the sweet scent of jojoba lifts with the steam.

His hole is slicked up, one of his thighs is around my hip, and I coat my dick before lining up my tip with the puckered flesh. Eli takes a deep breath and relaxes as I push forward. My tip pops past the tight ring of muscle, and he clenches around me as he groans an almost pained sound.

"Such a good boy. You can take it." I move my hand from his throat to cup the side of his neck, pushing farther in. Eli's fingers grip my wrists, but his dick is leaking for me. I'm sure it hurts a bit with the lack of prep, but he fucking likes it.

His body relaxes, and I slide the rest of the way in until my hips are flush with his.

"There's my sweet boy." I kiss along his clean-shaven jaw, nipping at his skin and teasing him with too quick kisses. "You look so pretty with your skin flushed red."

I pull back slowly, then snap forward quickly. He gasps, then moans, so I do it again. And again. And again. Speeding up until I'm pounding him into the wall and all I can hear is Eli. His throaty cries bounce off the walls of my skull to make an erotic soundtrack that will haunt my dreams.

I love the way my head clears when I'm inside him. Nothing matters like he does. The outside world, my demons, football, nothing compares to him.

Pulling out of him with no warning, I drop his leg and spin him around. His shriek of surprise making me chuckle. I use my foot to spread his and grip his hip to arch him the way I want him so I can sink back in. Eli lifts onto his toes and leans against the wall as I set a hard pace, his bubble butt bouncing off my hips with every fucking thrust.

"I'm going to fill you up," I say with my lips against his ear. "Then watch my cum run down your leg."

Eli shudders and reaches for his dick, stroking himself quickly.

"Use me. Make me take it, please." Eli's demanding words make my eyes roll back in my head. I sink my teeth into his shoulder and groan into his skin as I explode inside of him. His hole sloppy and wet with my cum has me shuddering against him.

"Fuck, please," Eli whimpers, pulling hard on his dick as I try to catch my breath.

I pull out of his ass and drop to my knees.

Pulling on Eli's hip, I swallow him. His hand falls away on a hiss and his cock throbs on my tongue. I bob quickly on him, taking him as deep as I can while I slide my middle two fingers into his slick hole and search for his prostate.

His ass cheeks clench when I find it, and his hips jerk forward, choking me, but I keep going as he fills my mouth with cum. I sputter at the amount, only losing a few drops before he slumps against the wall and slides down to the floor bonelessly.

I lick my lips and pull him against me so I can claim his lips. It's a deep, slow kiss that I feel to the marrow of my bones. This boy. I need him so fucking badly.

After our shower, I text Aaron that Eli is here, and he needs to be scarce. I'm not letting Eli out of this house until he convinces himself not to run again. There is shit I need to be handling, but I can't. He's the only thing I can focus on. I need to burrow as far into Eli as I can. I want the breath in his lungs to fill mine. I'm tired of drowning. For just a little while, I want to pretend that he's all there is.

Eli comes out of the bathroom in my shirt that hangs down to his damn knees. He stops when he sees me watching him and fidgets with the edge of the cotton.

"I should go," he starts, shifting his weight from foot to foot.

"No." He can't leave, not yet. I'm not ready.

"I'm sorry for you—"

"Stop," I bark the word louder than I intended, but I can't hear those fucking words from him. "Don't do that. Please."

Even from halfway across the room, I can see his lip tremble, and it guts me.

"I can't stay." He shakes his head, the wet curls flying at the movement. "I had to make sure you were okay, but it changes nothing."

My gut clenches at the resignation in his tone, and I hate that I don't know how to fight him on this. How many times can I tell him that he's worth everything and still have him not believe me?

"I just need some time to figure it out." The words aren't out of my mouth before he's shaking his head.

A phone notification sounds, and he squares his shoulders. "My ride is here."

"No!" Panic seizes my lungs as the darkness starts to creep back in. My hands shake as he moves to the door. I'm off the bed and rushing toward him when he reaches for the knob. I hit my knees with my arms around his waist, holding him against me.

"Please, Eli. I can't," I all but sob into the shirt.

"Asher." I can hear the tears in his voice, the emotion threatening to choke him. "Please let me go. I can't stay. If you ever loved me, please let me go."

"I need you." The sob finally breaks through, my pain dampening the cotton.

"I have to go, I'm sorry." His tears drop onto my arms as his body trembles while he tries to stay strong.

The door opens, and I dig my fingers into Eli's sides for just a second. It carves a hole in my heart that he needs to get away from me this badly, but I can't make him stay.

"Hey—" Aaron starts, and Eli loses all control, scratching and pulling at my arms to get away from me while sobbing. If Aaron didn't know before this moment that I was in love with Eli, it would be clear now.

I drop my hands, and Eli runs as fast as he can from me. I break down into a puddle of agony with only my friend to hold me together on the floor of my childhood bedroom. This room has seen more than its share of pain, so it makes sense that I lose the only man who will ever complete me in here too.

Twenty-Seven

ELLIOTT

My bare feet slap at the hardwood floors as I run from everything I've ever wanted. The tears in my eyes make it impossible to see, but I know where I'm going. Nothing in this house has changed since the last time I was here.

The pain in my chest is almost more than I can take as I rip open the front door and launch myself down the stairs and into Jordan's car.

"Jesus! What's wrong?!" she demands, but I crumble into myself and sob. Ugly, soul-deep pain pours from me. I can't be what he needs. I can't live a lie, but that doesn't mean everything in me isn't begging to try. I know it would destroy me in the end, but what if it saved him? Wouldn't my demise be worth it then?

Jordan doesn't ask any more questions, just drives as I purge. The sobs become full-on screams when the tears aren't enough to get it all out. I'm half bent over my legs, punching my thighs and ripping at my hair because I don't know what else to do with all the emotion threatening to choke me.

It's not fair. None of this is fair. I want him, but I would be his end. I can't bring him more pain. He thinks he can find a way through this, but I doubt it. I'm not worth it. All the bullshit he'll have to deal with on the team, the media, the fans. He'll be hated, and the hatred speaks louder than acceptance. I can't be the reason he loses everything.

By the time Jordan pulls into the parking garage of my building, my breathing is stuttering and I'm weak.

I hate this.

I wipe my face and climb from the car without a word. Jordan wraps her arm around my shoulders, and I lean my head on her. The ride up to my floor is silent, and she opens my apartment door, ushering me in.

I head straight for my bed without turning on any lights and cover my head in the blanket. A few minutes later, Jordan climbs in with me. She holds my hand in the dark, offering me comfort the only way I've accepted from her in the past.

But I need so much more.

Crawling toward her, I let her hold me. Tears ease from my eyes and onto her shirt. I didn't think I had any left, but she wraps her arms around me in a hug.

"I love him," I whisper in the dark cocoon.

"I know."

"It's not fair."

"You're right, it's not." She rubs a hand up and down my back.

We're quiet for a bit, and my body finally starts to warm, the racing thoughts start to slow. Should I go to the funeral?

The wake? Would it be worse if I did? With all those people around, it should be safe, right? No one would suspect anything. I grew up next door to him. Of course I would come pay my respects.

Will that be harder on me? Will it hurt him more if I go or if I don't? I don't want him to be alone.

Who the hell was that dude in his house? Did I ruin everything? Does someone know Asher's secret now? I didn't know anyone else was there, so I wasn't quiet. He had to have heard me. Will he make a scene if I show up?

Are he and Asher hooking up?

The thought makes my stomach turn. Did I help him cheat?

"Do you want to talk about it?" Jordan runs a hand through my hair, and I shiver.

"Not really."

"Do you want to come up with a plan?"

"A plan would be good." I sigh. Knowing what I should do will help ease the anxiety.

"If he calls or texts, do you want to talk to him?"

I roll onto my back and pull the blanket down to our shoulders.

"I want to talk to him, but I don't think it's a good idea. It hurts to be his friend. Seeing him with someone else will kill me."

Jordan nods and links our fingers together, giving me her strength.

"What about the funeral?"

"I feel like I should go, pay my respects." A knot clogs my throat. "After his mom died, he was so alone. I don't want that for him. It breaks my heart."

"Okay, we should go then." She squeezes my hand. "There will be enough other people there that you shouldn't have to talk to him if you don't want to."

"I'm scared."

She kisses my cheek and leans her head on my shoulder. "I know, babe. I'll help you get through it if you want me to. We'll see how you feel the day of, okay?"

Twenty-Eight

ASHER

The next few days are hectic. All the phone calls and arrangements that go into planning a funeral are insane. Since my father rubbed elbows with the elite, there are a lot of people who have reached out, sent flowers, and are asking for funeral details. Dad's attorney had a list of family members and contact numbers to call for when he died, so I'm leaving that up to him to do since I couldn't care any less.

Aaron is still hanging around, which I appreciate greatly. After being alone for so long, it's refreshing to have someone who cares. Maybe I didn't give him enough credit before.

I've tried to call Eli about ten times, picked up my phone to do it, but freeze before I can hit call. I'm afraid he'll just send me to voicemail or will only say something like "sorry for your loss," and that will gut me. So I back out before I can hear his voice.

Now I'm sitting in an uncomfortable chair, in a suit in

front of my father's casket. The room is empty except for him and me.

"I'm mad at you," I tell him, leaning my elbows on my knees. "I know you were hurting after Mom died, but so was I. I needed you, and you weren't there. You kicked me out of the house!" Folding my hands together, I press them to my forehead. "At thirteen, I had to grieve my mother while being basically homeless." I let the tears fall down my face. "I hate you for that. For not telling me that I was enough. That you still loved me."

Standing, I stare down at the peaceful face of my father. "But I forgive you because now I understand what it feels like to love so deeply you're consumed by it."

I place my hand on the closed section of the lid and close my eyes, letting go of the hurt his lack of attention caused me over the years. I could never do it to my own flesh and blood, but I understand being trapped in the hell that is losing your soul while it lives in another person.

After a minute, I wipe my face and leave the room. In the foyer is a crowd that I'm surprised by. I guess my father touched a lot of lives. There has to be over a hundred people here. How many of them are here to make sure he's really dead, though? How many of these people hated him? I guess it doesn't matter. The funeral director opens the doors and people make their way in. I stand to the side and shake hands, thanking people for coming, all the while hoping Eli shows up. If he does, will I be able to keep my shit together? Will I be able to keep up the fake guise that he's just a friend? I doubt it.

Once everyone is inside with only one chair left in the front row for me, the doors close and the ceremony starts.

All the chairs are full. People are lining the walls. I'm shocked.

And hurt. How did he have time to make an impression on this many people but never made time for me? Am I to blame? Did I need to go to him instead of waiting for him to come to me? Even when I would reach out, he barely spoke to me. I knew more about his secretary than I knew about his life.

A prayer is said, I get up and say a few words, but I honestly can't remember what I said, then everyone is excused. The wake is being held at the house, and I need to get back there anyway.

I leave the funeral, only a few people stopping to talk to me, tell me how sorry they are for my loss, he's in a better place, blah blah blah. I know they all mean well, but it's empty words. They mean nothing.

Aaron drives me to the house, parking in the garage next to Dad's BMW. I guess it's mine now, but I'll never drive it. I hate that damn car. It's mustard yellow, for Christ's sake. Why he had it painted that color, I'll never understand.

"You can take a minute. No one will blame you." Aaron grabs my arm and pulls me to a stop when I head straight for the house.

"What's the point? Will taking a minute make him any less dead? Will it make me any less of an orphan?" I snap, but I don't know why I'm so angry at him. It's neither fair nor his fault.

"Take a minute to breathe, man, so you don't blow up in there in front of people." He grips my shoulders tightly, forcing my muscles to relax just a little. "You can swing at me if it'll make you feel better."

I chuckle and shake my head, dropping my shoulders. "No, I don't want to fight you."

"Good, 'cause I'd hate to kick your ass today."

I snort a laugh and shake my head.

"All right, let's get a drink, then, huh?" Aaron says, opening the car door.

"Yeah, that sounds good." We enter the house, and there are snack tables set up all over the place. The caterers did a great job with the spread. At the door to my father's office, I hesitate. Even as a kid I wasn't really allowed in here. It's boring, gray walls, dark wood, and wingback leather chairs. A few bookcases, a locking file cabinet behind the massive desk, and his scotch collection. On his desk is a picture of him and Mom.

I open the liquor cabinet and pull out a bottle of Macallan Red Collection. It's aged forty years and about thirty-five thousand dollars a bottle. Aaron grabs glasses, and I pour us each two fingers because why the fuck not? We stare out the window overlooking the pool as we sip, taking the last few minutes before guests arrive to enjoy the silence.

"I really appreciate you staying with me this week."

"I'm glad it helped." He finishes his glass just as the doorbell rings.

I finish off mine and set it down with a sigh.

"Let's get this over with."

It's been hours of listening to people sing my father's praises. He was such a good man, helpful, caring. Some of my teammates have shown up to show support, which I appreciate. I guess I didn't realize how much they actually cared. I guess the perk of this is it leaves me less time to obsess over how to convince Eli I'm serious. I'll find a way; I just need some time.

I'm standing in the dining room, talking to some actress that I could not care any less about when I hear it.

"I grew up with Asher."

Spinning around, I pick him out of the crowd in a nanosecond. Those bouncy blond curls framing his face, the haunted look in his eyes, and the navy-blue suit cups him in all the right places. He's even wearing a pearl necklace that I'm sure belonged to Mom.

Necklace. *His necklace.* He left it on the island. Did he do that on purpose, or was he in such a rush to leave he missed it? I wish I had it on me now to give to him. Either way, he needs to have it back. She wanted him to have it. It was important enough for her to put in her will while she was dying.

His bright blue eyes lock on mine, and the next thing I know, he's in my arms and my lips crash onto his. I don't know who moved first, but it doesn't matter. My body comes alive with him so close, my heart beats, and for the first time in what feels like years, it doesn't hurt. I cup the back of his head to keep him with me, and he lifts onto his toes, leaning against my chest for balance with his arms around my neck.

After everything, he came today, knowing I would need him.

He's my entire world. My boy. Mine. Nothing matters but him and the way he fits against me. I can't let him go. Never again. We need each other. Our heartstrings are woven together, and once we touch, we're helpless against it.

Our mouths are a frenzied pairing, taking what we so desperately need from the other. Nothing exists past this. When we're together, we can't not touch.

Someone coughs and taps on my shoulder, making me jump. My head pops up and everyone around us is staring. Everyone. Teammates, celebrities, coworkers of my father. Embarrassment for losing control of myself in a public setting heats my face, and Eli shoves away from me, ducking his head to the floor. I grab his hand quickly and thread our fingers, pulling him back to me.

"Stop it," he growls in a hushed whisper, pulling on his hand.

"I am not ashamed of you." My tone is hard and loud enough for the people close enough to hear me, but I don't give a shit.

Eli lifts his eyes to mine, huge and vulnerable with fear and hope warring within the depths.

I open my mouth to tell him I love him and want him with me forever, even if it means losing my career, but Aaron speaks up.

"This is probably a private conversation that should happen later." He pats me on the back and steps closer, dropping his voice so only we can hear. "People will start clearing out soon."

He's right, this is a conversation for us to have alone, but that doesn't mean I have to like it. Keeping Eli's hand in mine, I continue on with the wake. People give me strange looks, obviously curious about the scene Eli and I just caused, but no one straight out asks. I'm surprised by it, to be honest.

Finally, people start leaving. From the corner of my eye, I see Aaron going around to our teammates and talking to them, probably telling them to leave first so people start clearing out. In less than thirty minutes, the guests are gone, and the catering crew is cleaning up.

Exhausted, I drag Eli upstairs. Aaron catches up on the landing, and I stop to introduce them.

"Aaron, this is—"

"Eli, I figured." He holds out his hand with a smile on his face while Eli looks back and forth between us.

"You told him about me?" He's trying to hide a shy smile but failing as he takes Aaron's hand to shake.

"Of course he did," Aaron says. "I'm Aaron."

"Nice to meet you." Eli shakes his hand, and it's adorable how awkward he is about it.

"Can we do this tomorrow? I'm exhausted." I nod to Aaron, and he waves us off.

"I'll handle the caterers." He motions over his shoulder.

Fuck. I forgot about all of that.

"Thanks."

Pulling Eli along behind me, I open my bedroom door and lock it behind us, then back him up to the bed.

"Asher," he starts, holding his hands up like he's trying to hold me off, but I don't give him the option to say anything else. I claim his mouth in a quick, punishing kiss, then pick him up under the arms and toss him back onto my bed. Quickly, I climb on after him, desperate to feel him under me again.

"Asher," Eli groans my name when I pinch his nipple and pull.

"You're not leaving me again, Elliot." At his full name, his eyes spring open and meet mine. "Do you understand?"

"I can't stay," he insists, and there's heat behind it like he wants to but needs to be convinced.

Laying down with half my body weight on him, my leg over his and my hand on his skin, I stare at him. The dark circles under his eyes are back, the glow in his eyes has dimmed again too. It hurts to see my boy losing himself.

"You can and you will." He shakes his head, tears filling his eyes that I brush from his cheeks with my thumbs. "Why can't you stay? What's holding you back?"

"You can't lose football for me," he says in a rush, his voice breaking. Eli covers his eyes with his arm, hiding from me.

"If that's what it takes to keep you, fuck football." I lift his arm and cup his cheek. "Will I miss it? Sure, but you are the most important thing to me. You. You are worth everything, and I am not giving you up again. I can't. I love you."

Eli sobs and buries his face in the crook of my neck. I wrap myself around him, turning on our sides so he can curl into me while he purges the emotions I know are flooding his head.

My boy is broken, and that breaks my heart. I caused some of this self-doubt, but I'll fix it. I'll make sure he never has a reason to question his worth again.

We lay together a long time, Eli's sobs quietening to sniffling, then to silence, but I don't rush him. I let him process what I've said, and when his breathing evens out and his body relaxes into sleep, I follow him. For the first time since I left the island, I fall into a deep, restful sleep and stay there all night.

The next morning, Eli is curled on his side facing away from me. As badly as I want to wrap myself around him again, I know I need to get up and get ready to head back to San Diego. The idea turns my stomach. I need him to come with me even though I'm going to minicamp.

Standing, I realize I'm still in my dress shirt and suit pants, though I had shed my jacket at some point apparently, since it's on the floor. I leave the room carefully and head downstairs to make coffee and to give me a few minutes to get my head together.

Aaron is sitting at the bar in the kitchen when I come around the corner, eating something that looks like a veggie omelet, I'm sure, since he went out and bought a ton of food not long after we got here. The dude is meticulous about his diet.

He looks up from his phone, his fork halfway to his mouth when he puts it back down.

"Hey, man." He nods, watching me carefully with tension suddenly tightening his shoulders.

"What?" I turn to face him instead of getting coffee first.

"The entire team knows about Eli."

Fuck.

That was not the way I want it to come out, but fuck it, it's done now. I don't know how to feel or what to think. I'm relieved it's out and I don't have to do it, but what now? How did everyone handle it? Am I going to get traded? Is it public now or just the locker room knows?

I lean against the counter and pinch the bridge of my nose while I try to wrap my head around it. I've hidden this part of who I am from everyone except Eli for my entire life. Now, just like that, it's out, and I can't get it back. Do I want to? No, I don't think so. I want Eli, and if this is what needs to happen for me to keep him, then so fucking be it. But will it be the end of my career?

Is this a life raft offering me safety, or an anchor coming to drown me?

"And? What now?" I finally ask in the silence of the room.

"It's hot news, but I expect it to die down soon. From what I've seen, there have been a few jokes that weren't really okay, but they got shut down quickly." He shrugs like my life isn't on the line and he doesn't have a front-row seat.

"Let me guess. Marshall and Collins?" Dudes are assholes who will try to exploit anything they deem as a weakness. We've gone at it a few times over the years.

He nods and picks his fork back up to shove food into his face.

"Where's the boyfriend?" he asks around a mouthful of food.

The term makes me smile, helps ease the stress of everyone knowing.

"He's asleep. Does just the team know or was there some-thing posted online?" I turn to grab a mug from the cupboard and fill it with coffee.

"Just the team as far as I can tell, though I'm not sure Tweedledee and Tweedledum will keep a lid on it for long."

That's a damn good point.

"Dude, did you sleep in your suit?" He eyes me with disgust. "How was that comfortable?"

"It wasn't." Eli's sleep-rough voice comes from the doorway, and we both turn to look at him. His curls are sticking up like he stuck his finger in a light socket, eyes puffy from crying, and wearing a rumpled suit. He's fucking beautiful, and he's mine.

"Coffee?" I ask as I grab a cup and fill it, leaving room for creamer.

He grumbles an unintelligible sound and shuffles toward me, only pausing to look in the fridge.

"What kind of monster doesn't have creamer? Not even half and half," he whines, which makes me chuckle.

"Hang on, I know a trick." In the pantry I dig around until I find a can of sweetened condensed milk and a can opener. Eli eyes me suspiciously as I come back and spoon some into his cup before stirring it around to dissolve. "You may want a splash of milk, but that should work."

He doesn't look convinced but wraps both hands around the mug and lifts it to his lips. Once the hot brew has hit his tongue, he pulls it away and looks at it with surprise and confusion.

"How did you know about this?" he asks, still inspecting his cup like I've performed magic and he's trying to figure it out.

I shrug. "It was something Mom used to do sometimes. I haven't thought about it until I came back here."

Aaron flicks his gaze back and forth between us, trying not to be obvious that he's watching us but failing.

Eli sets his mug down and looks up at me. "When are you going back to San Diego?"

Aaron freezes mid-chew, his eyes meeting mine.

"Today, actually." I clear my throat and put my cup down too. Eli's body language changes from open, if not hesitant, to rejected. His shoulders droop, and he drops his head. "We have minicamp tomorrow, but you should come with us."

Eli shakes his head, and his eyebrows pull together.

"Oh no, that's okay. Do you want any help with all this?" He motions around the room. I reach for his arm and turn him around, pinning his hips to the counter with mine, and lift his chin with my fingers.

"Come to San Diego."

His eyes meet mine, a little haunted and sad, but he's trying so hard to hide it.

"I can't be a secret." His voice is so raw it hurts my heart.

"My entire team already knows."

Eli pulls his head back away from me, staring at me like he's looking for something.

"What?"

"A few saw us kiss yesterday, so by this morning, everyone knows. My agent knows too. It's only a matter of time before it gets out, and I'm done caring if it does." I cup his cheek to make sure he can't turn away from me. "I'm not giving you up."

His eyes flick between mine a few times before he wraps his arms around me, burying his face in my chest and breathing deep. I hold him against me and kiss his forehead, whispering against his skin. "I'm going to keep you forever, okay?"

Eli nods and squeezes me tighter.

Twenty-Nine

ELLIOTT

After a quick pit stop at my apartment, we hit the road to San Diego. Since my bag was still packed from Black Diamond, I just grabbed more clothes and my important jewelry. My heart is heavy knowing I don't have the necklace from Mrs. Vaughn, but I haven't mentioned it. If I'm being really honest with myself, I'm afraid to. What if he's angry I lost it?

Since it's a Tuesday and early afternoon, traffic is moving along at a good pace. Aaron talks constantly, telling me stories from them being on the road for games. Asher is in the back seat with me, one of my legs tossed over his knee with his hand on my thigh, playing with the edge of my shorts that I changed into on our pit stop.

Asher's hand slides up my shorts to tease the skin of my inner thighs, and it takes all of my self-control not to react. Aaron is laughing about something in the front while my dick gets hard. It's uncomfortable and embarrassing but so fucking hot.

"Almost there," Asher tells me, looking out the window. My only thought is *thank fuck* because I need to come so fucking bad right now. I swear to God, if Aaron stays, I will jack off in the bathroom. I'm going to kill Asher for this.

Aaron pulls the car to a stop in front of a beautiful glass-walled building with sleek lines. He pops the trunk, and Asher grabs our bags. He gets the lobby door unlocked and looks back at Aaron.

"Thanks, man, see you tomorrow."

Aaron waves and gets back in the car. *Oh thank you, Jesus.* Asher marches us to the elevator and slams his finger into the button.

"I can't wait to feel you around me." Asher's rough words send a shiver up my spine, and my cock aches. Bastard. He knows exactly what he's doing. The doors ding open, and we step on. He hits the button for the fifteenth floor, and as soon as the doors close, Asher has his mouth on mine and my back against the wall.

I moan into his mouth while he swipes his tongue along mine. His body pressing against me is exactly what I've been craving for days.

All too soon, the elevator comes to a stop, and the doors open. We're both panting and red-faced when we step off, and I follow him to his apartment door.

The door closes behind us, and Asher is on me, slamming my back against the wood, ravaging my lips. I jump up and wrap my legs around his hips, grinding my cock against his and groaning into his mouth.

"Fuck me, please," I whimper as he carries me to the kitchen and sets my ass on the counter.

"Oh, I'm going to. Don't you worry, baby." He sucks on

my bottom lip for a second before backing away and looking in a cabinet. Reaching for something on a top shelf, he turns around with a container of coconut oil.

Asher sets the jar on the counter and leans on his palms next to my hips. His eyes are locked on my lips, and he presses his hard-on against mine, rolling his hips to pull a moan from me. He watches my mouth, denying both of us the kiss we want, even when I wrap my arm around his neck and lift my mouth to his.

My body hums with need. Not just for the orgasm I know is coming, but for him. For the connection I've only ever had with him. I want to feel his skin against mine, lose myself in him, because I know he'll catch me before I crash. For the first time in too damn long, I feel safe.

Asher brushes his lips over mine in too quick of a kiss.

"Lay back," he murmurs against my skin, pushing against my chest until I'm flat on the stone countertop. I shiver when the cold seeps through my shirt.

Grabbing my shorts, he pulls them down with my underwear and drops them on the floor, not giving a fuck. Asher lifts one of my legs to hook over his shoulder, then leans forward to lick up the underside of my cock. My back arches and my hips jerk at the sensation, a gasp escaping my throat. He runs his tongue around my head before sucking me into his mouth, gagging when he goes too far.

I can't stop the whimpers falling from my mouth as he sucks and bobs, twirling his tongue around me, and just playing with me. It feels fucking amazing, and I've been too long without him.

"Asher," I whine, tangling my fingers in Asher's messy hair. "Please."

His big hand cups my ass cheek, kneads it, then slaps it hard enough to sting. Every muscle in my body tightens as my dick throbs on his tongue. He hums around me, and I can't hold it back. I come in his mouth with no warning.

"Fuck. God. Jesus. Shit." My hands clench into fists as I try to think past the orgasm rocketing through me but fail. I didn't warn him. Fuck.

He doesn't stop sucking on me until I'm completely drained and sensitive.

Asher pulls off my dick with a pop, and it drops onto me with a damp slap while I pant.

"I'm-I-I'm sorry," I finally manage to get out in between breaths.

The sound of a jar opening and the top hitting the counter barely sinks into my head. Asher lifts me onto my side, and my leg straightens as he stands, no longer bent over his shoulder but against his chest.

Using just one hand, he grips my thigh until my knee bends, keeping my hips off the counter.

"Hold it," he demands, and I flex the muscles to hold myself up. Slick fingers slide between my cheeks and press against my hole. Asher watches my face as he pushes one finger, then two inside, pumping in and out of me. My eyes want to close, and my body is heavy from the orgasm I just had. It takes a lot of concentration, but I manage to stay in place.

"Such a tired boy, worn out already." Asher adds a third finger, and I groan. "Let's see if we can wake him up."

With his free hand, Asher pushes his clothes out of the way and grabs more oil to coat himself. I drag my teeth over my lip as I watch him stroke himself. My dick starts to twitch when his fingers pick up speed, pumping into me and stretching me for him.

"Hmm . . . getting sloppy, baby." He pulls his fingers out and drops my hips back to the counter, pushing me onto my stomach and lifting one leg to bend on the countertop. He moves me until my dick is pointing to the ground and my toes are barely brushing the floor. Asher smacks my ass cheek again, the sound echoing in the space. The heat from his palm soothing some of the sting, and he pushes into me. Not taking it slow, just all the way in until his hips hit my ass.

"You take it so well, baby," he groans, grinding deep inside of me and gripping my shoulder. "You look so perfect with your ass stretched around my dick."

I shudder, goose bumps breaking out along my skin at his words. He pulls out slowly but thrusts back in fast and hard, setting a brutal pace. He's fucking me so hard I'll have bruises from the edge of the counter digging into me, but I don't care. I want him to own me.

With one hand on my shoulder and one on my raised thigh, he takes everything he wants from me and turns me into his fuck toy.

"You're so fucking beautiful, Elliot." Asher lifts my face to his, not letting me look away from him.

Tears burn the backs of my eyes as he uses my body.

"My good boy." Asher drags his lips down my throat. "So perfect for me."

The words falling from his mouth are just as deadly as his dick. I don't know how long he fucks me. Time no longer has any meaning.

My dick wakes up with a vengeance, and I come again before Asher fills me with his own orgasm. We're both sweaty and spent, panting and tired by the end. He bends over, dropping his forehead to my back as he catches his breath.

"I love you, baby," he pants. "We'll figure this all out, okay?"

"Yeah," is all I'm capable of right now. His dick scrambled my brain. There are no thoughts past sleep.

Asher presses a kiss to my damp skin and slowly slides out of me. I hiss at the friction against the abused flesh, and he helps me down. The counter, cabinet front, and the floor are all a mess, but he doesn't seem to care, just lifts me in his arms and carries me down the hall.

"I've waited too damn long to have you in my bed," he grumbles into my neck, licking at my salty skin. "You're mine."

My heart flutters, and a lazy smile lifts one side of my lips as my eyes close. I barely recognize getting laid in a bed and covered with a blanket. A pressure settles on my chest as Asher lays on me, and I pass out.

The sun is rising when I open my eyes again. I guess we forgot to close the curtains when we came in here. The sky is full of color as the sun dips below the horizon. Asher has his thigh between mine and his head on my chest. I run my hand through his hair with a smile on my lips, loving the intimacy of this moment. It's easy and comfortable here where it's just us.

The silence is ruined with the insistent ring of a phone. Pretty sure it's mine. There are only two people who call me, Jordan and my mother. If I don't answer, Jordan will give it an hour and try again, but my mother will keep calling until I answer.

The phone stops for a few seconds, then starts back up. Knowing it won't stop until I answer it, I slide out from under Asher and make my way to the entryway with no pants on. That should probably be embarrassing, wandering around the apartment in nothing but a T-shirt that's long enough to be a dress, but I'm past the point of caring about it.

I find my phone in my pants pocket and answer it.

"Yes, Mother?"

"What the hell took you so long?" she demands like she has the right.

"I'm busy. What do you want?" I lean my hip against the counter, smirking to myself at the mess we made just a few hours ago.

"Where the hell are you? Why aren't there any boxes in here? It's a seller's market. You have until the end of the week to get your stuff out."

She's in my fucking apartment.

"First, get the hell out of my apartment. Second, I've been helping Asher deal with the loss of his father. I'm *so* sorry that's an inconvenience for you, but fuck off." My voice rises until I'm shouting. How dare she talk to me like this. I'm done being a punching bag for her, a pawn for her to use to get the public's attention. Done.

Footsteps sound in the hallway, and I feel bad for waking Asher. Sucking in a deep breath, I force myself to lower my voice. Mother is yelling into the phone, but I've pulled it away from my ear.

"You stay away from that boy! Are you really so selfish to ruin his life with your bullshit? You aren't worth his career! He has no family left. He needs to focus on finding a nice young woman to create a life with. You can't give him that, Elliot Martin! Leave him alone!" I know she's wrong, but she sure knows how to feed into every insecurity I have.

Asher stops in the doorway to the kitchen and watches me. He takes in the state of the kitchen and my lack of pants, reads my face like the words are written on my skin.

Self-doubt starts eating at me the longer she rants, pointing out all my flaws and why I'm not lovable, not worth it. It's so fucking hard to believe that someone like Asher can see past it all. I'm a mess. I have no direction. My mental health is in the toilet. I can't give him kids, and my family sucks. So, what do I have to offer him?

He stalks toward me and cages me against his body, lifting my chin with his fingers.

"She's wrong. Stand your ground. I won't let you fight alone."

With my eyes locked on his, I bring the phone back to my ear, and even with everything in me terrified to burn the only bridge I have left with my family, I speak.

"I'll be out in time, and you don't ever need to call me again." I end the call, and Asher takes it from my hand, chucking it across the room.

"Good boy." He cups my face and presses his lips to mine, our bodies melting together as I cling to him.

"Say 'I am worth it'." He holds my face so I can't look away.

"You're worth it."

Asher gives me a hard look.

"Elliot." My name is a warning, and his mouth forms a serious line. "Say it right."

"I'm worth it." My voice is so soft it can barely be heard.

"Louder."

"I'm worth it." My lower lip trembles as overwhelming emotions start to plague me.

"Again."

"I'm worth it!" I yell this time with a tear running down my cheek.

"I'm enough," he prompts.

"I am enough," I manage to get out around the lump in my throat.

"I am lovable," he prompts again.

My eyes slam shut, and a sob rips from the tattered parts left of my heart. Most of my life I was taught that I wasn't lovable. If only I was more like Marcus or Asher, then I would be. Boys have to be tough and not like *girly* things. They can't get emotional. I was never enough for my parents, never met any of my grandparents or aunts and uncles. The only people who ever loved me were Marcus, Asher, and Jordan.

"I am lovable," Asher repeats. "Say it."

I didn't know it would hurt so much to hear what I've always needed to. It's not fair that when you finally get what you need, it feels like a lie. The things you've craved to hear all your life feel like a punishment.

A thumb brushes over my bottom lip, and I force my eyes open to see Asher. His own face showing cracks in his heart while I deal with my own. His face is a watery blur, but he's not hiding the pain of watching me fall apart.

"You've always been worth it." He rests his forehead against mine. "I'm sorry I made you feel any less. I didn't feel like I was worthy of you, that you deserved more than I was when I left." A tear trickles down his face to disappear into his beard, and I lift my lips to his.

The kiss is salty and full of pain, healing, and understanding. There's no heat, no lust, just comfort, and in this moment, it's exactly what I need. With my eyes still closed and my forehead against his, I pull back enough to speak.

"I am lovable."

I can feel his lips lifting in a smile and his thumbs brushing the tears from my face.

"That's right, you are. I love you." He wraps his arms around me and lifts me off my feet. I let out a very undignified shriek and quickly wrap my legs around his waist while he chuckles. "Time for a shower."

Thirty

ASHER

The water is hot against our skin as we stand pressed together. Unhurried touches that have more to do with comfort than sex, slow kisses, and sweet smiles. The steam billows around us, blocking out the world. Reaching over his shoulder, I grab my body wash and squirt it right into my palm. I don't want anything between my skin and his as I wash him.

The warm, masculine scent is heavy in the damp air as Eli drags in a deep breath.

"You still use American Crew body wash?" he asks with a little smile.

I smirk at him and nod. "It's the best thing I've found to keep the B.O. under control with training."

Being in here with him, I can pretend for just a little while that I'm not about to face down my team. That my place isn't on the line. It's terrifying to think that I'll get traded or cut because I love Eli. It's bullshit.

So I busy myself with washing his back and butt,

kneading the muscles as I slick his skin with soap. He groans into my neck as I clean his hole and I lean my mouth down next to his ear.

"You're perfect." He shivers at my words and relaxes into my touch. I work my way down his body, taking special care with his inner thighs, kissing each of the scars. There's not an inch of skin I haven't touched by the time I'm done, including his face and hair. I worship his body the way he was meant to be loved.

"You need better conditioner," Eli grumbles as he looks at the bottles available and grabs one.

"Tell me what you want, and I'll make sure it's here."

Eli puts some conditioner in his hand and bends over so his hair is hanging away from his head. He combs the product through his hair with his fingers, careful not to get it too close to his scalp, then rinses it out. I love watching him. Even though I've known him since I was a kid, there are things like this that I didn't get to experience. These intimate moments are still new.

He looks at the bottles again. "That's as good as it's going to get for now. I'll make a list."

Eli reaches for the body wash and spreads the soap across my chest. My eyes don't leave his face as he washes me. I love the blush that tints his cheeks at being watched. He takes his time, asking me about scars he doesn't recognize, sharing memories and stories. His touch heals a part of me I didn't know was broken. That dark place in my heart with ragged edges that was abandoned by my parents and never enough to keep anyone is less sharp.

As I watch him, I can see the light is starting to come back into his eyes. With time, he'll be the vibrant boy I've always known him to be with no more dark circles under his beautiful eyes.

Eli does a thorough job of cleaning me, tracing his fingertips along the lines of my tattoos, and we rinse off. We're still touching and caressing when I shut off the water and grab us some towels. Being comfortable with who we are together is not something I've ever experienced with anyone. It's just more proof that Eli is the only one for me.

We dry off and shiver as we leave the warmth of the bathroom. I wrap my towel around my waist and kiss his temple while he stands naked in the room, drying his hair.

"I'll go get your bag." I hurry to the front door where I dropped our shit and hustle back to the bedroom. Aaron will be here soon to pick me up for camp, and as much as I'm dreading it, I know I need to get it over with. The longer I wait to see everyone, the more I'll blow it up in my head. It's better to just rip the Band-Aid off.

A sob comes from my bedroom, and I run full speed back to find Eli kneeling on the floor next to my dresser with something clutched to his chest that I can't see. Fear courses through me as I try to figure out what the fuck just happened. Did he get a text or something? What the hell would cause this kind of reaction from him?

I drop his bag and wrap myself around his back, holding him against me.

"What happened, baby?" He's rocking back and forth with tears streaming down his face, and it's scaring the shit out of me. "Talk to me."

It takes a minute, but I pull on his hand to see what he's got a hold of and pause when I see the satin bag with my mother's necklace in it.

"I thought I lost it," he manages to get out through the tears. The broken part of my heart that cracked when I found it on the island knits back together. *He didn't mean to leave it.*

"Let me," I tell him softly, taking the bag from his hand and pulling out the string of pink pearls. Opening the gold clasp, I hang it around his neck and fasten it. His hand immediately goes to the beads, running along the cool, smooth pearls.

I clear the knot in my throat and turn him around to hug him. "When I found it, I thought you were really done with me."

His head shakes as he holds me tighter. "I'm sorry I let my parents get into my head."

Cupping his face, I bring his mouth to mine, a tear running down my cheek. Our kiss is salty and full of remorse, love, and understanding.

"I love you," I say against his lips. "Nothing will ever change that. You were made for me and I'm not letting you go."

"I love you too," Eli says as he pulls back enough for his watery gaze to meet mine. "Please don't let me go."

"Never."

Eli wraps his legs around my waist and claims my mouth again, this time rocking his hips against mine. His naked body heats with a flush as he gets hard. This towel does nothing to hide my hard-on either. I drag my bearded jaw down his neck, loving the shiver that rocks through him.

The doorbell rings, and Eli freezes while I cuss.

"That's Aaron. I have to go." I kiss him quickly and pat

his ass for him to get up. He grumbles but does, his cock bobbing in front of my face as I get off the floor.

I quickly get dressed in workout shit, swipe some deodorant on my pits, and kiss a now dressed Eli on my way to the door. He's wearing one of my shirts he stole from the closet, and it's so big on him I don't know if there's anything under it.

"I'll be back tomorrow night. It's a quick minicamp to make sure everyone is here and to get an updated fitness and nutrition plan," I tell him as I pull open the front door.

"Hey, Eli, how's it going?" Aaron lifts a hand in greeting, and Eli nods at him before turning back to me.

"Okay. I'm sure I can find something to keep me busy." The smirk on his face tells me he's going to go digging into everything, but I just laugh and kiss him again. I have nothing to hide from him. He can dig through every crevice of this place.

"Love you, brat."

"Love you too."

Eli has a soft smile and pink cheeks as he closes the door, a look that's just for me. Aaron snorts as soon as the door is closed, and I shove him.

"Shut up," I grumble at him, but I can't hide the smile.

"That was adorable," he mocks.

"Keep it up and I'll beat your most yards in a single season record." I push the button for the elevator, and Aaron raises his eyebrows at me.

"Oh, you just woke up and decided to choose violence today?"

"Afraid of a little competition?" I smirk at him.

"Bring it on, my guy." He rubs his hands together and rolls his shoulders back. He thinks I can't beat him.

We ride it down and get into the car, making the quick drive to the stadium. The closer we get, the more my confidence fades, replaced with a heaviness that's never been there before. When we pull up into the parking lot, there aren't many news vans since this minicamp isn't open to the public.

With every step toward the locker room, a weight drops farther into my stomach until I'm ready to hurl. I don't know how this is going to go. I'm sure someone will say something about Eli, but how many? Will the room fall silent when I walk in? Will Coach pull me aside and tell me I'm being traded?

"I've got you, man," Aaron says with a squeeze to my shoulder as we approach the locker room door.

I suck in a deep breath and square my shoulders. *I will not be made to feel less for who I love.* Who I'm in a relationship with has nothing to do with my ability to play football. Anyone who thinks differently can kiss my ass.

We walk in and head to our cubbies to get changed into team apparel workout gear. The guys I pass say hi and fist-bump me. So far so good, I guess, but the troublemakers either aren't here yet or haven't seen me.

The locker room gets loud as it fills with players reconnecting after a few months off. Some guys are friends outside of here, but a lot of us are just associates; we work together and that's it, but feel the need to catch up when we're back together.

I pull on my cleats and lace them up as a shadow comes over me. My gut tightens knowing the confrontation won't be put off any longer. I don't hurry or look up until I'm done. You can't let them know they ruffle your feathers.

I stand up and give Marshall a bored, blank expression. He's a five-foot-ten, dark-haired prick with a pinched face and more muscle than brain.

"Lose something over here?" I cross my arms and face him.

"Yeah, my fucking appetite," he sneers.

"You need me to rub your tummy?"

Aaron stands shoulder to shoulder with me and snorts at my answer but keeps the laugh in.

Marshall takes a step back, disgust clear on his face. "Don't fucking touch me, fa—"

"Finish that sentence and it'll be the last one you say in this locker room," Coach's no-nonsense, cold timbre cuts him off, and I lift an eyebrow at the man in front of me.

Everyone in the room is silent, crowding around the space to watch it all go down. They all knew it would happen, but maybe not this early in the day.

While I knew this was probably going to happen when I came out, I hoped it wouldn't. We've come a long way for acceptance of the LGBTQIA+ community, but there are still these assholes that make it hard for all of us.

"First of all"—I crowd into his space—"liking men isn't contagious, unlike the VD you're normally sporting. Second, jocks don't do it for me. Never have. I have never looked at any of you with anything other than friendship." I move closer until my arms brush his chest. "Third, I'm not an asshole that sexually harasses people who aren't willing. That says a lot more about you than it does me." I stare at him for a second before turning my back to him to head toward the gym for warm-up. I'm pushing through the doors when I hear Coach speak to the entire room.

"I will not stand for homophobic slurs or offensive jokes about the LGBT community. If I hear even a rumor about someone causing problems, you'll be out of here by the end of the day. This team, this franchise, is better than that shit. It will not be tolerated. Am I clear?"

The room breaks out in a "yes, sir," and Aaron claps me on the back. I didn't know I needed the reassurance, but hearing Coach have my back is a huge weight off my chest.

Thirty-One

ELLIOTT

I t's been almost three months since I went to San Diego with Aaron and Asher, and I've never looked back. Not having to hide around the team is really nice. I'm invited to things for the significant others, allowed in the box for games. We're just careful in public, and that's fine. A lot of people aren't comfortable with PDA, so that doesn't bother me. Much.

Today is the first game of the regular season, and it's a home game. Asher has been gone for hours already, getting ready with the team, while I get ready to join the families and significant others in the box. I dig out a pair of lace thigh-highs with an attached garter belt and some sexy underwear. Asher loves me in lace and satin, skirts and tights. I love that he finds it attractive, and I'm not shamed for liking it too.

I find a pair of jeans with lots of holes in them for the lace to show through and pull them on, careful not to shove my foot through one and rip them even more. Standing in front of the full-length mirror in the closet, I check my reflection as I button up the jeans. They cup my ass perfectly and the flash of delicate lace is sexy as fuck.

I dig out a silk camisole in light blue and a navy velvet blazer to put over it. The air conditioning in the box is always too damn high, and I end up freezing. Today, I'll be warm. Hopefully.

There's a knock on the front door and a cheery Jordan calls down the hall.

"Get your ass out here and drink this abomination you call coffee!"

I smile at her comment and grab my favorite pearl necklace to add to my outfit. Once again, I check the mirror, fluff my curls, and slip on some ankle boots. I look damn good, if I do say so myself.

Leaving the closet, I stop and admire the black-and-white pictures that we had printed for above the bed. They're all pictures I took at Black Diamond. Some of them are of Asher, some of them of the beach or the trees, and somehow he managed to sneak a few pictures of me while I wasn't looking. They didn't turn out too shabby either.

I like to think of that time as the start of us. We've come a long way over the years, growing and being dealt shitty hands, but we made it.

My boots click on the wood floor of the hallway, and Jordan holds out the cup of iced double cream, double sugar coffee from Dunkin' Donuts. I grab the cup and take a big drink, the sugar settling in my soul.

"Perfect."

Jordan lifts an eyebrow at me, gives me a once-over, and whistles.

"Look at you!"

I flush a little at the compliment and shrug like it doesn't get to me.

"My boyfriend is an NFL star." I fake a snotty attitude. "I have to look the part."

She grins, giving me her true happy smile. She's been doing that a lot more lately.

"You look happy," she says quietly, wrapping her arm around me in a hug. "I can't tell you how happy that makes me."

"Thank you for sticking with me." I squeeze my eyes shut and wrap my arms around her back. "I know I was a shitty friend for a long time, but I know I wouldn't have made it this far without you."

She lets out a little sound that's somewhere between a breath and a sob.

"I always knew you had it in you; you just didn't believe it." Her voice breaks, and she swipes away a tear quickly when she stands up. "You weren't a shitty friend, by the way. I knew if I needed you, you would be there in a heartbeat. I never doubted that."

With a watery smile, I grab my stuff, and we head out to the game. She's coming with me today to meet some of the WAGs. I think she's a bit jealous that I've been hanging out with other people since she's still in LA.

We take an Uber so we don't have to deal with parking and traffic after the game, then wander through the tail-gaters to the stands.

At some point, I'll be comfortable wearing his jersey number, maybe once he's publicly out. I don't know. I expected this to be worse than it has been, honestly. The team and families know. I'm able to be who I am around them.

Jordan hooks her arm through mine and steers me toward the gates. Her ripped-up blue jeans, jersey, and combat boots make her look like a badass.

We get checked in and escorted to the box where there's catering set up and a bar.

"Elliot!" My name is shrieked in that way that only women can master, and I smile when I see Ashley coming toward me with her arms open for a hug. I give her a quick squeeze before stepping back to introduce Jordan. She's on the shorter side with long dark hair and piercing green eyes. She's sweet and funny and was the first to accept me into the group.

"Hey, Ash, this is my best friend, Jordan. Jordan, this is Ashley. She's married to one of the linemen, Hopkins." They shake hands and give each other those fake polite smiles that everyone does.

"How's your boy doing today? Get all his rituals done?" She waggles her eyebrows at me, and I laugh. All sports players are superstitious, and a lot of them have a ritual that revolves around sex. Asher's include a blow job before he leaves on game day.

During away games, he wants video call sex in the morning. I'm not complaining, it's hot as fuck.

"Of course, yours?"

She winks at me and starts to say something, but her little girl starts crying, and she leaves to take care of her.

"Aren't you mister popular?" Jordan comments after three other wives come up and say hi to me. She hands me a mimosa, and I hide my smile behind it as I take a drink.

"I was really nervous to meet them, but they've accepted me with open arms. Mostly."

Jordan lifts an eyebrow. "Mostly?"

I sigh and nod toward the seats so we can sit. "There's always one, right? Luckily, she stays away from me and doesn't make a fuss."

Jordan and I settle into our seats, and a group of wives moves toward us. One of the little boys, Carter, who's about three, crawls into my lap and plays with my necklace. I smile at him and offer him some fruit from my plate that he happily munches on.

"Carter, you have your own food," his mom, Bethany, sighs and offers me the boy's plate.

"Don't you know it tastes better off someone else's plate, Mom?" I smile at her, and she smirks as she rolls her eyes. She drops down into the seat next to me in case he starts acting up and she needs to intervene. I haven't had any problems with him, but other people have, so I understand the hesitance.

"How do you guys know each other?" Bethany asks me, motioning to Jordan.

"She's my best friend. Basically, she found me in a bar one night and decided to keep me." I smile and Jordan shakes her head.

"Not far from the truth. I knew you were one of mine the minute I saw you." She nudges me.

"You look familiar," Bethany says to Jordan who laughs.

"Yeah, my dad is a musician, but I didn't want to go that route. You might have seen pictures of me with him." She doesn't want to say who her father is. It's always the same questions once someone finds out.

"Oh, who's your dad?" Bethany asks, interest piqued. Shit.

"Jay Barker." Jordan sighs. As the lead singer of Sons of Chaos, a lot of people know his name.

Bethany's eyes widen. "Oh shit."

"I'm going to grab something to eat," Jordan says, quickly rising to her feet. "It was nice to meet you."

Bethany blinks and turns to me with embarrassment clear on her face. "I'm so sorry. I didn't mean to upset her."

"It's okay. Normally when people find out who her dad is, they start in with all the questions and sometimes people get crazy invasive." I rub a hand down Carter's back, and he snuggles into me.

"I can take him," Bethany offers, but I wave her off since I don't mind. I don't know if I want my own kids or not, but I love moments like these. I'm content to sit and cuddle the little boy for as long as he'll let me. Bethany gets called to talk to another girlfriend, and I'm left in silence for about a second before the door opens and Aaron's parents come in. The duo look around the room, and when Mrs. Thomlyn meets my gaze, a smile takes over her face. She nudges her husband and points toward me, then comes over. I stand to give her a hug, and she wraps her arms around me carefully to not disturb the sleeping toddler.

"Hello, dear." She kisses my cheek and releases me. "How are you?"

I can't hold back my smile. "I'm good. I'm glad you guys made it."

"Of course," she says and takes a water bottle from Mr. Thomlyn when he offers it.

"How are you, Eli?" he asks, wrapping his arm around me in a hug.

"Good, how are you guys?"

Mrs. Thomlyn chats for a few minutes about upcoming trips and makes me promise to come by for dinner soon, then they head over to take seats on the other side of the box with some of the other parents.

Jordan brings me a new drink and has a seat with her sandwich and fruit as the game kicks off.

My man is on the field, and my eyes are glued to his jersey. He's fucking impressive, shooting down the field to catch the ball thrown in his direction. He and the quarterback, Thomas, have such amazing chemistry out there. Reading each other's moves before they make them, it's like magic.

Everyone in the stands is on their feet as my man makes the first touchdown of the season. Pride blossoms in my chest as he does an end zone dance and points toward the box where I'm sitting. Everyone smiles and there's a collective "aww," but since cameras could be pointed at us, no one looks at me.

Jordan snaps a selfie with me, careful to crop out the sleeping child, and posts it on IG, tagging Asher and the team.

The game drags on; it's a close one so every play we're holding our breaths and hoping for no mistakes. By halftime we're tied 10-10, and everyone is nervous. Losing the first game of the season will be hard on the guys. They can overcome it, of course, but it'll be rough.

The door to the box opens, and Aaron's sibling, Brit, comes in with a backward hat covering their short bleach-blond hair, a jersey, cutoffs, and combat boots completing the outfit. Brit reminds me a lot of Jordan with them both having a "take no shit" attitude while being completely accepting of everyone. Brit is always late, if they show up at all, but I'm always glad when they do. We are opposites and I adore them.

Brit and Jordan eye each other for a moment, giving some flirty vibes that I'm here for.

"Elliot, how ya doing?" Brit nods to me and sits in the row directly in front of us but turns around to sit backward.

"I'm good, you?"

Brit lifts their chin in a nod. "You know how it is, fucking shit up and causing chaos."

I chuckle. "Sounds about right."

"Jordan." My friend sticks her hand out for the newcomer to shake. Brit lifts an eyebrow and looks Jordan up and down, teeth dragging over their bottom lip before sliding their palms together.

"Brit."

"It's nice to meet you." For the first time ever, Jordan sounds a little breathy. I'm forced to school my face and not gawk at her. I've seen Jordan flirt countless times, but she's never reacted like this to anyone.

Carter stirs in my lap and stretches, waking up and looking around for his mom.

"Hey, buddy." I rub his back and stand to take him back to Bethany. She reaches for the sleepy toddler, and I hand him off, stopping to grab a beer for Brit. When I'm on my way back to my seat, it looks like Brit and Jordan are having a moment, so I leave them be and watch the game via the TVs set up around the room.

Our guys are doing amazing, fighting for every point they earn and making the other team fight harder to come back. I'm so damn proud. It's kind of surreal to be here watching Asher play football. He's come a long way since I was sitting in the high school stands, cheering for him with Marcus next to me.

I drop back into my seat and hand Brit the beer. They take it and wink at me while lifting the bottle to their lips and taking a drink.

"You going to the I Prevail concert on Friday?" Brit asks, looking between Jordan and me. Jordan was making me go since Asher will be out of town for a game, but if Brit is going, I may be able to get out of it . . .

"Jordan is. You guys should meet up and go together," I offer, way too chipper.

Jordan looks at me completely unamused. "You're going."

"I hate you." I lift my glass and finish off my drink. "You have someone to go with. Why are you harassing me?"

"I have no problem going by myself, but you are not going to hole up in your apartment and mope because the boyfriend is out of town."

I roll my eyes, and Brit snickers, much like Aaron does. He's around a lot, having become Asher's new best friend. They roughhouse like teenagers, and while it's hilarious, it's also expensive since they crash into shit regularly.

We're down to the last two minutes of the game, we have the ball and are down by three points. We need a touchdown to win, field goal to tie and go into overtime. Everyone in the box is leaning forward to watch the game, on edge. Thomas drops back and throws the ball downfield in a Hail Mary pass. Everyone is on their feet, watching it fall right into

Asher's hands. The stands erupt in screams as he races for it and crosses into the end zone. The cheers are deafening as we scream and celebrate the win, everyone hugging each other and high-fiving as they set up for the extra point and pull ahead by four points.

My face already hurts from smiling so much, and my heart is pounding as adrenaline and excitement course through me. I'm jittery, hands shaking and my stomach fluttering as I watch the other team receive the ball and the clock run down to zero. The families start gathering their things and clearing out. All smiles and happy conversations. I hang back and wait to see if Asher is interviewed. I don't have to wait long.

Becca Walker, the local journalist who interviews players, shows up onscreen with a sweaty-faced Asher towering over her. Her long blonde hair is hanging down her back, the tips fluttering in the wind. She's so put together in her blue slacks and cream silk shirt.

"This was a tough game. What was the most important part of this game that you guys had to master?"

Asher is breathing heavy, chugging water before he answers. "The mental game. This was a team win. It took all of us staying focused and not letting falling behind get to us."

"You've had a difficult summer. How do you think that has affected your game tonight?" She shoves the mic back in his face, and a look comes over him as he stares in the camera. Unease squeezes my stomach as he answers the question. *Don't you dare . . .*

"My boyfriend was key. I was able to focus, process, and

grieve thanks to him being by my side and loving me through the hard times."

There's a buzzing in my ears, and I'm pretty sure the entire stadium has fallen silent. *I can't believe he just said that.* There are too many thoughts in my head to focus on any one specifically, but he's out. Officially out.

Becca looks momentarily stunned, staring at him.

"Thank you, that'll be all," Asher says with a big smile and jogs away from her toward the locker room.

I'm going to kill him. What the fuck? That wasn't the plan.

Someone has their arms around me in a hug. I blink a few times and realize it's Jordan.

"You good, man?" Brit asks with a hand on my arm.

"I-I," I start but close my eyes and take a deep breath. "I don't know."

"He loves you," Jordan says with her chin on my shoulder. "Enjoy it. It's going to be okay."

The wives and girlfriends give me hugs and high-fives, saying goodbye and telling me not to worry about the haters that will pop up.

I don't know what to think or how to feel right now. Am I excited for the secret to be out? Sure. I hate hiding, but what will the backlash be?

Thirty-Two

ASHER

I'm still buzzing when I exit the locker room, showered and dressed in a damn suit an hour later. Will Eli be pissed? I didn't name him, but it will take about two-point-five seconds for the media to connect the dots. He's probably freaking out, his anxiety making him overthink it and find every bad scenario possible.

Aaron walks out with me since he's meeting with Brit for a post-game dinner. We find Eli, Brit, and Jordan standing together at the end of the hallway we use to enter the building from the parking lot.

Eli has his back to me, and I run up behind him and wrap him in my arms. He gives a startled shriek that I love and slaps at my arm.

"Ass," he huffs under his breath while Brit and Jordan laugh.

"Hi, baby," I say into his ear, his back pressed against my chest.

"You're a dick."

I nuzzle the sensitive skin behind his ear and whisper, "I'll give you my dick as soon as we get home."

Eli flushes and smacks my arm while I chuckle.

"You ready to go?" Aaron asks Brit, rubbing his stomach. "I'm fucking hungry."

"Yeah, let's go. All I've had is some crackers and a beer." Brit shrugs, then turns to Jordan. "What are you doing this evening?"

Jordan flushes, which is the strangest thing to witness, but follows along with Brit and Aaron for dinner.

"That was weird," I comment, watching them walk away.

"Super weird," Eli agrees. "Jordan is never shy, but she's got a real thing for Brit apparently."

"Good to know."

I turn Eli to face me and lift his chin with my fingers, one arm still banded around him to keep him close.

"Are you mad?" Unease has wings brushing the inside of my stomach and making my hands shake. The last thing I want is for him to be angry at me.

He sighs and wraps his arms around my waist.

"No, I'm not mad, but a little warning would have been nice." He lifts onto his toes and presses a quick kiss to my lips.

A smile splits my face, and I lift him off the ground. He wraps his legs around my waist and arms around my neck.

"It wasn't planned, but she gave me the opening, so I took it. I'm not going to let every interview focus on my sexuality, though. I have a boyfriend I love, and that relationship has nothing to do with football."

Eli's smile is so bright it's blinding. I didn't know just how dark my life was until he came back and turned a light on. I wasn't living; I was barely surviving, but that's changed. He's changed my life for the better, and I honestly can't wait to see what comes next for us.

We make it back home after I call us an Uber, and the second we're inside the safety of our apartment, I start stripping off his clothes. His jacket hits the floor in the entryway. His shoes are left in the living room. Jeans are peeled off in the hallway, and I groan at the thigh-highs and garter underneath.

I drop to my knees and pull his black underwear down just enough to free his cock and suck him into my mouth. Eli grips my hair in his fist and thrusts against me. I've gotten pretty good at deep throating him over the last few months and rarely gag anymore.

His ass flexes as he moves, and I grip the muscle in my hand, pulling his ass cheeks apart so he shivers.

"Fuck," he whimpers, watching his dick disappear between my lips. Saliva and his precum drip down my chin and onto my shirt. I love how he leaks for me. He's panting as I press my fingers against his hole, slick with spit.

"I'm going to come, please." His grip in my hair tightens, and I swallow around him, my nose pressed against his body as he loses control of himself.

His moans and whimpers echo off the walls, only making them hotter. My dick is aching in my suit pants, and I rub my palm against it to relieve some of the pressure. I groan around Eli's spent dick, and he shivers as he pulls out of my mouth.

He straddles my lap, his body relaxed and limp. He kisses me, tasting himself on my tongue, and moans.

"You're so beautiful when you come for me," I growl

against his lips. "I'm going to see if you've got another one in you." I slide my hand over the delicate lace tights, fingering the edge of the thigh-highs, and snapping the bands holding them up.

He groans into my neck, sucking on my skin until I'm sure there's a mark. Eli has never left a mark in a place that was visible before. We've been careful for months, but now I want his ownership, his claim on me to be seen by everyone.

With my hand on his ass to hold him against me, I stand and walk us through the bedroom to the walk-in closet. The fucking thing is huge and has an armless, tufted accent chair in there. I usually sit there while I watch him get dressed, enjoying the way he moves and picks things out.

I grab the chair and set it across from the mirror and set him down on the light gray fabric. I strip out of my suit and grab the lube from the bedside table before coming back to him completely naked. He watches me stalk toward him with his lip caught between his teeth.

"Stand," I instruct, and he does so without question. I sit my bare ass on the chair and turn him to face the mirror while I strip off his underwear but leave the tights and satin shirt he has on. I love the way satin feels against me when we fuck. It's soft, delicate, and warm from his skin.

"Spread 'em." I tap his inner thigh, and he widens his stance, leaning forward to hold on to the edges of the mirror while I slick up my fingers and find his hole.

In the reflection, I watch him bite on his lip, eyebrows pulling together as I press one finger inside of him.

"More," he says quickly, and I smirk at him as I add a second finger, then a third quickly after. He groans, pushing back onto my hand. "Please fuck me."

I pull my fingers from his hole and coat my dick in lube. Sitting back in the chair, I scoot forward a little to make the angle better, then grab his hip and pull him back to me. Eli widens his legs so they're on the outside of mine and impales himself on my cock in one hard thrust.

The groan that rips from my throat is loud, but he doesn't stop. He's leaning forward, bouncing on me, taking what he wants from me. It's sexy as fuck to watch his body take mine, working me over.

Releasing his hip, I wrap my arm around his chest and pull him back to me, the satin is slick and warm on my skin.

"Feet on my knees," I demand. "Fuck me with your pretty hole."

Eli turns his face into my neck, his back arching as I watch in the mirror. My dick disappearing into his ass over and over as his cock bobs. He's hard again already, and I reach to play with his balls. His rhythm stutters at the touch, and he moans into my skin. Reaching down to his hole, my fingers spread to either side of my dick, pressing into the skin that's stretched taut around me.

His skin heats, and his breath is hot against my skin while his sounds fill my ears. It's perfect. He's perfect. My boy.

I love watching him in the mirror, how he takes me, how he loves it.

"Are you my good boy?"

"Yes," he whimpers, and I wrap my hand around his dick, jerking him off in time with his thrusts.

"Are you going to come for me again?" I tighten my hand around him as he grinds on my cock, making my eyes roll back in my head. "Fuck, baby, you're going to make me come. Your hole feels too good."

He shudders, his dick throbbing in my hand, and I thrust up into him. My balls draw up as tingles shoot through me.

"Fuck," he moans as his body tightens, and cum shoots onto his chest and stomach. The clenching around me pushes me over, and I fill him a few thrusts later. Eli collapses onto me, my dick still buried in him as we pant.

"I love you, baby," I tell him, kissing his temple.

"Love . . . too," he gets out between heavy breaths, and I chuckle at his lack of words. His feet have slipped from my legs to hang limply, his entire body boneless and tired. It's my favorite sight. I love knowing I did this to him.

After a few minutes, I sit Eli up and pull the shirt off over his head and use it to clean him up some, then carry him to bed where we both crash immediately.

A KNOCKING on the door wakes me up an hour later. Begrudgingly, I find some sweats and pull them on before answering the door.

Franklin is standing there in his dark blue suit, looking unamused as usual. I sigh and step back to let him in. He's going to rip me a new asshole and possibly quit.

"You're a real pain in my ass, you know that?" he starts before I even have the door closed.

I sigh and take a seat at the kitchen island on one of the stools.

"Yeah, I'm aware."

"What part of 'wait for us to have a plan together' did you forget?" Franklin paces the room for a minute, then stops in front of me with his hands on his hips.

"I'm sorry," I start, rubbing a hand over my face. "I didn't plan to do it tonight, it just happened, but I'm also not sorry. I'm done hiding Eli."

Franklin sighs and pinches the bridge of his nose. "Of course. I'm not saying it's better to hide Eli, that's bullshit. I just would have liked to be better prepared. We need to make a statement." He pulls out his phone and taps his password in before handing it to me. "Social media is in a frenzy over this. Make a post of you and Eli, nothing scandalous, you asshole, and just tell people what you're comfortable with. That you grew up together, fell in love, and are happy."

"So, no dick pics then?" I joke, just to get a rise out of him.

He pins me with a glare. "I swear to God, Vaughn."

I laugh but nod. Soft footsteps on the hardwood have me turning toward the hallway to see a sleepy-eyed Eli in my T-shirt and no tights. He must have pulled them off before coming out here since I didn't remove them before he fell asleep.

"Sorry if we woke you." I open my arms for him, and he comes to me, leaning his face against my shoulder as he stands between my legs. I wrap an arm around him, and he relaxes with contentment.

"Nothing scandalous, I'm serious. Both of you. Keep your damn noses clean for a while," Franklin tells us before picking up his phone and pocketing it. "Better yet, before you post anything, send it to me for approval."

"You got it," I tell him, and he huffs at me before turning to leave.

It's a peaceful silence once the door is closed, Eli and I just existing in the space. I run a hand up and down his back, and he wraps his arms around my naked torso.

"Oh, I forgot to tell you that your dad's lawyer dropped off some stuff on Friday." Eli pulls away from me to head into the living room, so I follow him. The couch is more comfortable anyway. I drop down, and he hands me a thick manila envelope and what looks like a blue ring box.

Inside the jewelry box is a ring I haven't seen since my mom was alive. The silver ring with a single white pearl that I don't think she ever took off. I forgot about this. She loved this ring, and my father used to complain because it was cheap, just sterling silver instead of gold or platinum, but she loved it. I remember one Christmas he bought her a "better" one, but she refused to wear it, saying she liked this one better.

My chest is tight with the memory. It's been so long since I remembered something about her. She's been gone for a long time, and I haven't had anyone to share the memories with that I've buried or forgotten a lot about her.

Eli curls up on the couch with me, wrapping his arm around mine, and leaning his head on my shoulder.

"That was your mom's, right?" he asks quietly.

I can't speak past the knot in my throat, so I nod and hand him the box.

"She loved this thing." He smiles at the simple piece of jewelry. She was like that. Simple. She liked the little things in life. The big house and name-brand clothes were all my dad, not Mom. She was fine in a Hanes T-shirt and Levi's.

I open the envelope, and along with a bunch of legal documents, there's a smaller envelope with my name on it in Mom's handwriting. I set the stack aside, and with trembling fingers, I hold the last words my mother tried to give me. The ache is back in my chest, trying to choke me. Did Dad know about this and keep it from me for a reason? Were there stipulations to giving it to me?

Eli threads his fingers through mine and squeezes, giving me unspoken comfort and courage to open the letter.

Asher,

My darling boy. The light in my heart. If you're reading this, I'm no longer with you. I'm sorry, baby. I have a lot of regrets, a lot of missed moments because I was distracted. I hope you know that was not a failure on your part, but mine. I love you so deeply.

You may not understand this now, but I'm leaving a few things to you that I want you to be careful with. The pearl ring I always wore on my right hand is my favorite piece of jewelry. It's not an expensive piece, pearl and silver, but it means the world to me. Pearls are created out of necessity. When a grain of sand gets into an oyster, the animal coats it in the same material the inner shell is made of to protect itself. Remember that even when some-

ANDI JAXON

thing comes into your life, trying to hurt you, there's something about it that can be beautiful. Growth, survival, perseverance is beautiful. Scars are proof of life and success, not failure.

Remember that if you ever find yourself lost in the dark, I am with you. You are never alone, even if you feel like you are. Your mind may sometimes lie to you, but I will always sit in the dark with you until you can find the light.

I hope you find someone you love that will sit with you in the shadows. Who can see the beauty in survival. And I hope you give them this ring. Even though the metal is dented out of shape, it tells a story too of living. It formed to the shape of my finger, a flat spot where it was pressed against the tools of my life.

Wrap your arms around the Cushings boys for me. Tell them I love them, always. Death will not stop that, and I will meet all of you again one day.

You, my boy, are a fighter. Use that spirit to take yourself as far as you can, to touch as many lives as you can. Never let fear dictate what you do with or how you live your life. It is yours. Set an example of how to live fear-

lessly. More people need to see it. Be unashamed of who you are and what your goals are. You have it in you.

Love always,
Mom

TEARS RUN DOWN MY CHEEKS, blurring her handwriting. I wipe at my eyes and read back over it. I can almost hear her voice in my head. Almost. Just a tease of it somewhere in the back of my mind.

Did she know back then that I was in love with Eli? That I would end up giving this ring to him? Because that's what's going to happen. When I find the right time to propose, I'm doing it with this. Nothing else will mean as much, and I know he'll love it as much as I do.

Eli sniffs, wiping at his cheeks, and I wrap my arm around him, pulling him into my lap.

"I loved her." His voice is muffled by my skin.

"She loved you just as much." I kiss his hair and hold him close. Eventually, I move the papers, take the ring box, and set it all on the coffee table so we can lay down.

"Do you remember when she taught me how to make cookies?" Eli asks, a smile in his tone.

I chuckle at the memory. They were terrible. "Yeah, I do."

He starts laughing trying to tell the story and ends up crying from laughing so hard.

"The smoke detector went off." He's barely able to get the

words out, and they're squeaky when he does. "Your mom comes running full speed into the kitchen while I stand there, oven mitts in hand, staring in horror at the oven."

I start laughing too, mostly because he's laughing so hard.

"They tasted terrible," I admit.

"They were black! I can't believe you tried one!" Eli shoves at my chest, wiping his eyes with the sleeve of the shirt he stole from me.

"My boy made them. Of course I was going to try one."

Eli rolls his eyes and shoves at me. "You're ridiculous."

"Ridiculously in love with you."

Epilogue

ASHER

It's been a crazy few months. After I came out on national television, it hit social media for a while, but another NFL player was arrested for drunk driving into a house the following week, and I became old news. Eli started taking pictures again. His camera collection is now like twenty cameras strong, and he sells framed pictures. He even got asked to do a gallery showing. It went amazingly.

The Thunderbolts won the Super Bowl in Tampa Bay, and now the team is relaxing after a long season. I managed no major injuries and beat Aaron's personal record for rushing yards. It was a good year for me.

Now, Eli and I are back on Black Diamond. He doesn't know it yet, but it's about to be more crowded. Aaron, Brit, and Jordan are here too, though Eli won't see them until later. It's all planned and ready to go. I'm nervous but excited for tonight.

On the beach at sunset, we sit with a dinner spread out on a blanket in the sand. It's just us on this little section of the beach. It's been fantastic to have this time with him. It's our own little world. Nothing exists here but the island.

"What do you want to do in the off-season?" Eli asks, popping a bite of pineapple into his mouth.

"Get married."

He chokes and coughs, looking at me like I've gone insane.

"What?" he wheezes between coughs.

"Get married," I repeat. Inside my pocket is my mother's pearl ring that I've been holding on to for this moment. I dig it out and rise to one knee. Eli's eyes widen and his cheeks pinken with emotions. I love that I can still surprise him.

"I love you, Elliot. With everything I am." I take his hand in mine, pulling him to stand with tears filling his eyes. "I want everyone to know that you are mine. Only mine. Our lives have been entangled since we were kids, and I will accept nothing less for the rest of our years. You're the only one for me. Perfect."

A sob escapes him, and he covers his mouth with his free hand.

"So, marry me, baby. Show everyone you're mine and I'm yours." I open the box, and he drops to his knees, quickly wrapping his arms around my neck, and crying into my shirt.

"Yes," he forces out between sobs, and I smile into his curls.

I pull the ring from the box and take his hand in mine, sliding it on.

"Perfect fit," I say before cupping his cheeks in my hands and kissing his trembling lips.

A loud whoop and a scream come from the bushes, and

Eli jumps, spinning to see Jordan, Brit, and Aaron racing toward us. A huge smile splits my face, and I laugh when he looks back at me with wide eyes. Eli wipes at his face and stands.

"What did you do?" he demands as Jordan wraps her arms around him, shaking him in her excitement.

"Congratulations!" she shrieks as Aaron slaps my back in a hug.

"Dude! I get to be your best man, right?"

I slap his back, watching Eli show Jordan and Brit the ring. Brit gives him a quick hug and a congrats before wrapping themself around Jordan.

Aaron releases me, and I pull Eli into me, wrapping my arm around his shoulders.

"How's tomorrow work for you?" I ask my fiancé.

"What?!" he yells at me, staring up at me in horror. "Tomorrow? Have you lost your mind?"

"Yes, tomorrow. And I'm only crazy about you."

"Uck. You are the cheesiest human I've ever met." Eli slaps at my chest while everyone chuckles.

"Tomorrow, you will be Elliot Vaughn. Tonight, go get drunk with Jordan and Brit." I grab his chin and lift his lips to mine in a quick kiss.

"What the hell am I supposed to wear tomorrow? I didn't bring anything fancy!" He's starting to panic over the details. *Oh, ye of little faith.*

"You really think I would plan all this and forget to bring you something to wear?" I ask him with a lifted eyebrow.

His face falls. "Oh no, what did you do?"

Jordan laughs and grabs his hand, pulling him down the beach toward the bar.

"Hey! Stay away from that damn bartender!" I yell, Aaron and I following after them.

"Holden is married, caveman!" Eli shouts over his shoulder. "But he does have weed lube. You ever gotten high off anal?"

What the fuck did he just say? Aaron runs into me when I stop short, my brain not understanding the words Eli just said.

"Hold up!" We hustle to catch up to the trio, who are now laughing hysterically. "Weed lube?"

Eli is wiping tears from his eyes from laughing so hard, holding his stomach.

"I never thought I would say that sentence," he wheezes.

"That dude has lube with weed in it? Like leaves? Is it chunky, because I don't think that would be fun?" Why am I questioning this? This leads to everyone around me doubled over in laughter, but these are serious questions. Eli, Jordan, and Brit walk away toward a different part of the island as Aaron and I head back to my villa while no one has given me answers. I expect Eli to get wasted, so I don't want to get too drunk, but we can hang out, eat, and have a few drinks. See if there are any basketball games on and wait for everyone to get back. Jordan and Brit have a villa on the next pier over from us, but Aaron is at the end of the same one we're on.

I find a game and pop the tops on a few beers, handing one to Aaron.

"You did it, man." He clinks the bottles together, and we both take a drink. "I'm happy for you."

"Thanks. I really appreciate you coming out here." I drop onto one of the velvet, shell-shaped chairs in front of the TV and take another drink.

"Of course, I wouldn't miss this for the world. You're family now."

I smile, a warmth spreading across my chest. Eli and I found ourselves a family in San Diego for sure. Aaron's parents are amazing and will be here tonight. They're the parents Eli always deserved and the ones I missed out on. Mr. and Mrs. Thomlyn accepted us with open arms, and we've been one of the kids since Thanksgiving when we were invited to dinner.

For a few hours, we just chill. Drink some beers, eat dinner that is brought to us, watch sports on the TV, and eventually go for a swim. The sun has long since set, and the water is lit up with lights under the villas while we fuck around in the water. It's fun, and we've both got decent buzzes going when the trio returns.

"Aaaashy poooooo!" Eli singsongs on the back deck, stumbling around as I climb up the steps with a grin on my face.

"Hey, baby." I wrap my arm around his waist to catch him before he attempts to step down a stair. "Feeling good?"

"Mmm," he hums, turning his face up to me. "I need you to fuck me."

A strangled cough sounds behind me, and I snort.

"That is my cue to go." Aaron grabs his stuff and heads out, promising to make sure Brit and Jordan make it back to their villa too.

"What were you drinking?" I back Eli up to a table on the deck and push him to sit, then lay back. His whole body doesn't fit, but I don't need it to.

Unbuttoning his shirt, I lift him up to remove it and open his shorts. Eli lays back down, and I lean over him, kissing and sucking on his skin while palming his dick through his underwear. With my hand under his jaw, I push his face up to give me better access to his throat. His Adam's apple bobs as I suck on it.

His back arches when I wrap my hand around his soft cock. I have a feeling he's too drunk, but I can still get him off. I kiss, bite, and suck my way down his torso, leaving a trail of red marks down his body. At the waistband of his blue underwear, I slide my tongue just under the edge and smile when Eli pants out a whimper.

"Make that sound for me again, baby." I lick under the band again, this time licking across his tip, and he groans, gripping his fingers in my hair.

I get the rest of his clothes off and eye his inner thighs, kissing each scar on my way to the short blond hair surrounding his cock. Dragging the tip of my nose up his sack, I nuzzle into the hair and breathe him in. Eli moans and pulls on his dick, but it's no use. His poor body is just not able to do what he wants with all the alcohol in his system.

I lick his hole, and my boy cries out for me. A sweet sound that shoots right to my cock.

"Hang on, sweet boy." I kiss his inner thigh and hurry inside to grab the lube. Dropping to my knees next to the table he's spread out on, I slick up my fingers and press them against his hole. Two fingers go in easily. I thrust them a few times, making sure there's enough lube, then hook my fingers to find his prostate. Eli's hips buck off the table, his hands gripping the edges as I stroke that pleasure spot.

"Oh fuck," he whimpers, riding my fingers.

"Are you going to come for me, baby?" I coax, speeding up my fingers.

"Hu. Ung. Fuuuck."

I chuckle and pull my fingers from him and find the lube again to coat myself. I press against him and sink into his hot hole in one thrust. Grabbing the backs of his knees, I push them into his chest and thrust again. When his eyes roll back, I know I've got the right angle and set a quick pace. I want to fuck him unconscious, and if I keep this pace up, I fucking will. My boy is greedy for orgasms, and I'm oh-so happy to give them to him.

"You look so sexy taking my dick," I growl, leaning onto his legs to arch his hips so I can get deeper.

"Oh god," he moans.

My thrusts get harder, pounding him into the fucking table as I take his body the way I want. I love how he takes me, so open and vulnerable. His body so responsive that I never have to wonder if he likes something I'm doing.

Eli trembles and cries out, arching his neck as he comes on his stomach while my hips slap against his ass.

"Good fucking boy." His hole tightens around me as he spasms the last of his orgasm, pushing me to my own. I come inside him, making his hole wet and sloppy, as goose bumps erupt on my skin. I lean on the table for a minute, my eyes closed as I catch my breath.

When I open them, Eli is asleep, his body completely relaxed. I smile to myself and run a hand over his messy curls before pulling out of him and picking him up. He grumbles a little but doesn't open his eyes as I wipe him down quickly and carry him to the bed. I lay down next to him, cover us up, and pass out with the love of my life pressed against me.

ELLIOTT

When my eyes open, it's bright outside. I vaguely remember stumbling back to the villa last night, but I don't remember losing my clothes. Turning my head, Asher is sitting up in the bed next to me, a steaming cup of coffee in his hand, flicking through his phone.

"Morning, almost husband." He smirks at me as I sit up.

"Morning," I mumble. Glancing down at my left hand, I smile at the pearl ring he placed there last night. At the memories that come with it and the promises. Over the last several months, he's shown how much he loves me by making me a priority. Even with his crazy football schedule, he never forgets to call or text me. I was never forgotten or shoved to the side. Not once did he ask me to dress a certain way or hide me. He embraces me the way I am and loves me for what makes me, me.

"Go get something to eat. I'm going to go get ready at Aaron's villa. Jordan will be here any minute." He kisses my lips softly and gets out of bed. "I suggest putting pants on before she arrives."

Shit. That's a good idea.

I grumble and grab a pair of shorts from the dresser and find breakfast on the table on the deck as Asher opens the door to let Jordan in.

Jordan joins me on the deck and picks at the breakfast with me. I'm anxious but not. It's the strangest feeling. I'm not worried about things going wrong for once. I just want to be his.

"How ya feeling?" Jordan asks, picking at a croissant. "You were white boy wasted last night."

"I feel better than I have any right to," I admit, eating a strawberry and looking out over the turquoise water. "I'm anxious but not nervous."

"Good. You've got about ten more minutes before you have to get into the shower," she informs me, checking her phone.

"What's Brit up to?" I ask.

"They have stuff to do today. You'll see them later." Jordan picks up a champagne flute and takes a drink of her mimosa.

"Okay, I'm going to shower. Do you know where my clothes are? Asher didn't tell me," I ask as I stand up.

"Yup. Go shower and I'll get it all laid out for you." She smiles at me, obviously very proud of herself.

I huff but go and shower. I make sure to get my hair dealt with, applying the products I'll need to keep it from frizzing too much in the breeze. Once I'm dried off and my hair has been scrunched, curled with a brush, and plopped to dry for a bit, I head into the bedroom with a towel around my waist and find a long, cream satin sheath dress with a high neck and bare shoulders. It's gorgeous.

I cover my mouth with my hand as I stare at it.

"It-it's—it's perfect." Tears well up, but I let them fall down my cheeks as my best friend hugs me.

"I would like to take credit for it, but it was all Asher," she admits with her arm around my shoulder.

Next to the dress is a matching set of lace thigh-highs and garter. Asher has a bit of an obsession with those, which I am happy to oblige him.

"Thank you isn't enough," I whisper, staring at her.

"Thank you is never needed." She kisses my cheek and puts her hands on my shoulders. "Okay, time to get beautiful."

I grab my underwear and lotion up all my skin before pulling on the tights. Jordan holds out the dress for me to step into and zips it up. It fits like a dream. How did he get it so right? The silk is cold on my skin for a moment, and I love when it warms. There's a slit up my leg to mid-thigh that shows off the tights, and I smile to myself knowing it will drive Asher crazy.

Jordan curls her hair and pins it back away from her face. Her makeup is lighter than her concert look, but still striking and beautiful with winged black liner and lashes. Her dress is a teal blue with gray underneath that swirls around her knees when she moves, and she has one fishnet fingerless glove. She looks beautiful.

Her teal flip-flops make me raise an eyebrow.

"Really? Flip-flops?" I ask.

"They're just to get to the beach."

We're about ready to head down to the beach when there's a knock on the door.

"Knock, knock, party people!" Brit announces, wearing light gray suit pants, a white button-up shirt that's open at the throat with the collar popped, and teal suspenders.

Turning toward the door, I'm caught off guard to see Brit and Aaron's parents.

"Oh my god! What are you doing here?!" I hurry toward them, lifting my dress so I don't trip over it, and wrap my arms around Mrs. Thomlyn.

"Oh, you sweet boy, like we would miss this?" Her arms come around me, holding me tight. "Absolutely not."

Once again, my eyes fill, and I tell Jordan to grab some tissues because I know the day is going to be filled with waterworks.

Mrs. Thomlyn holds me at arms-length to get a look at me.

"Oh, honey, you look so beautiful." She cups my cheek. "I have something for you to wear today."

From the pocket of her teal flower-covered dress, she pulls out something wrapped in tissue paper and opens it.

Inside is a sapphire tennis bracelet. She puts it on my wrist at the same time Jordan drapes my favorite pearl neck-lace around my neck.

"Something old." Mrs. Thomlyn touches the pearls. "Something new." She taps on my dress.

"Something borrowed and something blue," she touches the bracelet. "You're all set."

Mr. Thomlyn steps up in the same outfit as Brit to give me a big bear hug and squeezes more tears from me.

"You look lovely, and I would be honored to walk you down the aisle if you would like."

My throat clamps closed, so all I can do is nod.

"All right, my guy, I need the ring." Brit steps forward, palm open.

I force myself to swallow and manage a smile. "Are you the ring bearer?"

Brit bows, not moving their hand. "At your service."

I slide the ring off my finger and watch them put it on their pointer finger and shove that hand in their pocket.

"Time to roll," they announce, and we head outside after Jordan, and I find the white flip-flops Asher has supplied.

As a unit, we walk down the pier, across the beach to a little setup where Asher and Aaron are in matching outfits with Brit, except Asher doesn't have suspenders. Asher looks sexy as hell, all dressed up and put together. Are they also barefoot in the sand? Something about that is enticing. A watery smile lifts my lips as I watch both of them. Asher put so much planning into this.

They are standing next to a man I've never met.

I stop when I see the strange man in blue jeans, cowboy boots, and a blue plaid shirt with snap buttons with the sleeves ripped off. I am so very confused.

"Where the hell did you find him?"

Brit purses their lips for a minute before saying, "He fixes toilets and can get ya hitched. Apparently." Brit shrugs. "Look, Asher gave me forty-eight hours to find someone, and there weren't a ton of options. Some dude named Holden was available, but Asher said, and I quote, 'not a fucking chance,' so . . ."

"He's huge!" Jordan says under her breath, and she's not wrong. The man is built like a brick building, tall and solid. "I think his arms are bigger than my head."

Mrs. Thomlyn clears her throat. "I'm sure he's a very nice young man."

"We ready then?" the officiant hollers in some kind of southern accent, and Jordan snorts.

"Line up, come on," Mr. Thomlyn tells us, and we all kick off our shoes. Brit heads the line, followed by Jordan, then the Thomlyn parents and me. I can't take my eyes off Asher, though. There's no mask, no hiding the love he has for me. His eyes sweep over the dress he picked out, only hesitating on the slit for a second before he meets my gaze again. I've been living with him for months, and I still can't believe this isn't a dream. The only boy I ever wanted, ever loved, loves me back. And not only does he love me, he wants the world to know.

Not to mention the family we've created. The love and acceptance I feel right now is more than I ever expected. These people dropped what they were doing to fly to this island to be here for Asher and me today. I don't know how much warning he gave them, but knowing him, it wasn't much. My own parents wouldn't have done it, but these people did. They're my family now. The family I choose and who choose me. Blood means nothing when you have love and respect.

Music starts playing behind me, "You Are the Reason" by Calum Scott, and my eyes tear up again as I stare at Asher. He has a tear running down his cheek, and I want to swipe it away. Brit starts toward Asher and Aaron, handing the ring to Aaron, then standing next to him.

Jordan goes next and steps to my side, then I head down with the parents I deserved growing up. With love and acceptance wrapped around me like a shield, I head to my destiny.

Mrs. Thomlyn kisses my cheek, and Mr. Thomlyn gives

me a side hug, then they step aside.

"Y'all'er here 'cause these two wanna get married," the mountain of a man starts as Asher and I face each other.

"You look better than I had pictured," Asher says, and I can feel my cheeks heat.

"Ya do look mighty pretty," the officiant says and clears his throat. "My name is Devon and I'mma be your officiant," he announces. "Everyone cool with these two gettin' hitched?" He looks around for a split second, then nods. "Good. You got vows or some shit?" he asks Asher and me.

Asher is trying very hard to hold a straight face but is failing. Tears are falling down his cheeks from laughter this time, and I'm about to break too.

Aaron is shaking, trying to hold in his laughter, and Brit isn't much better.

"This is the best wedding I've ever been to," Brit says, and Aaron loses it, doubled over with laughter. "Dude was a solid choice."

"You gotta problem?" Devon points at Aaron with a serious set to his face. "Tough titties."

That does it, now we're all laughing. I wrap an arm around my stomach as I turn away from the man and laugh. I don't know where they found this guy, but he's perfect.

"Anyway, y'all got vows or what?" Devon points to us. The wind picks up, making his open shirt flap around his body.

Asher is wiping his laughing tears away and straightens up. "Yeah, I got something."

I turn back to my soon-to-be husband, and he takes my hand, sliding the ring back on my finger.

"Eli, I've loved you since before I knew what that meant.

My entire life has led me to this moment. The universe kept pushing us together, but I was too stubborn, too dumb, to listen. I lost us time together, but never again. You're it for me. You have always been it for me, and I can't wait to see what life has in store for us."

There's a knot in my throat again as I stare at this man who is promising me his life.

"That was real pretty," Devon drawls, and I snort.

I turn to Jordan, realizing I don't have a ring.

"Does Asher have a ring?"

Jordan winks at me and hands me a simple white gold band.

"It's just a place holder until you can pick one for him," she tells me.

"Asher. The last few months have been a whirlwind, and when I try to think about how we got here, I can't remember it all, but that's always been us. You came into my life like you had always been there. You held all of me in your hand, and I didn't know it until it was gone. In the last ten months, you've healed me more than I thought was possible. I figured I would be broken for the rest of my life. Cast to the shadows of the world where light never shines, but you brought the light to me when I couldn't find my way out of the dark. You showed me what it feels like to be loved the way I deserve, and I can never thank you enough for that." I slide the ring on his finger, and he laces our hands together.

"Real nice," Devon says with a serious nod. "I announce y'all as husband and husband. You may kiss the groom."

Asher grabs me, hauling me flush against him, crashes his lips to mine, and tips me backward over his arm.

He's mine. I'm his. Asher and Elliot Vaughn. Forever.

ACKNOWLEDGMENTS

I am beyond honored to have been invited to participate in this world. I've made friends and found a group of authors in my genre that I connect with for the first time. You guys are never getting rid of me now.

Honestly, this book would not have been possible without a few people who held my hand, talked me off the ledge, and helped me brain storm. JR, Riley, and Ashley, you guys are the MVP's of putting up with my shit. You all deserve gold stars.

Kayla, my alpha reader and SIL, you know I would be a mess without you. You are invaluable to my process.

My betas, Jessi, Kate, Melissa, JJ, thank you for all of your feedback. You guys helped me polish this dumpster fire until it shined.

Kari, my PA, the brains behind the operation, I can't begin to tell you how much I love having you behind the scenes keeping me on track. Don't ever leave me.

My hubs and Momma for taking over kid duty so I could write, making sure they didn't starve, and making sure they had clean clothes while I holed up with my computer. Appreciation isn't enough.

Finally, you, my readers. I couldn't do this without each

and every one of you. I hope you enjoyed the ride these boys took me on while writing them.

-Andi

ABOUT THE AUTHOR

Andi Jaxon and is one of the most random people you will probably ever come in contact with. Her favorite accessory is rainbows (she has glasses, shoes, wardrobe, and accessories), big hoop earrings, and fake eyelashes (she only recently learned how to put them on). She always has coffee on hand so she can try to keep up with the three minions she's created.

Want to know more about Andi Jaxon? Follow her on social media or subscribe to her mailing list to receive the latest information on new releases, sales, and more!

www.andijaxon.com

Made in the USA
Columbia, SC
03 August 2024

39930979R00200